P9-CJW-596

COLD FLORIDA

COLD FLORIDA

A Foggy Moskowitz Mystery

Phillip DePoy

This first world edition published 2016
in Great Britain and the USA by
SEVERN HOUSE PUBLISHERS LTD of
19 Cedar Road, Sutton, Surrey, England, SM2 5DA.
Trade paperback edition first published
in Great Britain and the USA 2016 by
SEVERN HOUSE PUBLISHERS LTD

Copyright © 2016 by Phillip DePoy.

All rights reserved including the right of
reproduction in whole or in part in any form.
The moral right of the author has been asserted.

British Library Cataloguing in Publication Data

DePoy, Phillip author.
  Cold Florida. – (A Foggy Moskowitz mystery)
  1. Missing children–Florida–Fiction. 2. Seminole
  Indians–Florida–Fiction. 3. Detective and mystery
  stories.
  I. Title II. Series
  813.6-dc23

ISBN-13: 978-0-7278-8575-3 (cased)
ISBN-13: 978-1-84751-683-1 (trade paper)
ISBN-13: 978-1-78010-739-4 (e-book)

This is a work of fiction. Names, characters, places and incidents
are either the product of the author's imagination or are used fictitiously.
Except where actual historical events and characters are being described
for the storyline of this novel, all situations in this publication are
fictitious and any resemblance to actual persons, living or dead,
business establishments, events or locales is purely coincidental.

All Severn House titles are printed on acid-free paper.

Severn House Publishers support the Forest Stewardship Council™ [FSC™],
the leading international forest certification organisation.
All our titles that are printed on FSC certified paper carry the FSC logo.

Typeset by Palimpsest Book Production Ltd.,
Falkirk, Stirlingshire, Scotland.
Printed and bound in Great Britain by
TJ International, Padstow, Cornwall.

PART ONE
Fry's Bay, Florida, 1974

ONE

It was two in the morning, the middle of February. I was signing my time card, but I could barely read the handwriting I was so tired. Then the phone rang. I said something rude to it, but it rang again anyway. I looked at the door to my crummy office. It seemed very unsympathetic to my situation. It stayed closed. The phone rang a third time, and I picked it up.

'He's not in,' I said.

'Nice try, Foggy,' Sharon said. 'But this is important.'

I squeezed my eyes shut and then opened them again. I imagined how nice it might be to lie down on the top of my desk. I would only have to move a couple of folders in the right direction to make a nice pillow. The light in the room was hurting my eyes. The hum from that fluorescent tube was stopping up my ears.

'Still there?' Sharon said impatiently.

'Define *there.*'

'OK,' she said, 'you have to go to the hospital.'

'Good idea,' I told her. 'I'm very run down lately.'

'Hasn't hindered your sense of humor,' she said, without the slightest hint of levity. 'Somebody stole a baby. From the neo-natal care whatever-you-call-it.'

'Stole a baby?' I rejoined. 'At two in the morning? This close to Valentine's Day?'

'Hmm,' she mumbled and I heard her rustling something on her desk. 'I guess it is almost Valentine's Day at that.'

'Isn't this more of a police type of a situation?' I asked her.

'The baby's mother is missing too,' Sharon said right back. 'She's a junkie, and the baby's addicted too because the mother shot up while she was pregnant. Shot up, apparently, all the time. So now she's gone, and the baby's gone, and the police are called thence, but they also want someone from our little branch of crime-fighters on the scene, because they're defining it as "an endangered child" case. So, tag. You're the only one on duty at the moment.'

'Technically speaking,' I began, hoisting my time card up to the phone as if she could see it, 'I already signed out.'

'Technically speaking, I'm five-foot-eleven, but does anyone call me *willowy*? No. I get *scarecrow* a lot.'

'I always think of you as willowy.'

'Not the point.'

'It's not?' I asked, somewhat disingenuously.

'The point is,' she sighed, 'that just because you think it, that doesn't make it so. You think you're off. But you're not.'

'Nietzsche or Kant or one of those German types,' I said, very reasonably, 'and I, would disagree with you. They always like to tell you that the only thing that makes it so is that you think it's so.'

'Have them call me tomorrow,' she snapped, 'and we'll discuss it, but at the moment?'

'I'm going to the hospital.'

'I told them already that you're on your way. So hurry. Don't stop for coffee.'

I hung up without saying anything further about German philosophers.

I looked around my office and took a second, a brief second, to reflect on my lot in life. How, I asked myself, did I end up here? My office was the size of an elevator car, no window. My desk was made of plywood. The walls were painted some color that wasn't even bright in 1947 when it was applied. The floor was a blond carpet that had so many stains everybody thought it was an imitation Pollock – a bad imitation. There was nothing on any wall, unless you'd counted the smudges. And the guy who'd worked in the office before me was a two-pack-a-day smoker who'd died of lung cancer, so the place smelled like an ashtray in a bus station.

The entire building was just as bad: a squat, concrete two-story, painted pink. It was a box with windows and a flat roof that

leaked. And I was on the second floor. The sign out front said
Child Protective Services because Congress passed Public Law
93-247, the *Child Abuse Prevention and Treatment Act*. The act
came with a little bit of federal funding. The only job I'd had in
Florida before that was as a sort of private investigator. But the
romance of that job had worn thin after a while – nearly as thin
as my bank account – so a nice government paycheck seemed
just the ticket. Also, for reasons too nefarious to disclose, it was
the perfect job for me. It helped me to atone for past
transgressions.

Previously, I had been happy-go-lucky in Brooklyn: the
halcyon days, before 1971 – a long three years earlier. Sometimes
this happy-go-lucky me, my former self, would emerge from the
place in my brain where I'd buried him. When that happened,
the little man who used to be me, he taunted me.

'You used to be the best four-wheel booster in Borough Park,'
he would say. 'Free as a bird. What happened to you?'

The beauty of stealing a car in a mostly Hasidic neighborhood,
of course, was that the cops didn't give it as much attention as
they would have in, say, Brooklyn Heights.

'You were only caught twice,' he said, the guy in my head,
'and one of those times all you had to do was apologize to a
guy named Schlomo, and Bob was your uncle. He let you cop
a walk.'

'Yeah,' I explained, also in my head, 'but the second time I
got caught, I was on my way to the slam. I was only able to
avoid it by slipping out of the cop car under very dire circumstances and hiding out all the way to Florida. Florida is where
you made me come to! And now, somehow, it got to be 1974!'

That would usually shut him up, the little guy in my head.
For a while.

As I was leaving, I happened to catch a glimpse of myself in
the dirty glass part of the door. I needed a shave, and a haircut,
and a new suit, and, to be honest, a fair amount of plastic surgery.
But was that going to happen? The beard grew fast. The hair
looked better longer. The suit, well, it used to be Brooks Brothers,
but at this point it looked like the brothers had fought over the
thing before going their separate ways. And that face: seriously,
I used to catch clocks trying to avoid eye contact. Still, it was

the face I was given, and it certainly belonged to a guy who would call himself *Foggy*. So there I was.

I decided to walk to the hospital. It was only five blocks, and I thought the air and the exercise would wake me up. The wee hours of the night were always quiet in our little berg. This particular night the streets were slick because of the rain and shiny because of the moon, which was full like a big white snowball. Which, by the way, they never saw around those parts: snow. Still, it was plenty cold, and I got the shivers, which made me walk faster. Because I was from parts north, I always underestimated the ability of a cold night in Florida to ice me up. I never wore an overcoat. I always thought to myself, *You're from Brooklyn! What do you need with an overcoat in Fry's Bay?*

These were the thoughts I was having as I walked along the chilly, wet streets toward the hospital. There was no other idiot out of doors. Everyone else had sense enough to come in out of the rain. Still, it was my job, and I tried not to complain.

I rounded the corner of Broad Street and saw the *Emergency* sign for the hospital a block away. It was all red and misty, hanging in the air above an empty parking space where ambulances might hang out. I had to prepare myself to talk to night nurses about a stolen baby and a junkie mother. I was not an overly sensitive guy but, still, a conversation like that took a moment of steeling up beforehand.

I was wet, so I shook off a little before I sauntered in through the emergency door. I was greatly relieved to see Maggie Redhawk at the nurses' station. I knew her, she knew me. That was going to make things a little nicer.

Maggie Redhawk was a fifty-year-old woman of what she said was *mixed ethnicity*, which meant she couldn't decide if she wanted to write *African-American* or *Native American* on her census form. She and I had bonded because of my somewhat unusual looks. She thought I looked more like a Seminole than she did. Now, in fact, I was actually almost entirely a Russian Jew in the heritage arena. But, to Maggie, I looked a little like a Seminole, and we had several discussions about the lost tribes of Israel. We mostly talked about other things such as the weather and, on this particular night, a missing baby.

She saw me walk in. She was dressed in her usual hospital uniform, so large on her that she looked like a big white pillow with a black wig on.

'So,' she said. 'You're wet.'

I nodded. 'Yes. And I am also cold.'

'You're here about the missing baby.'

No small talk. That was interesting to me because Maggie was a big one for the small talk.

'I am,' I told her. 'And the missing mother that goes with her.'

'The baby's the problem,' she allowed, 'because, if it doesn't get its medication in just about three hours, it's dead.'

'That is a problem.'

'We ain't really got time to kid around, Foggy,' she told me, more serious than I had ever seen her.

'So tell me about the mother,' I said, sidling up to the nurses' station.

The emergency waiting room was about as per usual for that time of night. It was not much bigger than a living room. Four or five guys were bleeding in chairs under very harsh fluorescent lighting. The place smelled like rubbing alcohol and vomit. The floor was smeared with the black traces of gurneys and wheel-chairs and heel marks. And Maggie smelled like powder, a nice white scent.

'The mother's a junkie, like I said,' Maggie told me matter-of-factly. 'Had the kid in her apartment. A neighbor reported it. They both would have died otherwise.'

'She came here when?' I asked.

'Last Thursday, not quite a week ago.'

'So, this baby,' I concluded, 'it's really in bad shape.'

She nodded.

'All right.' I rapped my knuckles on the countertop between us and made as to leave.

I was halfway to the door before she objected.

'Wait. Where are you going?' she wanted to know.

'I am going to the apartment of the mother with all due haste,' I told Maggie, without turning around. 'It seems like a good place to start.'

'Her apartment?' she queried. 'And where do you think that is?'

'I'm guessing,' I told her, my hand on the door, 'that it's the address listed beside her name on that paperwork in front of you. Right where it says "patient's residence".'

'How the hell—' she began to ask me.

I didn't hear the rest of her question, because I was already outside and on my way to the address of one Lynette Baker, an apartment on Pine.

Another nurse passed me as I stepped on to the sidewalk. 'Tell Maggie that I can read upside down. Tell her I'm not as stupid as I look.'

The nurse looked up, caught my face, recognized me, and smiled. 'Yeah, I'll tell her. But I think she probably already knows the second part. I mean, it would just be cruel if you actually *were* as stupid as you look.'

'Comedy after two in the morning,' I rejoined.

'You have to do something to keep from crying,' she said, shoving on the door to go into the hospital, 'don't you?'

I nodded, even though she didn't see me, because I figured she had a point.

TWO

S hortly after, my fist was saying *blam* on somebody's door. It took a while, but somebody answered.

'What?' she wanted to know.

'You're the concierge of this establishment?' I held up a badge.

Now, if she looked at it too good, I'd maybe have to wade through half an hour's worth of explaining what a task force was and sometimes even what a battered child was, though I always found that the phrase was fairly self-explanatory. If she was sleepy, she might mistake my badge for a cop badge, and everything would be Jake.

She squinted past the door chain. 'Oh. You're here about the junkie.'

'After a fashion,' I confessed.

She unbolted her door. She was dressed in a fright wig and chenille bathrobe. Her feet were adorned with the dirtiest slippers

I'd ever seen. She reached up to a nail by the door for a ring of keys.

'Come on.' She muscled past me, down the hall, and up a flight of splintery stairs.

Even though it was pressing three o'clock in the morning, there was a stereo on somewhere, playing *Los Tigres Del Norte* very softly. My Spanish was rusty, but the song was about a woman who shot a drug smuggler and stole his money. Somewhere else gave off the smell of cooking onions, and it made my stomach growl. A woman was crying in D-7 as we passed her door. The shower was running in D-9. The super stopped at D-11 and shoved the key in the door without knocking.

'This is her place,' she said loudly. 'But she ain't in, I can tell you.'

'How do you know?'

'Because she's in the hospital.'

She flung the door open. Immediately a stench assaulted my considerable nostrils that made me think maybe I was in a slaughterhouse.

'What the hell is that?' I asked haltingly.

'What?'

'That smell?'

'What smell?'

'OK,' I said, trying to ignore it.

'After you,' she said.

I took a tentative step into the lair, and was presented with something worse than the smell: the scene that was causing the smell. The dump was a one-room affair; sometimes they call it a studio. There was a sofa, a side table, a lamp, a large photograph of a penguin hanging on the wall, and seventeen years' worth of accumulated garbage. In addition to the empty pizza boxes and moldy cottage cheese containers, there was a significant amount of blood and guts on the sofa. My guess was that our girl had her baby right there.

I took one step farther in, and I could see the stove and fridge side-by-side to my left, and a bathroom without a door on it. The sink was filled with dishes and the tub had water in it.

There was a window, but it had plastic over it, to keep out the cold I was guessing.

'You hear the ruckus a few nights ago?' I asked, trying not to look anyplace in particular. 'The baby being born?'

'Me? No. It was Gerard.'

'I see. And where is Gerard?'

'D-10,' she told me. 'Right across the hall. But he ain't in either. He's still working. He's a stripper. A male stripper. You ever hear of such a thing?'

'Yes,' I said. 'Now, about Lynette.'

'She's a junkie.'

'You already told me that.'

'She's always late with the rent.'

'And yet, you let her stay.'

'It ain't my place,' she said, rolling her eyes. 'I get to live here for free, and all I gots to do is take in the rent, notify people about this and that, and call the cops on a regular basis.'

'You call the cops last Thursday night when Lynette . . .?'

'Gerard came to me,' she sighed. 'I went to the cops, yeah. But I knew there was something more to it. You don't bleed that much just from having a baby.'

'You've had a baby?'

'No,' she said, adjusting her chenille robe, 'but I seen it on the television.'

'I'm going to look around in here now, for a minute,' I said, swallowing.

'Help yourself,' she told me. 'I'm going back downstairs to have a little nightcap.'

'Perfect.'

She left. I closed my eyes. I tried not to think about the scene in that room when the baby was born. I was just hoping to find something to tell me where the girl, the junkie, Lynette Baker might be hiding.

I opened my eyes, and all of a sudden I could have kicked myself for not asking what the baby was named. It would be nice, I thought to myself, to be able to say the baby's name to the junkie mother. Sometimes when you personalized things, a junkie would soften up. A little.

I took a moment to stare at the picture of the penguin on the wall. It seemed hilariously out of place, though I did not, at that moment, feel much like laughing. I decided that it was the only thing out of place in the dump, so I should start by examining it more closely. Sometimes you got lucky.

I took the few steps farther into the apartment that were necessary for me to grab the picture frame. I lifted the picture off the wall. There was a nail and a sizeable hole in the wall around the nail, like somebody had hit the nail so hard that the nail went all the way in and the hammer left an indentation, a little crater. Otherwise, there was nothing hidden on the wall.

I looked at the back of the picture. There was a very old slab of corrugated cardboard that was held in place by four finishing nails, one in each corner. I bent two of the nails a bit and slid the cardboard out of the way. A postage-stamp-sized baggie dropped to the floor. It was sealed with scotch tape and almost completely flat, but it had a nice white powdery substance in it. I scooped it up and pocketed it. Then I saw that, written in very light pencil in the corner of the backside of the cardboard, it said *Jody* and gave a telephone number.

Like I said, sometimes you got lucky.

I looked around, found the phone, and dialed the number. Just like that.

It rang maybe fourteen times before a very disgruntled female voice said, 'What?' into my ear.

'Lynette,' I said calmly.

There was a pause, after which the person said, 'What about her?'

'I'd like to speak with her.'

'Me too,' the voice said. 'She owes me money.'

'So, you have to be Jody,' I said politely.

'I don't *have* to be,' she insisted.

'OK,' I allowed, 'maybe you *want* to be Jody, because I hear that I might purchase some interesting *memorabilia* from you.'

'What?'

I got the impression that Jody was just about to hang up.

'I call it memorabilia,' I hastened to say. 'I know some people just call it trash – in fact, that's just how Lynette described it to me. "It's all *junk*," she said to me. But never the less, I am interested. And I am a somewhat significant collector.'

I could hear her smile. 'I get it. That's good. But, OK, look:

I don't sell to dealers. I'm strictly a neighborhood operation, you understand.'

'I hoped I might have a look-see, like, now.'

'I'm sleeping. It's three in the morning.'

'If I like what you have,' I told her softly, 'I could buy out your entire inventory. But I'll be gone by dawn, back to . . . back out of town, you understand.'

'Christ,' she mumbled, mostly to herself.

I heard her light a cigarette.

'I would like to come over right now,' I pressed.

'Yeah.' She coughed. 'OK. But I'll have to ask you for a minimum purchase no matter what. You know, for the inconvenience.'

'For the inconvenience,' I agreed.

THREE

On my way to Jody's address – a number she would only whisper, as if someone might overhear – I stopped by the all-night donut shop to pick up something sweet for Jody. Junkies liked the sweets. The place was called *Donuts*, so that you would know exactly what they sold without any guesswork.

I walked into the place and was not surprised to see seven or eight other people there, eating donuts and drinking coffee and generally minding their own business. This was a popular place with the late-night set: kids out after curfew, drunks trying to sober up before going home to somebody, even the occasional police person endorsing a time-honored cliché.

The shop always smelled nice, like fresh donuts, even when there were none. And the lighting was not too harsh, which I liked. Also, whoever owned the joint had installed a jukebox that contained only jazz from the cool school. This frustrated some of the younger customers, who complained that there was no music they liked. Generally, everyone else told them to beat it if they didn't like it, and generally they did. This left the place in a sort of pristine time capsule. As I sidled up to the counter by the cash register, the tune *So What* was playing. This was not

only a fine Miles Davis tune but also a relatively correct philosophical attitude, in my opinion.

'Foggy,' the woman at the cash register mumbled, after the
briefest possible glance.

She was, perhaps, sixty years old, five-foot-nothing, red of
eye and rouge of cheek. Once, maybe, her hair had been red, but
now it took something called *henna rinse* to make it stay that
way. I knew about that because she complained, almost every
night, about how it made her hair wiry. Her face was a road map
and filled with details about what she had done in her past.
The donut shop, she said, was only a rest stop for her. Just a
place marker in the progress of her journey. But she'd worked
there since 1952. Her name was Cass.

'Yes, Cass,' I admitted, 'it's me.'

She didn't look back up from her newspaper. 'You're off
work late.'

'I'm not off at all,' I said to her, 'in that I'm still on.'

'You're still on?' Still, she did not look up. She was dressed
in the same shabby pink waitress uniform that she had worn
since 1952, when she got here looking for a job and a place to
hide.

'I'm still on,' I repeated, 'and I would like half a dozen.'

'What are you working on so late?' She was irritated with the
whole idea.

'Tell you later.' I tossed down a buck, which was nearly twice
as much as six plain sugar donuts cost.

She didn't touch the bill. In fact, she didn't even seem to look
at it. She hauled herself off her chair, and I could actually hear
her bones creak. The ashes dripped from her cigarette down on
to the floor, and when she turned away from me I could see that
her hairnet had a very large hole in it.

'They ain't fresh,' Cass said over her shoulder. 'Lou's drunk
again.'

'When were they made?'

'Midnight.' She said it like it was the Middle Ages. 'Lou left
right after that. He was out in the alley and then he didn't come
back.'

'Still,' I told her, 'a couple of donuts can be good at this time
of night.'

She resumed her tortoise-like forward motion. 'Coffee?'

'Two, please.' I tossed down another buck. I knew it was way too much, but Cass could use the moolah, and the state paid me double for overtime. I didn't mind sharing.

Cass was back with a white paper bag and two cardboard cups in relatively short order. I made as to leave and she coughed.

'Your change,' she growled.

'What change?' I asked her, pushing through the door and back out on to the street.

The rain had stopped completely. I was still wet, but the hot coffee cups were keeping my hands warm, so the shivers were more or less gone.

Inside of five minutes, I was gently kicking at the bottom of the door in an apartment building only very slightly nicer than the one where Lynette most recently had her baby.

I saw the peephole darken. 'Get lost!' said a very male voice.

'OK, I can try,' I answered reasonably, 'but it won't be that easy, because this is a small town and I've lived here already three years. I know the place pretty well.'

'You the guy?' the voice was asking me – obviously Jody making her voice very deep.

'I am the guy. It's Foggy Moscowitz. I got coffee and donuts.' I held up the same so that she could see the truth of what I was saying.

There was a slight pause in the conversation, and then I heard a chain on the inside of the door start to move. As this happened, I heard her saying, in her normal voice, 'I could go for donuts. I could go for donuts *real* good.'

The donuts had changed her attitude, which had been my plan. The door edged open. Jody looked me up and down, then she peeped out into the hall. Two seconds more went by, and she stepped aside to let me pass. She was wearing a giant gray sweatshirt and nothing else that I could see. It came halfway down her thighs, but it seemed pretty short to me. Her wiry blond hair was pulled into two ponytails, one on either side of her head so that she looked like a demented Kewpie Doll.

I handed over the bag of donuts. She shoved her hand down in it, fished one out, and crammed the whole thing into her mouth.

I held up the coffee. She nodded, picking out her second donut.

'Save a couple for me,' I told her.

She turned away, and I thought she was pretending not to hear me because she was already grabbing a third.

Jody's place was just as depressing as Lynette's, but at least there was no blood on the sofa, as far as I could tell. Still, I preferred to stand. There were scattered newspapers and magazines everywhere. A cruddy yellow sofa was backed up to the window, which looked out on to an alley. There was only one other chair. There were bookshelves, but they had as many candles and whatnots on them as they did books. I thought there might be a kitchenette off to the left, but it smelled like very old cabbage. And what do you know: there was a picture of a penguin on the wall over one of the bookshelves. It was the exact same picture that was hanging in Lynette's apartment.

Jody collapsed on to the sofa, seriously tearing into a fourth donut. I still preferred to stand, but I set both coffees down on the table in front of her. This was generally called a coffee table, so I inferred that it would be appropriate. However, on this particular table there was a scale, a measuring spoon, and other items that a police officer might refer to as *paraphernalia.*

'Is that a photo or a drawing, that penguin?' I asked, pointing to the picture.

'It's a photo,' she said, around a mouthful of donut. 'I took it. It's my photo. I made copies. I used to sell my photos at that gallery on Biscayne, but they closed.'

'Where did you take that photo?' I asked, suspiciously. 'There are very few penguins in this part of Florida.'

'It was at the Lowry Park Zoo over there in Tampa. They got this place called Fairyland with all these concrete statues of nursery rhymes and a big maze that you can only get to if you go over a giant rainbow bridge.'

As luck would have it, I knew the place. The way she described it, it sounded like a junkie vision, but in fact there really was a great big rainbow bridge and a bunch of concrete fairytales. Still, it dated from 1957 and was currently a bit on the seedy side.

'Lynette has a picture just like this,' I said casually.

'She likes penguins.' Jody gave me the kind of shrug that told me something. It told me that a shrug was central to her philosophy of life. 'I gave her a copy.'

'I have to find her.' No point beating around the bush. 'Tonight.'

'Damn it,' she whined, shifting around on the cruddy yellow sofa. 'You're a cop?'

'No,' I told her in a voice that she had no choice but to believe.

She sat up and looked at me for the first real time. 'No. You're not a cop. I see that. What then?'

'Lynette had a baby a few nights ago.'

Jody's eyes got wide. 'I *thought* she was pregnant!'

'She and the baby are missing. If I don't find them in a few hours, the baby will die, and I'll have to fill out all kinds of paperwork. So please, tell me where she is.'

'But you're not a cop.'

'I'm a concerned citizen.' I squinted, trying to control my irritation. 'Where is Lynette?'

'Why are you looking for her?' Jody complained. 'You her dad?'

'I look like her *dad*?' I was offended. I was by no means a kid, but I did not have *dad* written anywhere on me.

'You look a little like one of them Indians from over on the nation, but you got a better suit and a sharper edge. Plus, you ain't from around here.'

'Where am I from?' I wanted to know.

'Yankee Land,' she said, oozing disgust.

'OK, but now you have to tell me where Lynette might hide out.'

'Why are you asking me?' she said in a voice that was twice too loud. 'Do I keep up with Lynette?'

'Well,' I reasoned, 'I know she was here earlier tonight.'

It was a guess, but a good one. Where would a junkie go after a few days of deprivation, especially if she thought the cops might be watching her own place?

'She wasn't here,' Jody told me, but she didn't even bother to make it believable, or maybe she wasn't capable of lying in a convincing manner.

'She came here, you sold to her, and she split. But to where? Family? Girlfriend? Father of the baby?'

Jody slumped down. Her sweatshirt rode up and I could, unfortunately, see that she was sporting no undergarments of any sort. A gentleman should always avert his eyes. I considered averting mine all the way to Pittsburgh.

'Pete's,' she mumbled, after the merest of pauses. 'She might be over there.'

'The billiards parlor on third?' I asked.

'She ain't got no family. And who the hell would be a father to *her* baby? I didn't even know she was pregnant, for sure. But sometimes she goes over there after she shoots.'

'Where else?' I asked, looking into the kitchen.

'She knew this guy who lived across the hall from her, Gerard,' she sneered. Apparently she did not care for Gerard.

'The male stripper?'

She gave me the once-over. I could see it out of the corner of my eye. 'You don't look like a sissy. How would you know about Gerard?'

'Anything else?' I sighed.

'That bastard Indian, Lou Yahola. He was friends with her.'

'Lou at the donut shop?'

'Damn, Jackson, you do get around. How you know Lou?' Jody somehow managed to make these sentences sound like she was impressed, while she was actually insulting me. Or maybe I was just forming a bad impression of the kid.

'It's a small town,' I told her.

'But you and me never met,' she said.

'We travel in different circles,' I told her.

'So you don't want to buy none of my – what's that you said? Memorabilia? I liked that. That was clever.'

'I don't care to make a purchase.' I reached into my pocket and fetched the tiny baggie from Lynette's apartment. 'But, so it shouldn't be a total loss for you, I am returning merchandize for which you have already been paid.'

I tossed the baggie in her general direction, still trying hard not to look right at her.

'So who do you work for, really?' she asked me, ignoring the dope in her lap area.

'I work for the county,' I said quickly. 'I look out for kids, little kids.'

'Really?' she asked, in the softest voice she had yet used.

'Really,' I confirmed, turning to head for the door.

'They pay you for that?' she wanted to know. 'The county.'

'Yes, but the money is not my primary motivation.' I reached out for the door handle.

I heard her stand up behind me. 'What is, then? Why you do it?'

'Yom Kippur,' I mumbled.

'The Hebe Holiday? That's today?'

'The actual day,' I explained, as I opened her door, not looking back at her for fear of turning into a pillar of salt, 'is the tenth day of Tishri. But I got a lot of *atonement and repentance* built up to do, so for me it's every day – for a while.'

'I don't understand.' She started to say more.

But I didn't hear the rest because I closed the door behind me and headed down the hallway toward the street.

FOUR

I didn't want to backtrack because I thought it would make me lose momentum. So I wasn't returning to the donut shop or Lynette's apartment right away. I figured Lou was drunk or sleeping one off, and Gerard wasn't home yet. So I kept going forward; headed over to Pete's Billiard Emporium.

The place dated back to the cool-cooler sixties when everyone referred to it as a *go-go*, and it was set up with a sort of 1920s look; bent wood chairs, flapper dresses nailed to the wall, a mirror ball, just like in Chicago nightclubs of the bygone era. Currently, in the seed-seedy seventies, the joint was much the worse for wear. Tougher locals would hang out to drink, gamble on pool, and then whack each other with pool sticks. I knew about the place because the guy who ran it was a good cook.

It didn't take me long to get there, but I was wishing that I had the coffee I left on Jody's table because my chill had returned. Then my stomach complained because thinking of the coffee reminded me that once there were donuts, and now there were none.

So I was very happy to clank into Pete's because the place was very warm, and there was a smell of cooking onions. I headed immediately for the bar.

Pete's was pretty much like a lot of joints in that part of Florida, or a lot of bars anywhere, I guess. The smell of stale beer and too many cigarettes would have been overpowering if drinking and smoking did not clog up most noses. Add the smell of onions, and I didn't mind it so much. The floor was always a little sticky, but it was old wood: dark and somehow dignified. The place was a big cube. You walked in the door and the bar was on your right, dining tables on your left. About halfway back, the bar and dining area ended, and the rest of the place was littered with pool tables. Those tables were not in any particular order. They were willy-nilly. The ceiling was twenty feet from the floor, and so dark that it was impossible to see, especially in the dim light. The bar had brightly colored, backless, spinning stools. It was supposedly a replica of the bar in the Cotton Club in Harlem in the old days. I knew this because it said so on a big sign behind the cash register. Otherwise, anything that might suggest an air of the Roaring Twenties had been expurgated, or tamed to a very dull roar indeed.

It didn't look like the kind of place where a pregnant junkie would hang out, and there was no young girl in evidence at all, so I began to wonder why Jody would have sent me there.

Behind the bar was a guy called Fat Tuesday. He was called that because he came from New Orleans and his name was Martin Craw, but he went by Marty, so that his name sounded like *Mardi Gras*, which anyone would know was the French way of saying 'Fat Tuesday.' This seems like a long way to go to get a nickname, but I never said so because a person known as *Foggy* ought not to throw stones.

Fat had three strands of hair, which he was careful to arrange across the top of his otherwise bald head. He was a fairly large individual, but he had thin, delicate hands. As long as I'd known him, he was always dressed in the same blue T-shirt and black jeans that were both covered by the World's Messiest Apron. It actually had those words written on it.

I slid on to one of the few untattered stools at the bar.

'Foggy,' said Fat the barkeep, sauntering my way.

'Fat,' I replied. 'I am looking for Lynette Baker.'

'Who?' he mumbled.

'OK, in that case,' I said quickly, 'I have got to eat something fast.'

'I have just the thing, already prepared.' He leaned forward. 'You know good brisket when you see it?'

'Do I know good brisket?' I asked him. 'Me, who had Shayna Moscowitz for an aunt, whose every Shabbat was occupied by the best brisket in five boroughs? Are you actually asking me if I know brisket?'

'I'm asking if you know *good* brisket,' he insisted, 'because I wouldn't want to waste this last little bit that I got on anything less than a connoisseur.'

'Look,' I said, as seriously as I ever got, 'a brisket must be braised, and it must take several days to cook over the lowest possible heat, and it must be moist enough to fall apart when you try to get it on to your fork. If it's not like that, do *not* taunt me with it.'

'Oh,' he assured me, 'it's like that.'

'Wait,' I added, 'I'm not finished. I hope it is cooked with the onions I am smelling.'

He nodded.

'And it must be sliced so thin you can see through it.'

'I could read the newspaper,' he claimed, 'through the thickest piece I got.'

'And!' I held up a finger. 'It must be sliced *against* the grain!'

'Please,' he snarled. 'Now you're insulting me.'

I sat up straight, elbows on the bar. 'I prefer a sweet sauce.'

'I make mine with Coca-Cola, ketchup, honey, and red wine.'

'I think I might cry.' I closed my eyes, like I was praying. 'This is almost exactly what my aunt used to use.'

'All the better people do,' Fat Tuesday said softly. 'I deem you worthy of my cuisine. Comes with little round potatoes and a dinner roll.'

He launched himself away without another word, lumbering toward the kitchen. I took the opportunity to amble toward the pool tables. There were three guys talking very quietly, not playing pool beside one of the tables. There was another guy asleep on top of another table. Otherwise, the billiards business was nonexistent.

When the unholy trinity saw me coming their way, they shut up and looked confused for a moment. Then one of them grabbed a pool cue like he'd been playing all night.

As I got closer, I could see that these were just kids. None of them was over sixteen. One seemed scared, the other two did everything they could to look tough.

I was more afraid of a teenage boy than anyone else in the world, because I remembered quite well what *I* was like as a teenage boy. I'd been willing to demonstrate my anger to nearly anyone, and in the most decisive manner. The problem was that this anger was unmodified by experience. That is to say, a boy of sixteen doesn't realize that whacking a person really hard with a pool cue might actually kill that person. Said boy would also not realize that, if the whacked person does *not* die, he would be in a mood to reciprocate. Either way, someone was bound to get hurt. A slightly older person would know this and would be somewhat more judicious.

So I hoped to obviate any pool cue whacking whatsoever by saying, 'Jody sent me.'

This was a gamble, because maybe they didn't know Jody.

After the briefest possible pause, one of the kids said, 'Jody who?'

'Yeah,' I answered him, 'I usually like a knock-knock joke too, but I'm in kind of a hurry. If Lynette's baby doesn't get its medicine in a little over two hours, it's going to die.'

This was a better gambit, I thought, because even if they don't know Lynette, what kind of a person was going to hear that a baby might die and not do something about it?

'Yeah,' the kid with the pool cue in his hand said, clearly hopped up, 'well that's crap, man. Lynette's in the hospital.'

One smiled. The other two nodded, like they had me over a barrel.

'OK,' I said, turning back toward the bar and the smell of brisket. 'You told me what I wanted to know. You do not, in fact, know where Lynette is. She absconded from the hospital several hours ago. Jody thought she might be here. I see that she is not.

I'm going to have my brisket in a hurry, and then I am going to find Lynette and her baby.'

'Lynette left the hospital?' I heard one of them ask. 'Why'd she do that?'

But I didn't answer because Fat was bringing the brisket from the kitchen.

FIVE

S even minutes later, the brisket was gone. I motioned to Fat, without speaking. He came to stand before me.

'You ate that too fast to enjoy it,' he whined.

'I'm in a hurry,' I told him. 'But I hope you'll accept the following sentence by way of apology. If you had a little more facial hair and a little less Christianity, you would actually be my Aunt Shayna. This is the extent to which your brisket achieved perfection.'

Fat blinked, and I thought he might be blushing. 'I'm honored.' He was genuinely moved.

Before I could go on to tell him just how much I regretted rushing through his fine cookery, I noticed Fat's expression change, and I tensed up. A second later, I was aware that someone was standing behind me, and almost instantly after that, I was flanked on my right and left by two members of the Caucasian Boys' Club trio. The one to my left did the talking.

'We don't like it that you're looking for Lynette,' he said, trying to make his voice deeper than it actually was.

'Yeah,' the one to my right affirmed.

I felt a distinctive metallic punch in my lower back. I had felt such a sensation before. It was a pistol.

Fat rolled his eyes. 'Boys,' he said, in a very soothing tone, 'leave the nice man alone. He's digesting.'

'I said,' the kid to my left told me, 'we don't like it that you're looking for Lynette.'

I nodded. 'Fat,' I said philosophically, 'I must apologize for what is about to happen.'

Fat stared me in the eye and seemed to understand. 'OK,' he told me affably. 'But don't make too much of a mess. It's been a long night already.'

'I completely understand,' I said.

Then, without further discourse, I jabbed my fork into the trachea of the boy to my left.

Before he could figure out what had happened, I twisted my left arm behind me, grabbed the barrel of the gun in my back, turned it, and shoved off from the bar with my feet. I pushed so hard that I flew up and backward and came down hard on top of the kid who was behind me holding the pistol. Meanwhile, the genius to my right was gawking, trying to understand what had just happened. Before he could do anything else, Fat cracked his head with a baseball bat produced from behind the bar.

So, to sum up: the kid to my left had a fork in his throat, the jackass underneath me had the wind knocked out of him, and the one to my right was a fountain of blood, teetering precariously toward the barroom floor.

I jumped up fairly quickly for a man previously referred to as *dad*. I had in my hand a .44 Auto Mag Pistol, which was a surprise.

'Look,' I said to Fat, whose baseball bat had already disappeared. 'This is an AMP.'

'It is?' He stared.

'This is unusual,' I said. 'They only made – what? – three thousand of these things a couple of years ago. Then the company went bankrupt.'

'Huh.' He studied the gun. 'Where did junior get a thing like that?'

'I'd like to know that.' I looked at the kid with the head wound. 'What do you think made these kids so playful? Is it me?'

'Boys will be boys?' Fat suggested.

I nodded. 'P.S. You know I could have taken care of this by myself, right?'

Fat smiled. 'I don't like people disturbing my dinner trade.'

'OK.' I leaned over and jerked the fork out of the kid's Adam's apple. Blood gushed. Before I had to ask, Fat produced a couple of bar towels. I took one and wrapped it around the kid's neck.

'Here,' I said to him, taking his hand and making him hold

the towel on his throat. 'Just hold that there for a little while. You'll be OK. Although you might not talk so good for a while.'

I turned to the one with the head injury. He was a mess. Fat got another towel and gave it to that kid.

'Put it to your head where it hurts,' he said very loudly to the kid.

The kid took the towel and then fell down hard on the floor.

'But seriously, what makes three perfectly nice neighborhood kids act in such a reckless fashion?' I asked Fat. 'These particular assailants, they've been in here before?'

'Oh, yeah,' he told me. 'Nearly every night.'

'Are they always this much trouble?'

'It's the times,' he told me, haplessly. 'In a world where Richard Nixon can get elected to a second term, anything rotten can happen. I believe that these youths got no hope.'

'Maybe not,' I said, staring at the pistol in my hand, 'but they've certainly got the fire power. This thing? Short recoil, rotary bolt – designed to give you a lot of power in a semi-automatic. The question I'm asking is less philosophical than your answer. I merely wonder why high school kids need this kind of artillery.'

'Oh.' That was all he said, and then he reached for the phone.

He dialed only three digits, and after a second he said into the receiver, 'It's Marty over at Pete's. Yes – again.'

He was silent for a moment, then looked at me and winked.

'Bar fight,' he said. 'Three high school kids. Two of them need an ambulance, I think. Nobody else in the place. It's closing time.'

I pocketed the AMP and headed for the door.

'No,' I heard Fat say as I touched the handle. 'Just them three. It's been a slow night. What? Yeah. Probably the weather.'

SIX

The weather was indeed something to make a person cranky. The chill in the air, the general dampness of all things, and, to be honest, the month – they all combined to make any citizen moody. Tourist season was long over, so the stores that depended on them were rarely open. This meant that the owners of these stores, and their employees, were beginning to wonder how far the wolf was from the door. It had always been my observation that when it was cold and wet, a lack of money was a double curse. I was certain that when April came, and it started getting warm and sunny, things would pick up, and the world wouldn't seem so glum. But not everyone shared my effervescent optimism.

I was, however, feeling a bit pinched by the clock. It was tough knowing that, if I didn't step up my inquiries and find a nice conclusion fairly soon, this would be a very unhappy story.

So I double-timed it back to the donut shop. By the time I arrived, it must have been nearly four in the morning. No one was evident in the shop, not even old Cass. But the door was open, so I let myself in.

'Cass?' I called out.

There was a grouchy kind of moan from the back, and Cass appeared through the doorway between the kitchen and the counter. She was scratching her arm and yawning. Her donut shop hat was askew.

'Why don't you go home, for God's sake,' she whined.

'I want to,' I agreed, 'but first I've got to find a baby – and also Lou, as it happens. I have to find Lou Yahola.'

'What for?' she mumbled.

'Do you know where he is or not.'

'I already told you,' she groused. 'I think he went home drunk or something.'

I shifted my weight to one side. 'Is there any chance that you'll tell me where he lives?'

'Do I know?' she shrugged and headed back into the kitchen.

'What are you doing back there?' I called after her.

'I'm trying to catch forty winks before the breakfast crowd, if you don't mind.' Her voice was already dusted with sleep.

I took the liberty of slipping quietly behind the counter. I rummaged around in a space underneath the register and, after finding a knife the size of a broadsword and a club that could kill a horse, I found a hand-printed piece of paper that said *Contack Sheet*. I took that to be a misspelling, since it had Cass's name on it. There was also a phone number on it, followed by several other such entries, including one for *emergensees*. One of them said *Lou* and gave a phone number.

I reached for the phone behind the counter and dialed.

The phone at the other end rang at least ten times. I stopped counting after that because I was fixing myself a bit of coffee while I waited.

By and by, the phone made a very harsh sound and a voice said, 'What the hell?'

'Lou,' I answered quickly, 'it's Foggy. I hate to wake you, but there's trouble, and you're in it.'

I figured this was a way to keep him from hanging up.

'Trouble?' he sniffed.

'I have to come over right now,' I said, even more urgently. 'Where's your place?'

'Now?'

'Lou, would I be awake at this hour of the night if it wasn't a matter of life or death?'

'Life or death, huh,' he said, but he sounded suspicious. 'Well. Then I guess you better come over.'

'Where?'

'Baker,' he answered. 'Top floor, number seven, on the right, but the number ain't on the door. You gotta count. This is about Maggie Redhawk, right?'

What I said to that was, 'Um.'

'Right. Come on.' And he hung up without further discourse.

Baker Street was close by, but it was really more of an alley than an actual street. It got its name because it was at the back end of what used to be a large bakery in Fry's Bay. It went out of business after WWII and the building had been entirely abandoned since 1952. Kids hung out there sometimes, mostly for nefarious purposes, though they were relatively harmless. Most of the real crime in Fry's Bay happened in less obvious places.

I shivered a little as I hit the narrow part of Baker, and picked up my pace getting to the only resident establishment in the area, a building that had the word *Bread* on it. The word was in big faded red letters, but some angst-ridden poet had filled in the *B* with black paint so that it more resembled a *D* making the name of the building *Dread*. I assumed they did it because it was harder to turn the word *Bread* into the word *Lonely*.

I was inside the hallway shortly, and it was no better than being out of doors. It was just as cold and nearly as damp. It was a short hall with nothing in it but a long stairway up. I couldn't even tell what color it was because the lighting was so bad.

I ascended the stairs as quickly as I was able, but my legs were complaining about the lateness of the hour all the way up.

At the top of the stairs, I found a slightly longer hallway, and it had doors. There were eight. I assumed that the last one on the right was number seven, as per Lou's invective, and I trundled in that direction.

Before I got there, Lou flung open his door and stepped into the hall. He was in a T-shirt, plaid boxer shorts, and thick grey athletic socks. And there was also a small silver pistol in his left hand.

The pistol was not particularly pointed at me, but the fact that he had one at all gave me pause.

'Foggy.' He said nothing more.

'Lou,' I told him, 'you have a pistol in your hand. Everyone wants to point a gun at me tonight. Before midnight it must have been several years since I even saw a gun. Now, tonight, I've already seen two.'

'Well,' Lou responded, 'it's that time of year. You know, *Valentimes.*'

That's how he pronounced the word.

'Yes,' I agreed, 'this is a particularly depressing season. Still. Do you really need the gun?'

He didn't move from his place. 'Depends,' he said.

'On what?' I wanted to know.

'What is it that wakes me up out of a sound drunk at this time of night?' He shifted his weight. 'You said it's life or death, but whose life? Or, more importantly, what death?'

'You know about Lynette Baker.'

'She's not dead,' he said right back. 'She had a baby. She's in the hospital.'

'Alas, she is not. I've just been in the hospital.' I shoved my hand into my coat pocket, partly to appear nonchalant, partly to feel the somewhat larger pistol I had there, just in case.

'That's what I thought.' He sighed. 'That damned Maggie.'

'Look, Lynette took her baby away from the hospital, and the baby needs medicine, like, now. That's the death I mentioned.'

'Oh.' Lou looked confused.

'So I'm in kind of a hurry.'

'Sometimes I forget that you're legit.' He rubbed his eyes. 'I mean, I've known a few shady characters, and you seem more like a crook than a cop.'

'Currently,' I explained, 'I'm not either one. I'm just looking for Lynette Baker.'

'And her baby.'

'And, more importantly, her baby,' I concurred.

Lou sighed very heavily. I couldn't tell what he was thinking, but his little silver pistol was on my mind. I saw in his face a couple of hundred nights just like this one; he was drunk, someone was pestering him, he was trying to figure what to do. A junkie only wanted dope at that time of night. A drunk usually wanted trouble. To prove that point, Lou raised his little silver pistol and aimed it right at my head.

'The problem is,' he told me, in a worried kind of voice, 'that you have no idea what you're getting into.'

'I don't?' I moved my hand very slowly in my pocket, but all the while I was thinking, *Is my gun loaded? Did I switch on the safety? Does it have a problem of any sort, such as a pull to the left or right, which could be very irritating?*

'No, Foggy,' he assured me in a very sober-sounding manner, 'you don't.'

'Well then,' I said reasonably, 'I won't get into anything. All I want is the kid. And I don't even really want that. I just want to see that the kid gets medicine and doesn't die. If the kid dies, Lynette is in for a bad time and I'm in for loads of paperwork, which I hate. Whatever else it is that I might have stumbled into, I don't care. You're a murderer, you're a slaver, you're Satan, I don't care. Mazel tov, seriously. Here's the deal: kid plus medicine equals me disappearing, right? So come on.'

He hesitated. That was good.

'No,' he said very slowly, 'I'll get into a world of crap.'

'I see.' He was obviously on the horns of a dilemma. 'So how about this, I'll just tell you what I know, anything that comes into my head, and then maybe you'll want to tell me something. How would that be?'

'I–I don't know what you're saying.' But he lowered the pistol. 'I don't see how that will help.'

'Well,' I allowed, 'maybe it won't. But sometimes I get lucky. So here I go. Lynette went to the hospital a few days ago after she had a baby. They gave her morphine for the pain, which was fine by her. Sadly, the baby's sick, so they had to keep everyone in the hospital for a while. Lynette began to ask for the morphine but since she was out of the woods in the baby-having department, they nixed the dope. So she grabbed the kid, skated away from the hospital, and went straight to Jody. My feeling is that you know Jody. Lynette bought stuff from Jody and shot up, which then made her want a donut. How am I doing so far?'

Lou's shoulders slumped. I took this as a sign that my nimble guesswork had been at least partially accurate. And there it was again: the luck.

'But the baby was wailing. Lynette, by this time, was in a very calm state, but she could still tell there was something wrong with her newborn tyke.'

Lou's eyes darted for a split second into his apartment, and I realized that I was something of an idiot.

'Wait,' I said, 'I think I might have gotten my order of things wrong. She left the hospital, came to you, to the alley behind the donut shop, and asked you to keep the kid while she went to score because the kid was making such a racket. And now you have the baby, it's asleep or unconscious, and Lynette is solid gone.'

Lou looked up, and I was very surprised to see tears in his eyes.

'I can't wake the little thing up,' he said, and I could tell that he was about to blubber like Baby Huey.

'Let's have a look.' I moved so quickly that he was startled, which was bad. He twitched and his gun went off.

The gunshot from such a little piece was more like a firecracker than a firearm, but I was still momentarily taken aback. I checked for a second to see if I had any holes in my suit. I did not.

'Sorry,' he said, and he blushed. 'You want some coffee? You look tired.'

The gun had been pointed at the floor, and the floor had a nice hole in it.

'I could use a cup,' I told him. 'I've been up since dawn so I'm nearing the twenty-four-hour mark. I take a spoon of sugar.'

Lou turned and stumbled into his pad. I followed.

Of all the wrecks I had seen that particular evening, his place was the worst. It looked like someone was using his living room as a landfill. I could find no discernable furniture under the garbage, there was nothing on the walls, and he only had a single, crummy lamp for light. The lamp was made from an old bottle of Chianti, the kind with straw around the bottle.

Lou ambled toward the kitchen area; I stood my ground in the living area.

'Where's the kid, Lou?' I asked, sighing.

He shuffled my way and handed me the cup. I took it and drank half in one gulp. It burned my mouth a little, and it had way too much sugar, but I didn't care.

'Where's the kid?' I asked again.

He pointed with his pistol, like it was stuck to his hand.

'She's back there,' he said softly, and headed for what I could only imagine would be the bedroom.

I followed, and the bedroom was no better than the other room, except that I could see a bed. All around it there was a sea of papers and pizza boxes and items of clothing. The television was on with the sound way down low, and by the blue light of the screen I could see that Lou had cleared away a kind of halo in the middle of the bed around a very still baby.

I zipped over to the nipper and put my hand on its chest. There was a little tiny cricket of a heart still beating there, and I instantly figured the kid for a trouper. I looked up at Lou, and the tears were streaming down his face.

'Lynette said she'd be back in half an hour, but that was I don't know how long ago,' he managed to tell me between sobs.

'At the moment, I couldn't care less where she is,' I explained to Lou, scooping up the kid. 'She could drop dead, but I have to take this little thing back to the hospital.'

'I–I don't know,' Lou said. 'I promised Lynette I would keep it here.'

'Do you want it to die, Lou?' I said sharply. 'Is this what you want?'

'No, but you don't know what's what.'

'As I have already explained,' I shot right back, 'I don't care what's what. Out of my way.'

'No,' he said hesitantly, 'I don't think I can do that.'

Suddenly the little silver pistol was right in my face, and me with an arm full of baby.

'Put it down, Foggy.'

'It's going to die, Lou,' I told him, in no uncertain terms.

'Put it down, and go get its medicine. That's what to do. You put it down, and I'll stay right here, and you nip over to the hospital, get a can of the medicine or whatever, and zip back here. That's what to do.'

He was shaking a little. Maybe he was cold, or maybe it was the DTs.

'OK,' I agreed. 'Good idea. That's just what I'll do.'

I set the baby back down in its halo. It didn't move a whisker. I straightened up, shook my head, and turned around.

'Lou,' I said, looking straight into his eyes, 'I like you. You make a nice donut, you're apparently something of a good guy, and I know you're trying to do the right thing.'

He nodded. 'I am.'

'So I'm sorry.'

'Sorry about what?' he asked me.

I took a deep breath. With the back of my hand I slapped the pistol out of his fist. It clattered against the wall and went off again. I produced my gun, the gun I got off the kid in the pool hall, and, sure enough, the safety was never on in the first place. I put the gun next to Lou's kneecap and squeezed the trigger. The gun made a very loud noise and, a split second later, so did Lou.

There was blood and gunpowder on my pants, and a pretty uncomfortable mess all over Lou's leg. Before he could stop screaming, I hit him in the side of the head with the butt of my gun. I bopped him pretty hard, but it only startled him. He stopped screaming and looked right at me. He had a kind of *Why did you do that?* question in his eyes. I popped him again harder, and those eyes rolled back. He dropped to the floor of his bedroom on top of a mountain of dirty clothes.

I put the gun back in my pocket and grabbed up a sweater from right where Lou was lying. I wrapped it around his bad knee real tight. Then I rummaged a bit to find a pair of pants, and used those to do the same thing over the sweater. This was not my first time performing such an act, so it only took twenty or thirty seconds.

I hopped right up, turned around, scooped up the kid again, and spied a phone by the bed.

In a flash I dialed the direct number for Maggie Redhawk at her nurse's desk. It took a minute, but she answered.

'Maggie—' she began.

'I got the kid,' I interrupted her. 'I'm coming right now. It's not moving, but it's still got a heartbeat. And send an ambulance right away to the apartments on Baker, top floor. I'll leave the door open. Lou Yahola's bleeding bad.'

'Foggy?' she said, a little slow on the uptake.

'I'm coming right now,' I said again. 'Have the medicine ready, OK?'

I hung up before she could answer.

SEVEN

I ran like a football player over the wet streets, only I was carrying a comatose baby in my arms instead of a pigskin. I felt like I was in a dream. The lights were vague, the moon had gone behind clouds, the air was cold and damp as a crypt.

After a couple of blocks I could hear a rattle in my throat, and I was wheezing like a broken concertina. I couldn't figure why I was so winded, or why the street seemed like an appealing bed.

Another turn and I could see the lights of the hospital. I was completely done in, and I couldn't see straight. I squeezed my eyes shut to try and clear the cotton balls out of my head. I thought maybe I could manage to yell before I went down, and someone from the emergency dock might hear me. Maybe.

Somehow, I kept running. I could hear the clop of my Florsheims on the pavement. In the distance, the noise of the hospital was beginning to get clearer. Then, like a lighthouse keeper or a sea captain's widow, there was Nurse Maggie Redhawk. She was standing at the double doors of the emergency entrance, and she was barking out orders. I couldn't hear exactly what she was saying, but for some reason that gave me the extra juice to kick into the last few yards and, before I knew it, I was handing over the little package of baby to a gaggle of medical personnel.

Maggie and I managed a bit of eye contact, just before I sank into the Dead Sea.

By the time I swam back to the surface, it was day. I was lying on a gurney near the nurses' station and the light was killing me. I was covered up with a sheet, but it wasn't over my face so I figured I wasn't dead.

I sat up. I couldn't understand why I had passed out, or stayed out for so long. And the worst of it was that I felt like I had a hangover, only without the benefit of having had a nice evening before.

I threw my legs over the side of the gurney and noticed, with no small bit of pique, that I had torn the right knee of my pants. As I was running my index finger over it, I heard a familiar, if unusually agitated, voice.

'Who do you think you are?'

I turned my head in the direction of the question and realized that my neck was stiff as a statue.

'This is a question?' I asked her back.

Maggie Redhawk appeared at my side with a hypodermic in one hand and a little white paper cup filled with pills in the other.

'No, I mean,' she said, clearly angry, 'who do you think you are?'

'Should I check my wallet?'

'You can't run around all hours, get in a fight, shoot a guy, and run five blocks in the cold and damp,' she growled. 'Not at your age!'

'My age?' I looked around, imploring strangers. 'Why is everyone talking about my age? I'm not even forty!'

'But you're supposed to be an adult,' Maggie said.

'And anyway, how would you know I got into a fight?'

'It's a very small town, Igmo, and I'm a very large girl.' This was her explanation, given to me whilst she was shoving the sleeves of my suit coat and shirt up, and sticking me with the needle.

'What's that?' I asked. 'What are you shooting me with?'

'It's a B-12,' she said. 'You'll feel better. I already gave you an antibiotic and a pain shot.'

'That's why I slept?'

'No,' she said. 'You slept because somebody gave you enough tranquilizer to knock out Secretariat. I think it was Seconal.'

So Lou gave me more than sugar in my coffee.

'Seconal? You gave me a blood test?'

'You're not really the type to faint like a girl,' she said, without the slightest hint of humor. 'And I smelled red cedar on your breath. You eat a closet last night?'

'Seconal smells like cedar?'

She finally looked me in the eye. 'I got lucky. It was a guess.'

'Well, sometimes a person can get lucky,' I agreed. 'So what time is it?'

'After noon, just barely.'

'What're these pills?' I took the little paper cup from her fingertips.

'You have to know everything?'

She wiped off the place where she gave me the shot, and my sleeves fell back into place.

'I just don't want to feel out of it all day,' I told her. 'I have a hair appointment.'

She glanced at my pate. 'Seriously? That hair? Take the damn pills.'

'All right,' I acquiesced, 'but I have stuff to do today.'

I popped back the pills without water and swallowed.

'Such as?' she wanted to know.

'Such as where is Lynette Baker?' I ran my hand through my hair in an attempt to make it look less like a bird's nest.

'Why do you care?' Maggie said in a much softer voice than she had been using. 'You saved the baby. That was your job. Go home. Christ.'

'The baby's OK?'

Maggie shrugged. 'The baby's alive. Which she wouldn't be if you hadn't got her here. The fact is, things don't look that great for the long term. The kid was unconscious for a while, probably has some brain damage – I mean, on top of whatever other problems she's got thanks to having been born with heroin in her blood.'

'Well.' I hopped down off the gurney and straightened my clothes. 'This is why I want to find Lynette Baker. I'd like to pop her in the head first, and then I'd like to see can I help her out of the hole she's in.'

'I see.' Maggie sounded highly suspicious. 'You're a Samaritan.'

'In fact,' I retorted, 'I am more Sephardic, but that has very little to do with my quest. I have paperwork, and I have a boss, and I wish to get both off my back as soon as possible.'

'You should go home and sleep.' Now she sounded weird not mad anymore – something else.

'I just slept, Maggie,' I said, lowering my voice. 'What's up?

'What do you mean?' She wouldn't look me in the eye.

'I mean, why don't you want me to find Lynette Baker? Last night—'

'Last night,' she whispered, 'I wanted you to find the baby. I'm the nurse in charge. You think you're the only one with a boss and paperwork? That's all there is to it. You found the baby. Job well done. The rest of it . . .'

I looked around. I took a breath. This is what some people will tell you when you're about to do something stupid: count to ten or take a deep breath. You'll keep yourself from saying something you could regret. So I changed my tack.

'How's our friend Lou Yahola?' I asked her calmly.

'How do I know?' She was really straining to avoid eye contact at this point. 'He's gone.'

'He's not here? He got shot. He really ought to be, you know, in the hospital.'

'He was here,' she said, so soft I could hardly hear. 'He was treated in emergency and then he left.'

'He left?' I asked her. 'I shot his knee. He couldn't walk.'

'Someone came to get him.' She started to leave.

I took her arm. 'Who came to get him, Maggie?'

'Tribal Council,' she said, squirming out of my grasp. 'He's in the swamp somewhere – holed up. He's gone, Foggy. They have Lynette too. I shouldn't have told you anything. Forget it. That's your best bet. Go home, and I mean it.'

She moved very quickly back to the nurses' station and busied herself with something or other right away. I could tell by looking at her that I wouldn't get anything more on the subject. Maybe not ever.

EIGHT

S o, as I walked out of the hospital on a mild day in February, I had to wonder why the Tribal Council of the Seminole Nation would be interested in a pregnant junkie and a donut cook. It made no sense. I continued to think that it made no sense all the way back to my office. So, when I walked through the main door, I must have had a look on my face that betrayed my quizzicality. I knew this because Sharon, the aforementioned boss, got a look at me and stood up behind her desk.

'Foggy?' she says. 'What the hell's the matter with you?'

'Why do you ask?'

'You look like you can't remember your name, your suit's torn, and you're a mess. You ought to be at home in bed.'

I lumbered into her office. It wasn't that much different from mine, only in slightly better order. She had pictures on the walls: a sunset over the sea and a big turtle swimming under water. Sharon herself was forty or so, dressed in the only thing she ever wore: a smart charcoal gray woman's suit, a starched white blouse, and expensive black flats. Her hair was up on top of her head a little like a bubbling fountain. God only knew what held it in place that way.

'Well,' I admitted, 'I am a bit puzzled, since you asked.'

I took a seat in one of the two ratty chairs opposite her desk.

'What's going on in that troubled brain?' she wanted to know. 'I hear from my sources that you had quite a night. You stabbed a kid in the throat, shot a drunk in the knee, ran ten blocks, passed out, and still managed to save the kid. Thank God nobody had any kryptonite.'

I had long since stopped wondering how Sharon knew the things that Sharon knew. Her *sources* were, in my estimation, most likely from the nefarious underbelly of our little hamlet. The thing was, she always knew things, and she was always right. So I always told her everything, because I figured she'd find out anyway.

'I have a few troubling questions on my mind,' I said, as I bit my upper lip.

'Such as?'

'Such as: A: Why did three teenaged hooligans menace me at Pete's? B: Why did Lou Yahola pickle me with Seconal? And most of all C: Why did the Seminole Tribal Council abscond with the very wounded Lou Yahola and, even more surprisingly, a recently pregnant Lynette Baker?'

She leaned back in her chair. It creaked like a haunted house. 'That's a mouthful.'

'And I just hit the high points. Why did Maggie Redhawk want me to leave it all alone? Why was young Lynette Baker so anxious to get out of the hospital once she had her baby? I mean, the tyke was barely conscious and Lynette was still messed up. It had to be against whatever better judgment she had left. I mean, what is she so scared of that leaving the hospital in her condition, with a very sick newborn, seemed like the best idea?'

'You mistake her for someone in her right mind,' Sharon suggested. 'She's a junkie. She just wanted dope.'

'That's what I thought at first, but now maybe I think she was scared. Scared out of her wits.'

'You could smell it, I guess.' Sharon knew me. She sighed very dramatically before she said to me, 'What are you going to do about it?'

'I mean to find out what's going on,' I answered, leaning forward to stand up. 'Don't you think? On the clock?'

'Well,' she told me, looking straight into my eyes, 'that seems to be who we are. You really ought to go home and forget about this and go to bed. But you have to do what you have to do, so do it.'

'Thanks, Sharon,' I said, and I meant it.

I was up and out the door before she could change her mind.

I headed back over to the hospital first, but I knew I had to be careful what I did there. Something bad was up with Maggie, so I had to play the whole thing a little carefully.

I did my best to saunter into the emergency room. It didn't take. The second Maggie saw me, her face clouded up.

'Foggy,' she began, really irritated. 'Didn't I just get rid of you?'

'What? I want to talk to the kid who jumped me last night at Pete's. The one with the fork wound in his neck. I just want to make sure he's OK.'

'You just want to make sure he's OK,' she repeated, only with the sarcasm dialed way up.

'I got a conscience,' I told her.

She didn't seem to believe me.

'I assume that the kid is here,' I stood my ground, 'and not off hiding in the swamp with Lou and Lynette.'

'He's here.' Her face was made of granite. 'Fat didn't mention that you were the one who jabbed the moron, though.'

I raised my hand. 'That was me.'

'He said the kids was in a fight, and he broke it up,' she sneered. 'You guys should really get your story together, just in case the local constabulary wants to know.'

'They've been here?' I asked as casually as I could manage to. 'The cops?'

'Oh, yes. Deputy Rodney and that other idiot.' She let that sink in before she said, 'But they're gone now.'

I tried not to let out my breath too loud. I was, in general, wary of law enforcement in any form.

'So can I see the kid with the bad neck?' I asked.

'No.'

'Can I see the baby that I saved last night, at least?'

'What do you want to do that for, seriously?' she had to know.

'I saved a baby, for God's sake,' I snapped back. 'How often does a guy like me do that?'

'I guess,' she allowed, begrudgingly.

'Look, you said earlier,' I told her, attempting to get on her good side, 'that the little guy's got problems.'

'Little girl, but yes,' she told me.

'Little girl,' I acknowledged. 'So, what problems?'

'Well,' she said, a little more seriously, 'like a lot of these girls who use heroin when they're pregnant, Lynette had a premature rupture of the membranes.'

'I don't know what that means,' I admitted.

'The bag of water that holds the fetus broke too soon,' she said flatly.

'There's a bag of water that holds the fetus?' I repeated, because I didn't quite believe it.

'Yes, dumbass.'

'First you call me an igmo, then you call me a dumbass,' I said, 'but this is the first time I have ever heard about a bag of water around a baby. How did the little guy breathe?'

'Little *girl*,' she insisted.

'Did I have a bag of water when I was a baby?'

'Yes.' She was very impatient with me by this point in the conversation.

'So how did I breathe, I'm asking.'

'You didn't,' she told me. 'You had water in your lungs. You got oxygen from your mother – assuming you had one.'

'So you're saying that I was, like, a fish before I was born?' I asked her. 'I had water in my lungs?'

'You weren't like a fish, but you lived in water for nine months,' she said.

'How is that possible?'

'It's the miracle of life,' she said, more irritated than ever. 'Do you want to see the teenager you stabbed in the neck or not?'

And that was the point of my sojourn into the miracle of life. It was a diversionary tactic to get her riled so that she would want to get rid of me, and also in order that she wouldn't think I was too interested in anything about Lynette Baker. But it was, nonetheless, an interesting diversion.

'OK,' I answered. 'If you say so, I'll look at the troubled teen.'

She hiked her thumb in a sort of obscene way, pointing down the hall. 'He's in room A-Eleven.'

'A-Eleven,' I repeated.

She softened. 'And then, if you want, you can go on down the hall – that's where the neonatal care is.'

I smiled, I nodded, and I was off.

The hallway smelled like rotten meat and hairspray. I tried not to think about what that would mean.

I veered gently into Room A-11, and there was the kid with the bandage on his neck, sleeping.

I stood at the foot of his bed and looked at him for a second. Asleep, he looked like he was about ten years old.

I kicked the leg of his metal bed really hard, and he woke up.

He saw me and tried to sit up. Sitting up hurt, so he went back down.

'What?' But that was all he could say, and it barely sounded human.

'You jumped me last night,' I said softly, 'and all I want to know is why.'

He closed his eyes.

I kicked the bed again, only even harder than before.

He jumped, and his eyes flew open wide.

'You get to be in this nice clean hospital bed thanks to me,' I explained to him, 'while the rest of your little youth gang languishes in jail. So, you're welcome.'

He tried to talk again, but he just couldn't.

'You see that you're really messed up,' I continued, 'whereas I am not only in the pink, but also not going to jail later on. So you realize that you're in trouble and I'm not. Next you realize that I can do almost anything to you and get away with it. So you can save yourself some real pain by just telling me why you and the Hardy Boys menaced me last night. Just a quick couple of sentences, and I'm gone, like a ghost. Right?'

He took a moment to think. I could see that he was unaccustomed to the process. But in the end, self-preservation triumphed. He reached for a pad and pencil that someone had placed on the nightstand beside his bed. He scribbled, then set the pad down on his chest and closed his eyes, like the entire effort was too much for him.

I stepped around the side of the bed and glanced down at the pad. It said, 'Jody called. Told us to hurt you.'

I nudged his arm. He moaned and opened his eyes again.

'Why?' I asked.

He struggled for the pad, and then wrote another couple of words.

The words were, 'For dope.'

'No,' I said very patiently, 'not what was your payment. Why did she *want* you to do it?'

He wrote, 'Protect Lynette.'

'From what?'

'Water,' he wrote, and he tried to write more, but a shadow in the doorway of his room seemed to stop him.

I turned around, and there was Maggie Redhawk, chart in hand, smiling a smile that I wouldn't wish on the last cop who arrested me.

'I figured out what you did,' she said. 'It took me a second, but I got it.'

'Got what?' I asked innocently.

'You put a trick whammy on me. You distracted me, and I let you come see this menace to society.'

'I just wanted to see was he getting the proper care and feeding,' I said.

'Uh huh. So, see?' she said, trying to be casual. 'He's fine.'

I turned to the kid. 'You're fine?'

He closed his eyes.

'He's not going to be able to speak properly for a while,' Maggie continued, fussing into the room, adjusting things like sheets and pillows and the bottle of fluid that went into the kid's arm. 'And when he gets out of here, he's going to jail.'

'Fat is a fairly unforgiving sort,' I said, sympathetically. 'It's really best not to start anything in his place.'

The kid never opened his eyes, and I thought maybe he was asleep.

'So,' I said to Maggie. 'Can I see the baby now? The baby whose life I saved?'

She shook her head like she was fed up with me, but she motioned for me to follow her.

Down another creepy hall where one of the florescent tubes was out, I could feel the anxiety as clearly as I could hear the padding of Maggie's hospital shoes. I couldn't tell if it was coming from her or the general air of the hospital. Then it occurred to me that a place can hold on to the things that happen in it. Not exactly like a haunted house, more like an echo. Just because you can't hear the echo any more doesn't mean that the molecules of every sob or sigh or wince of pain don't hang around in a hospital hall, bouncing back and forth off the grungy paint and the scuffed-up floors. This, I thought, was the anxiety I was sensing. With a capital A.

I turned a corner, however, and got a whole new level of horror. I saw big windows along one side of the new hallway, and behind those windows I saw tiny little babies, all of them hooked up to machines like something out of a science fiction movie. It really got to me. There were five infant creatures, all of them looking like elf remnants. The lighting was low, and the place was quiet as a crypt. I had kind of expected at least one of the things to be crying.

'They all look like some sort of horrible experiment,' I mumbled to Maggie.

'It's a little like hell, yes.'

'These little muffins,' I said, trying to whisper, 'are they all – what? Premature? Sick? Junkie babies?'

'All sorts of weird problems,' she told me. 'One of them was born with omphalocele.'

'What's that?'

'Born with a lot of the organs on the outside of the body,' she said.

'What the hell?' My voice was a little louder than it should have been. 'Organs on the outside? Like, what organs?'

'Intestines, liver, spleen, that sort of thing.'

'Why the hell would you tell me something like that?' I stared in at the babies. 'How am I supposed to sleep tonight?'

'You asked.'

I stood still for a second, but my mind was roaring around like a rocket.

'I admit it,' I told her. 'This gives me no small amount of trouble in my mind.'

'What I do,' Maggie said, a little sweeter than before, 'is try to think about one thing at a time. If I think about all the awful crap I got to do just today, I could go nuts. So, for instance, right this second I'm showing a guy the neonatal care unit.'

I took quite a deep breath.

'So, which one is my kid?' I asked her.

She looked for a second and said, 'See the one with the red bandana close to her head? That's her.'

I saw the one she meant.

'Where did she get the bandana?' I asked.

'Don't know for sure,' Maggie said stiffly, 'but it looks like the one Lynette Baker had around her wrist at some point.'

'So, wait, does that mean Lynette saw the kid since I brought it back here?'

'No. It's probably something she left with Lou Yahola,' she

suggested, 'and it was just in the bundle you scooped up, right?'

I didn't answer.

NINE

I left the hospital wondering why Jody the drug dealer would care so much about Lynette? Enough that she'd call down hooligans to rain on my parade? And that was just one of my questions. They were beginning to pile up.

Here are the questions, in chronological order, as they affected me: First, why did Lynette abscond from the hospital with a sickly newborn? Second, why did Jody send me to Pete's Billiard Emporium to be menaced by teenagers? Third, why did Lou Yahola dose me with Seconal? Fourth, why did the Seminole Tribal Council want Lynette and Lou? Fifth, why did Maggie Redhawk care so much about getting the baby and then care not at all about anything else? In fact, sixth, why did she advise me to leave off in general?

The sun was still high in the sky and doing its best to warm up the sidewalk, but the cold wind off the ocean was putting up quite a fight. I shivered a little, but maybe, I considered, I was hungry again. When I didn't sleep, I got hungry like crazy.

Now in Fry's Bay, the real place to eat, for my money, was Yudda's Crab Palace.

Yudda's was only a five-minute walk from the hospital. You just had to head toward the docks and, before you knew it, you could smell the barbecue, fresh fish, and salt water.

I liked Yudda because he had an eclectic palate. He had a tuna wrapped in wet seaweed, dredged in flour, then dipped in egg, and finally covered with white cornmeal. He deep fried this and called it, right on the menu, 'Southern Fried Sushi.' And while I believe that this insulted both of the cultures it evoked, it was also delicious beyond compare. Especially with the honey mustard and soy dipping sauce. But Yudda was always trying something new. The grilled zucchini in deviled crab was a disaster. The golden skate wing stuffed with grits was delectable. It was about fifty-fifty on the culinary front, which was fine by me as long as you knew which fifty to eat and which to leave alone.

This particular day was a Thursday, and Thursday was always monkfish. Now, if the monkfish was fresh, it was better than lobster, but if it was old it was worse than garbage.

I always steered clear of the monkfish.

Within minutes I was in Yudda's place, these various food items still on my mind. The slant of sunlight through the diner window gave the whole place a kind of cathedral-like ambience, even thought it was only the size of a railroad car. There were five booths, five tables, and five seats at a kind of bar. Everything was wood that Yudda had salvaged a long time ago from God-knows-where. The smell inside was like you were in the middle of an old barbecue oven. The ceiling was only the underside of the ancient rusted tin roof.

The great man himself was standing at the door, a cup filled with Brunswick stew in one hand, and a thermos of martinis in the other. Beside him was Myrna, his sometimes girlfriend, sipping from a paper cup.

Now, Yudda did not have a liquor license but, if you brought your own into his place, he wasn't going to stop you from drinking it.

'Jesus, Foggy,' Yudda said to me as I took a seat at the first booth beside the door. 'You're supposed to be dead.'

I took this very well, I thought. I said, 'You see, news travels fast when it is both bad *and* wrong. I'm not dead.'

'OK.' Yudda lumbered over. 'But somebody told me that you got poisoned by Lou Yahola, and then he shot you. They said you died in the street, and now Lou is dead or hiding out in the swamp.'

'Who told you this?' I asked. 'I find this amusing. In fact, I did get poisoned, but I shot Lou, not the other way around. He's not dead either, by the way. But we both had a rough night.'

Myrna wiped her hands on the dirty yellow apron she was wearing and leaned forward on the counter.

'You don't look so bad, considering,' she said. 'That's a nice suit, it's just a little beat up. Yudda didn't mention that we also heard you saved some baby from a fate worse than death; Lou Yahola's cooking.'

'Well,' I explained to them both, 'as it happens, I did save a baby – and nobody's dead. Although, I have been pronounced dead before, only not here in Florida. This was back home in Brooklyn. This is why I find it a little amusing that you should bring up the subject.'

'I assume that a story goes with that,' Myrna said.

Myrna was wise to me. I often came into Yudda's Crab Palace offering up the jive. Sometimes it was good for a drink. Every once in a while, I got a free meal out of it. I did it because it made me colorful, and I enjoyed being the interesting outsider from Brooklyn. It was really my only shot at participating in the community at all. I was a Yankee Jew Criminal, the only one of that kind in Fry's Bay. So, my only shot at being accepted by the locals was to take what made me different and turn that into what made me fascinating. This kind of understanding or insight into my own behavior was something I got from several years of Freudian analysis. I originally undertook such an endeavor to discover why I liked to steal cars, which I never figured out, but the entire enterprise did have some advantages.

'Now, where to begin?' I asked.

I stalled Yudda and Myrna in the telling of my story in order that they would be tantalized, which was something that often made a story better. Also I figured I might get my luncheon comped if I drew things out. It was always worth a shot.

Unfortunately, Yudda was way ahead of me.

'You're going to have the grilled shark steak with spicy steamed rice and purple slaw,' he said. 'It's the best we got today. Nothing's too good for a guy who saved a baby and came back from the dead.'

'So that's settled,' I said, sitting back in the booth.

Yudda took a seat at the bar facing me, and Myrna leaned on her elbows. Yudda set down his cup of stew, but took a healthy slug from the thermos of martini.

'All right,' he said. 'We're ready.'

'All right,' I told him, 'and stop me if I've told you part of this before, because it's a very long story and I wouldn't want to repeat anything.'

'Or tell us the whole thing in one sitting,' Yudda intoned, heavy-lidded. 'God forbid you should run out of material.'

'Do you want to hear how I got dead or not?' I asked.

'Tell,' Myrna said impatiently.

'Well,' I muttered, slumping down somewhat. 'I believe that I told you I was busted twice for car theft. Which, incidentally, was a very good percentage, considering how many fine automobiles I boosted in my youth. The first time—'

'Was a very nice rabbi who dropped the charges if you said some kind of prayer,' Myrna interrupted. 'Skip on down to the second time.'

'Second time,' I picked up immediately, 'was the kicker. I would rather not say what happened to get me nabbed, but nabbed I was. I was riding in the backseat of a cop car doing about seventy because the circumstances were dicey, and it was a very crummy night, with thunder and lightning and a blinding amount of rain. It was maybe three in the morning, and all of a sudden, out of nowhere, *wham*! A Buick the size of a bulldozer knocked the cop car into a roll. I mean, we rolled over maybe five, six times – I couldn't say exactly, because I passed out after the first few. Now, I have no idea what happened immediately after that, or what was up with the cops or the Buick, but here is what I can tell you: I was pronounced dead at the scene.'

'And you know this how?' Yudda asked me.

I leaned forward, my eyes drilling into his. 'Because I woke up in the morgue.'

Yudda's eyes widened. 'The morgue?'

'With my shoes off and a tag on my toe!'

'Holy crap,' Myrna whispered.

'In a normal world, when a man like Foggy Moscowitz gets killed, he stays dead. But apparently, I had other options.'

'You woke up in the morgue?' Myrna had to repeat.

'Covered in blood.' I nodded. 'My leg was killing me. My vision was blurred, like I was under water. My hair was a mess. My recently laundered white shirt was torn. My nice blue silk tie was bloodstained. My new gabardine suit was a wreck. But I was alive.'

'Unbelievable.' Yudda shook his head. 'Only you.'

'I squeezed my eyes shut, see, thinking maybe I was dreaming.

I was hoping the place would somehow turn into my room at the Magellan Inn. When that didn't happen, I sat up to take my first real look around the joint. It was dark and cold.'

'Naturally,' Yudda said.

'There wasn't much to the room,' I went on. 'Three tables side-by-side. I was on the middle one. The walls were painted some sort of industrial green, the kind of color that was supposed to be soothing and cheerful but only ended up being depressing.'

'Most of the customers there in the morgue,' Yudda said to me, 'what do they care about the color of the walls?'

'I agree,' I said.

'So come on, what happened next?' Myrna's voice was impatient.

'What do you think?' I asked. 'I hobbled my ass over to the double doors, leaned hard, popped the dead bolt, and stumbled into the night.'

'And Foggy Moscowitz,' Myrna said, clasping her hands aside her face, 'was born again.'

'In the non-Christian sense,' I assured her.

'But here you are,' she said.

Yudda took another swig from his thermos. 'You got a line of crap that could reach all the way to Europe, you know that? That what brought you to Florida?'

'Well, a couple of other things happened after that,' I declared, 'but that was the beginning of the story, yes. Swear to God.'

'OK,' he told me, hefting himself off the barstool, 'but you'll pardon me if I don't stand anywhere near you in a thunderstorm.'

Myrna brought my luncheon and silence prevailed in Yudda's Crab Palace for the ensuing twenty minutes.

TEN

When my meal settled, and a good meal it was, I decided that it might be best to retrace my steps from the previous night, which I hated doing. I liked to move forward. I had always found that, when you moved back, you were liable to bump into something you'd rather forget about. But there didn't seem to be much else to do.

So I offered to pay Yudda, just for show. He made the mildest of protestations. I quickly acquiesced, before he could change his mind, and I was out the door with my wallet safely in my pocket.

Despite my better judgment, I headed toward the apartment of Jody the pusher.

It was a sunny day, and the gloom of the previous night seemed to be lifting. It was even warming up. Somewhere in the air there was a hint of spring, which came early in Florida, I learned. In the part of Brooklyn where I was from, you could wait until June for a warm day. Maybe it was that way all over Brooklyn, I wouldn't know. I stuck pretty close to the neighborhood whenever I was there. But in Fry's Bay, it might be nice by the end of February. This was a reason that a great many people from Brooklyn wanted to come to Florida, though it was not my primary motivation.

At any rate, I ended up at Jody's door. I checked my watch and discovered that it was after one o'clock in the afternoon. I thought she might be up. I knocked on the door, and heard cursing and stumbling from inside the apartment. Then I heard what sounded very much like the click of a handgun. I felt in my pocket, like a reflex, only to discover that the pistol I'd pulled off the kid in Pete's was no longer with me. I decided that I would worry about that later. At that moment, I only stepped away from the door, a little to the side. I thought I would not present a perfect target should anything happen to go off.

'Jody?' I sang out, nice as you please. 'It's Foggy. From last night. Remember?'

'Who?' she mumbled.

'You know,' I reminded her, 'I brought you donuts? And then you tried to have me beat up over at Pete's?'

Jody did not make a sound.

'Jody, believe me,' I told her, 'I never carry a grudge. So you can put away the gun that I heard and we can just talk. Leave the door closed if you want to. Closed and locked. I only want to ask you a couple of questions.'

'Why would I want to talk to you?' I could hear that she was irate, although I couldn't figure why.

'Because I'm trying to help Lynette,' I said, 'same as you.'

'Help Lynette,' she repeats. 'That's a laugh. Since when did *my people* ever get any good out of the kind of help *you people* talk about?'

'*You people*?' I asked, incredulously. 'Just who do you think I am?'

'Listen, dickweed,' she growled. 'My father was a soldier in the army, a deserter from Korea, locked up in the Columbus stockade. He escaped and got as far as our swamp. He almost died, see? But he was found by a Seminole woman, my mother, who took him in, nursed him back, saved his life. And what do you think was her reward? He knocked her up, slapped her around, and took off. I never saw his face. This, to me, is the perfect example of the relationship between your people and mine.'

'Hang on, sister,' I snapped back. 'I don't know who you think I am, but *my people* were slaves before *your people* even existed. You got a bad couple hundred years with the white man? Try five thousand! That's what we got, first with the pharaohs, then the Cossacks, then the Nazis, and then somebody killed Lenny Bruce! We can't even have Lenny Bruce!'

'Who?' She was nearly screaming.

'Doesn't matter!' I matched her volume level. 'The point is, I am not *your people!*'

'Says you!' And she fired her little pistol right through the door.

If I had not been standing slightly to the side, the bullet would have gone right through me. As it was, the bullet kept on going until it got to the opposite wall in the hallway.

I decided to keep still and see what she would do. I noticed that no one stirred from any other apartment; no one called out, no disturbance of any sort presented itself. As the seconds ticked by in silence, I came to the conclusion that a little gunfire in the middle of the day might not be such a rare occurrence in the place. I took a closer gander at the smeared, battered wall where Jody's bullet had come to rest and, sure enough, there were maybe three other holes like the one she had just made.

Then I heard strange noises in her apartment and realized that

Jody was absconding via some rear egress. That kicked me into high gear. I raced down the hall, out the door, and around the back of the building, in under ten seconds. But it was not fast enough. I surmised that the open window I saw was the one in her apartment, and the still-trembling fire escape was the means by which she had achieved the roof. Not the alley where I was standing. In short, Jody was gone.

I had a second or two in which to ponder this question: where was the gun that had been in my pocket – the one I had taken off the kid the previous evening at Pete's? And that brought up several other questions. For example, if the cops showed up at the hospital the previous evening the way Maggie Redhawk said they did, why was I not at least questioned by them? First I stabbed a guy in the neck, and then I shot a guy in the knee. This, under most ordinary circumstances, would provoke at least a curious question or two from the local constabulary. So I was forced to wonder: what gives?

ELEVEN

S ince I got no answers from Jody, I decided to continue my hapless re-creation of the previous night's events by taking myself to Pete's Billiard Emporium.

In the light of the afternoon, it did not look so good. Some things – old buildings, semi-romantic landscapes, certain faces – are always best left to moonlight. The old joint looked very much like a tired hooker asleep on a park bench in the warm afternoon sun. I considered coming back when the sun went down, but I saw Fat through the window and I figured I might as well go in.

The contrast between the light of day and the dark room was, for a second, blinding. I couldn't see a thing, but I heard Fat say, 'Foggy. Jesus. You had a night. Did you know some people are telling other people that you're dead?'

'So I heard,' I told him. 'How do you suppose such a rumor – so obviously untrue – gets started?'

'Well, I can tell you,' he said.

His image was coming into view as my eyes adjusted to the dim light at the bar. He was smiling.

I sat. 'By all means, and maybe a nice cup of coffee?'

'Absolutely,' he said.

He moved to the coffee machine, poured me a big white mug of mud, and zipped it across the bar to me like it was a beer. The cup turned – almost a pirouette – and the handle spun perfectly toward me so that I could pick it up and sip.

'You know the hooligans who were in here last night?' he asked me.

'I do. I have some questions about them, as a matter of fact.'

'I have some answers,' he said. 'But first let me tell you that they have friends.'

'Hard to believe.'

'Be that as it may,' Fat told me, 'the friends got wind of their little party here – don't ask me how – and, before you know it, some of these so-called friends were out and about, looking for you. Looking to even the score. And what do you think happened?'

'I couldn't tell you,' I admitted.

'One of these extracurricular cohorts saw you running like an idiot through the streets with a baby in your arms, and then this guy saw you tumble to the pavement, and he went back and told everyone that you dropped dead!'

'I'll be.' I sipped my coffee, which tasted terrible. 'But that's the way these rumors get started.'

'It is,' he agreed.

'About that,' I said, squirming a bit on my stool. 'Maggie Redhawk told me that you saved my bacon by telling the cops *you* were the one who stabbed the kid in the neck with a fork.'

Fat nods. 'You don't need any legal trouble, Foggy,' he said softly. 'I know what you been through. Besides, the cop who *investigated* was that moron Rodney Weaver. I would mess with him just on general principles.'

I sat there for a second trying to decide if I was grateful or suspicious, because I couldn't ever remember anyone lying to the police on my behalf – although it was widely known that Rodney Weaver was, in fact, a moron. I didn't have time to complete these thoughts because Fat started up again.

'You know the drug dealer Jody Boyd?'

'This is the first I heard her last name, but I do know her, only slightly.'

'She's the one who started the ruckus last night. She called those kids. They're kind of her, what would you say? Local distributors, I guess is how you'd put it.'

'They're in business with her?'

'A little. I think she gives them free dope in exchange for, like, a little legwork and some protection. They seem to like her.'

'Hmm,' I said, almost to myself. 'Look, you wouldn't know if those boys were Seminoles, would you?'

He looked at me like I was nuts. 'You didn't know that? Christ. Half the people around here are full or part Seminole. And the rest of us are from out of town. I don't think there's but ten people in Fry's Bay from the original white settlers.'

'Huh.' This seemed to me an appropriate response. 'So then I guess I shouldn't feel so much like an outsider.'

'You?' He shook his head. 'I don't know. White people take you for a Seminole, the Seminoles take you for white. You're a man without a country, brother.'

'Oh. Well, there you go.' I was only a little deflated. 'But to return to the point, those kids last night, *they're* Seminoles?'

'Yeah.'

'OK, so let me ask you this: what do you know about the Seminole Tribal Council?'

'You don't want to mess with them, I can tell you that.'

'Why?'

'The Seminoles are the only tribe in America that never signed a peace treaty with the U.S. government. Technically they're still at war.'

'OK, but about the Council,' I went on, because I was not at war with anybody that I knew of.

'Some time in the 1950s, the Seminole tribes got together a Tribal Council and a Board of Directors. This was after they already filed a claim to get back their land. They've been waiting for that for a while.'

'Get back their land?' I ask. 'How long have they been waiting?'

'Since 1947. They lost it in, you know, the 1800s.'

'Lost it to who?' I wondered.

'The government. The U.S. government.'

'Wait.' I tried to clear this up in my head. 'The government took their land? No, that can't be right.'

'I understand that this is exactly how *they* feel about it.'

'Oh.'

'The Tribal Council,' he said, 'these men are tough as cuss; they got the patience of Job and the guts of a Kamikaze.'

'Aside from the fact that you are mixing too many world cultures in one sentence, I get the picture.'

'No, you don't,' he told me. 'They live way back in the swamp. Don't nobody know what they do back there. You hear all kinds of things. And if you go in yourself? You get all eat up by an alligator the size of a Cadillac. Seriously.'

My eyes were completely adjusted to the light in the room by that point, and I could see that Fat had a worried look on his face.

'You're nervous about the fracas here last night,' I surmised, 'because you don't want trouble with the Council.'

'Bingo,' he told me, tapping three times on the bar.

'Well then I am doubly grateful to you,' I said, 'for taking the rap – for telling the policemen that you stabbed the kid.'

He shrugged, but did not look me in the eye.

And I was still suspicious because I thought that there was more to this than he was telling me. So I made a bold – or possibly foolish – play.

'Can I see the phone for a second, Fat?' I asked. 'I have to call the boss.'

He reached under the bar for it and plunked it down in front of me.

I dialed.

'Sharon? It's Foggy. Look, that business we discussed in your office? It does involve the Tribal Council. I'm wondering if someone can dig up a few names for me. You know, who to contact on the Council. Just so I can close up the file and give you that report you were asking me for.'

Sharon did not even bother to respond. She could tell I was making a play. How she could tell this was a mystery, and it fell under the heading of all the things I did not know about Sharon. But I knew she was writing something down, because I could

hear the scratching of one of her razor-sharp pencils on some
pad of paper.

'OK, then,' I said, like she had told me something. 'I'm coming
right in.'

I hung up and slid the phone toward Fat.

He looked like he was going to say something, but he didn't.

Instead, I said, 'You're from New Orleans, right?'

'Born in Desire,' he confirmed, 'not far from the Florida
Projects.'

'What's that,' I asked, 'the Florida Projects?'

'Public housing,' he said. 'Funny, don't you think? I left Florida
to come to Florida.'

'Yes,' I said, without a hint of humor. 'Funny. So how did you
end up in Fry's Bay?'

'Korea,' he said. 'I joined the Army to get away from a woman
by the name of Marie. She had a little baby that she said I gave
her, and she wanted to give it back. So I went to fight for my
country.'

'In Korea.'

'I was only sixteen, but I was big for my size. I stayed over
there for two years, got shot twice before they sent me back.
Last thing in this world I wanted to do was let Marie get a hold
of my Army pension. So I come here to hide out for a little
while. Go by the name of *Fat* instead of Marty. When I left home
I was a beanpole. Nobody would ever think to look for me under
the name of *Fat* in a little backwater hole like this. I am cool as
a cucumber here.'

'But, my friend,' I said, 'it has been nearly twenty years since
Korea. That's more than a little while.'

'Turns out I like it here,' he said.

'I guess you got along with Pete OK if you've been here that
long.'

'Yes, well.' He smiled. 'There ain't no Pete, see? That's what
the sign said when I bought the joint.'

'You're the owner?'

'Shh!' he said, even though there was not another soul in the
place. 'Keep it down. I don't like people knowing that. I like to
have somebody to blame, just in case there are complaints. "The
toilet quit working? Oh, I'll ask Pete, but he's pretty stingy with

the money, that bastard." "Bastard," they say, and then they say, "Thank God you're here, Fat. Gimme another beer." See?'

I had to smile. 'I do see.'

For some reason, this made me like Fat a whole lot more – maybe I felt some odd kind of kinship made out of funny nicknames.

But I was still suspicious of him, completely.

TWELVE

Now, despite what I told Fat, I did not go back to the office. On my continuing odyssey, I meandered back to the donut shop. I was still full from the fine fish I got at Yudda's, but I wondered if Cass, who always seemed to be there, might know more than she was letting on. She always seemed to be a person who saw more than she said.

So, through the donut door I went, and sure enough, there was Cass behind the register.

'You again?' she said. 'In the middle of the day? People will say we're in love.'

'What do people know?' I shot back. 'Some people were saying I was dead this morning.'

She gave me the once-over. 'You don't look that good, but I wouldn't say you were deceased.'

The way she said the last word it sounded like *diseased*.

I took the first stool at the counter, nearly in front of her. 'So. Cass. You've been here for a number of years now. In Fry's Bay, I mean. You've been acquainted with Lou Yahola for a while.'

'Yes.' That's all she said.

'And you know a thing or two,' I went on.

'Why would you say that?' she asked me, offended. 'I don't know Juke.'

'OK,' I admitted, 'I don't know what that means.'

'Well.' She pulled her faded blue sweater around herself and shifted in her seat. 'I don't like to get a reputation.'

'A reputation?' I repeated.

'As somebody who knows a thing or two.' She shot me the fish eye.

'Ah,' I said, suddenly understanding. 'Got it.'

'The secret to a happy life,' she sneered, in stupendously unhappy tones, 'is to let well enough alone. The less you know, the more you stay out of trouble.'

'Yes, all right,' I said, 'I guess I would have to agree with that.'

She nodded once very hard. 'Damn right.'

'Sorry I brought it up.'

'But I *could* tell you a thing or two,' she confided, much softer. 'You can bet on that.'

I blinked. I felt it was the least I could do.

She drew her folding chair a little closer to me, scraping it across the rock-hard linoleum. 'For instance.'

'Lou Yahola,' I suggested.

'Exactly,' she confirmed even more softly.

She glanced at the door to make sure no one was about to come in, and then leaned across the counter toward my face.

'Lou?' she said in a whisper. 'He's not just a donut cook.'

'He's not?' I asked. 'What else is he?'

'He's a medicine man.' Her eyes darted everywhere for a second. 'I've seen him levitate.'

'You've seen him *what*?'

'Float. I saw him float in the air. Twice. Swear to Christ.'

'Here in the kitchen?'

'No,' she went on, 'outside!'

'Outside where?' I began, then I thought better of it. 'Wait. You believe that Lou Yahola can float.'

'I don't believe it,' she said, and her voice was a little spooky, 'but I've seen it.'

'You have.' I didn't know what else to say.

'And he's got other tricks too,' she swore.

'Cass,' I sighed, 'I'm not going to mess with you. This sounds crazy. You sound crazy saying this.'

'Yes, I do,' she agreed. 'That's why I don't tell anybody. That's why I don't like it to get out that I'm a person who knows a thing or two. What happens? When they think you know some-thing, they ask you about it. And when you tell them? They don't believe it. That's my lot in life, and I know it. Even when I was young, I knew stuff that other people didn't know, and I would tell them about it. And they would never believe me. Why the hell do you think I ended up in Fry's Bay, Florida, in a God damned donut shop? I sang with George Shearing, did I ever tell you that? I was all set to record with him. Nineteen fifty-nine. And then that bitch Peggy Lee muscled in. I told him that she'd leave after one album. And she did! But he didn't believe me, and by then she'd ruined my chances.'

I stared at Cass. She had her eyes closed and her eyebrows raised way high and looked about as crazy as you could get.

'Peggy Lee ruined your chance at fame and fortune,' I said, 'and dumped you off in Fry's Bay.'

She opened her eyes. I wouldn't have said that she was crying, but her eyes were misty. The look on her face would have broken the heart of the toughest mob guy I knew. 'Sounds crazy, right? You think I'm not aware of that?'

So I realized, in that moment, that I wasn't going to get a bit of help from poor old Cassie. In fact, she was the one who needed help, and more than I could give her. So I did what anybody would do when they accidentally hit a hornet's nest. I backed away.

'So, it's a tough break, I'll admit,' I told her, mustering a bit of theatrical sympathy. 'But you make the best of it, I guess.'

She leaned back with a weird smile on her face. 'I guess.'

'Anyway.'

'Lou Yahola is in trouble,' Cass said, without looking at me. 'He's drunk at work a lot, but he's never messed up like this.'

'Like what?' I asked.

'Like hanging on to a baby and dosing you with Seconal and getting shot up.'

I nodded. 'News travels fast.'

'Cops were in here earlier. That asshole Rodney.' She sniffed. 'Asked about Lou. Asked about you.'

'Me?'

'I didn't tell them a thing.'

I took a look around the old donut shop. A cold February day in Fry's Bay, Florida. The place was warm and smelled like hot donuts, which is a smell you never get tired of. Sure, it's small.

And the clientele was not exactly your finer citizens. But Cass? I liked her, despite her obvious troubles, or maybe even because of the fact that she was nuts. Who could say? I thought to myself, *There but for fortune, that's me.* And then I thought, *What makes you a big shot? You think you're not in the same boat? Your office smells like crap and cigarettes, and it's a quarter the size of this donut shop.*

Thinking these things made me even more inclined to give Cass a break. So I told her, 'Thanks, Cass. For not mentioning anything about me to the police, I mean.'

She looked up at me. 'You'd do the same for me, right?'

I nodded, because I would at that.

I figured I was batting zero. Jody shot at me and got away with it. Cass turned out to be nuttier than a Georgia pecan farm. Lou was gone, Lynette was gone, and the baby who started the fracas was just fine. So what was I doing? I had to wonder, *why couldn't I just leave well enough alone?*

As I stepped outside the donut shop, I was thinking that I might just go home and sleep until, like, Passover.

Such, alas, was not my fate. At the exact moment I stepped off the curb, lost in thought, a bright red 1965 Corvette squealed around the corner and headed right for me, roaring like a very angry bull.

I managed to jump out of the way just in time, but the Corvette popped a tire on the curb and there was a mighty brouhaha. The busted tire made it impossible to steer the car, so it careened into the side of the building next to the donut shop – a shoe store that had been closed for a while. The guy driving the car was cursing like a banshee and saying words that even I did not know. He tried to back the car up, but the engine was stalled. He screamed at the top of his lungs and jumped out. I saw him, eye to eye. This made him even more upset, and he rushed me, like he was trying to tackle me. But he was so distraught that I only had to jump a little and he flew past me. As he did, I popped him one in the back of the skull, hard as I could, and he skidded, face down, across the pavement of the sidewalk. His nice grey suit got all messed up, and he didn't move after that.

Cass appeared in the doorway of the donut shop.

'What the hell is going on out here?' she wanted to know.

'A guy tried to kill me with his car,' I said, 'and then he got mad at *me* for not dying.'

Cass looked down at the mess on the sidewalk.

'This guy?' she asked.

'Yes.'

'How'd he get like that?' She pointed her loafer in his direction.

'He came at me, so I bopped him in the head.'

She stooped down just a little. 'Oh,' she said, 'you shouldn't have done that. That's going to make him very mad.'

'I should have let him knock me over?'

'Better that than what's going to happen when he wakes up,' she said, straightening up.

'What's going to happen when he wakes up?' I had to ask.

She looked at me hard. 'He's going to kill you.'

I stared down at him. 'He is? Why? This was his fault.'

'No, you misunderstand,' she said, backing away into the donut shop. 'That's McReedy. His *job* is to kill people. You should run.'

THIRTEEN

I didn't wait around to decide if Cass knew what she was talking about. Things were clearly moving in the wrong direction – what with people trying to kill me with their cars – and I began to think that maybe I needed a drink to settle my nerves. Maybe I would just quit my investigation and spend the rest of the day in drink. When I drank I got reflective, and I figured I needed a good bit of reflection before I did anything rash. So I headed back to Pete's for a Hot Tom and Jerry.

Now, Tom and Jerry was a drink that Fat didn't know before I taught him how to make it, but on a chilly day it was just the ticket. It consisted of a good portion of heated whiskey, along with a nice dash of bitters. You added a circle of lemon, a pat of butter melting into it, and enough sweet vermouth to make you forget that you were drinking too much whiskey. This was

not my recipe for a Hot Tom and Jerry. I got it from a guy named
Red Levine when I was a kid in Brooklyn, but that would be
another story.

Suffice it to say that I was looking forward to my Hot Tom
and Jerry just as the day began to cloud over and the chill wind
picked up from the bay.

It was still early in the afternoon, but as I walked into Pete's
I could see that the place was doing a selectively brisk business. I
counted seven or eight customers at tables and booths. There was
only one guy at the bar. Most of these were faces I recognized,
though there was no one I knew too well in the crowd. This was
perfect to me, because I would not be bugged by someone wanting
to be friendly, but I would not be spooked by a joint packed with
strangers.

I took a seat at the end of the bar and Fat shook his head.

'You again?'

'Yes,' I admitted, 'I'm getting that a lot today. I have been
making a particularly circular path so far.'

'Recidivist,' he sneered good-naturedly.

'Guilty,' I allowed, 'but you can make all my cares and troubles
go away.'

'A drink, perhaps?'

'If you insist,' I told him. 'How would you feel about a Hot
Tom and Jerry?'

'Ah,' he says wistfully, 'your Hebrew Manhattan.'

And with that he set himself in motion on his mission of
mercy.

I settled into a seat at the bar far enough away from the other
guy there to be respectful of his privacy. He gave me the nod, a
little sadly. I commiserated with a kind of a hapless shrug, and
there you were: bar etiquette observed.

Alas, before Fat could deliver on his promise of the aforementioned elixir, the sky blackened and gave forth with a mighty
rumble, the presage of cold rain. Likewise, the doorway of Pete's
Billiard's Emporium was darkened by the biggest slab of goon
I had ever seen. This guy had to weigh two-eighty, and stood
close to seven feet tall. He actually had to duck and turn sideways
a little just to get through the door. His midnight hair came down
to his shoulders, and he was wearing a gigantic silk shirt,

un-tucked, and black jeans. Behind him came a dandy in a superior sharkskin suit with a tie that cost six months' rent. Suit-guy's hair looked short at first, but then you could see it was actually in a long braid down his back.

They took over the entire joint just by walking in. They didn't even look around, neither one of them. They got a bead on me and motored right for my barstool.

I considered jumping over the bar and scrambling out the back door, because they appeared to mean trouble, but there was Fat, his back to me, entirely blocking even the whisper of such an exit.

So I took a deep breath, tried to stay calm, and wondered if my relatives in Brooklyn would ever find out what happened to my remains, because I had a very sinking feeling about what was about to happen. The swell dresser was a boss, and the goon was muscle like I had never seen before in my life, and I would have given five to one that I wasn't going to get out of Pete's alive.

I put my hands on the bar so that everyone could see I had no weapon. I let my shoulders sink down, relaxing the neck muscles.

The goon sat down on my left, and the dandy sat on my right.

'Hey, Fat?' I said in as steady a voice as I could muster. 'Maybe you better make three of those.'

'Three?' he railed, turning.

When he saw who was sitting with me, he froze, and then all the color left his face. He spilled half my Tom and Jerry because his hand started shaking.

I turned to the dandy. 'Unless you'd like something else. I'm having a Hot Tom and Jerry.'

The dandy smiled. 'Ask Fat why he's not going to serve me anything.'

I turned to Fat.

Fat said, 'I'll give you any goddamn thing you want, Mister Redhawk.'

Mister Redhawk kept smiling. 'Well, that wouldn't be legal, would it, Fat?' Mister Redhawk turned to me. 'It's still against the law in the state of Florida to sell liquor to an Indian.'

'Yeah,' I agreed, 'and it's always been illegal for a Jew to eat pork, but how many bacon, lettuce, and tomato sandwiches do I have in a month?'

'I'm not sure that's comparable,' Mister Redhawk said philosophically. 'One's a government law, the other is a religious observance.'

'No, see, it is comparable,' I told him. 'It just depends on
whose authority you're worried about.'

'Ah,' he agreed, tapping the bar with his knuckles, 'I was told
that you were smarter than you looked. I see that it's true. You
understand what I'm about to tell you before I even open my
mouth.'

'Maybe.' I glanced at Fat. He was still holding the un-spilled
half of my Tom and Jerry, and he was frozen in his tracks.
'Could I have what's left of my beverage, Fat? I think I'm going
to need it.'

'I'm about to tell you, Mr Moscowitz,' Mister Redhawk said,
as if I was not talking to Fat at all, 'that we live in a morally
relativistic universe. And that while you owe allegiance to certain
government authorities with regard to your job, you also must
follow the dictates of another power.'

I nodded. I thought it would be best if I kept my mouth shut
for a minute. It showed respect. Or at least I hoped that's how
Mister Redhawk saw it.

Mister Redhawk blinked and, without taking his eyes off me,
said to Fat, 'Are you going to bring Mr Moscowitz his drink, or
were you thinking of spilling the rest of it too?'

Fat instantly thawed, and the Tom and Jerry was set in front
of me in less than two seconds. I looked down at it.

'Sure you won't join me?' I said to Mister Redhawk.

Mister Redhawk just smiled.

I inclined my head in a more or less accepting way, grabbed
the drink, and tossed it back. It was a little too hot, and it burned
my tongue and my throat, so I closed my eyes, but I figured that
was a good thing. It distracted me for a second.

When I opened my eyes, Fat was gone.

'Now,' I said, a little hoarsely, 'tell me about this other authority
to which I must acquiesce.'

'I am not the director of the Seminole Tribal Council,' he
began. 'I am, as it were, the power behind the throne. I am not
here with you now in any official capacity. But I am here. You
see me. I see you.'

I nodded.

'Say it out loud, please,' he told me softly.

'Say what, exactly?'

'Tell me that you see me.'

I set down my empty glass. I understood what he wanted me to do, because it was not unlike what a lot of mob guys in Brooklyn wanted you to do; look them in the eye and really listen, so you'd know how serious they were. I turned a little more squarely toward Mister Redhawk. I leveled a look directly into his very strange eyes.

'I see you,' I told him, sober as a judge. 'I hear the words that you're saying.'

'Good,' he said, and I could see that he relaxed a little.

I could also feel that the goon to my left also released a bit of tension. I took this as an excellent sign.

'Then here is what I am telling you,' Mister Redhawk continued. 'I am telling you that the baby you have rescued belongs to our tribe. She is the keeper of certain . . . spiritual properties which we value and which we need. You have done us a valuable service, however inadvertently, in rescuing the baby from the troubled mother, and I am here to thank you.'

My turn to relax. 'Well,' I said with a big sigh, 'I have to tell you, that isn't how I thought this meeting was going to go when you walked in the door.'

'I'm not finished,' he said. 'We haven't talked about everyone.'

'You haven't yet told me anything about Lynette,' I answered back, 'or Lou Yahola. And you have them both, I understand.'

'We're taking care of the mother. She's infected with these drugs from your world, and we're cleansing her. She'll be fine. Lou is another matter. He's lost his way. He has a gift, or, really, many gifts. But they frighten him, and he doesn't know what to do. His is a more difficult case. We're helping him too, but that may take a bit more time. He's very confused.'

'So, you're not mad at me for shooting him in the knee?'

'He told us that you had to do it, because he was trying to shoot you.'

'That's true,' I said. 'But sometimes a plea of self-defense does not get you off the hook.'

'No one's angry with you,' Mister Redhawk assured me.

'Well, I hate to disagree with you, Mister Redhawk,' I said

very deferentially, 'but someone is very angry with me. Someone very recently tried to kill me with a red car.'

'Ah,' Mister Redhawk said, 'yes. I meant to say that no one on the Council is mad at you. McReedy is another matter.'

I sipped a little air and said, 'News does indeed travel fast in a small town.'

'You misunderstand,' he said. 'Very few people in this town know about McReedy's attempt on your life. Cass called us after he tried to kill you. She's worried about you.'

I stiffened up at that news, and tried to sit very straight on my stool. 'Cass called you?'

He nodded sympathetically. 'I can see how you might be skeptical about that, but Cass knows Lou, and I am Lou's emergency contact. She's called me before, but it was always about Lou.'

I remembered the *Contack* Sheet and the *emergensee* number, but I couldn't see how that made any sense.

'Cass doesn't know me or like me good enough to call in the Marines because some guy's car jumps a curb,' I said before I thought better of it. 'And unless you were around the corner when she called, you would never have gotten to me so fast. I mean, this McReedy character, he like, *just* tried to bop me – five minutes ago at the most.'

Mister Redhawk did not seem offended. 'You are an exceptionally smart and observant man, Mr Moscowitz, but your observations are limited by a certain perception of reality. To understand me and my ways you would need a perceptual shift, a re-evaluation of your *dasein*. And that sort of education? It takes a lifetime. Or two.'

'OK, I only understood about half the words you just said, but I get that you and I come from two different worlds. I get that part. I also get that you know more about me than I do about you. I can only guess why this is true, but it has something to do with the fact that you're related to Maggie Redhawk, or is that just a common name in the Seminole way of things. Like Smith. Or Greenbaum.'

'It's good to have a sense of humor,' Mister Redhawk allowed, although he wasn't laughing. 'But I can tell you that Maggie is my sister. We're very proud of her. She can ride two horses at once.'

'She lives in both worlds,' I translated. 'Yours and mine.'

'To answer your question,' Mister Redhawk continued, 'let's have Philip put his hand on the bar. Philip?'

Mister Redhawk's moose-like companion laid his paw, palm down, on the bar in front of me. It was the size of a rich man's dinner plate, and the fingers were as big as fat cigars.

'Have a look at that hand for a moment, would you,' Mister Redhawk said. 'If all you could see were the fingers, you wouldn't think there was any relationship between them. But if you looked deeper, or, in this case, a few inches lower, you could see that they're all attached to a fairly large palm. They're all related. That's the illusion of people in this world, Mr Moscowitz. They all appear to be unconnected fingers, but upon a more accurate observation, they all work in concert: the fingers, the palm, the hand – and the fist they can make.'

The moose clumped his hand into one gigantic fist, and it was bigger than my head.

I looked at Philip for the first time. He had a sweet face, not at all the kind of menacing gob a lot of muscle guys had, at least not where I came from.

'You know that Philip means *lover of horses*,' I told him.

He nodded, a little sorrowfully. 'That's how I got my white name,' he admitted, and his voice was as deep and beautiful as a bassoon. 'I was big even when I was little, and the other kids, they told me I was part horse. I said I didn't mind because I loved horses.'

'But you did mind,' I commiserated, 'because they were making fun of you. Listen, when you're known by the name *Foggy*, you understand a thing or two about sticks and stones.'

'What?' Philip says.

'They say sticks and stones can break your bones but names can never hurt you,' I answered him. 'I disagree. I'd rather have the stones.'

He nodded, and put his hand back in his lap. 'Yeah,' he said real soft, not looking at me. 'Me too.'

'Good,' Mister Redhawk said, 'you're bonding. That's nice. But not the point of my visit.'

I turned back to the man. 'Sorry.'

'First,' he began, now completely business, 'forget trying to

find Lou or Lynette. And when we take the baby out of the
hospital, which we will do today, forget about that too.'

'I hear the words that you're saying,' I told him, very
deliberately.

'Next,' he went on, 'don't worry about McReedy. Philip will
take care of that.'

'OK,' I said hesitantly, 'but could I ask, who is McReedy?'

Mister Redhawk sat back a bit. 'Yes. It's a little amazing to
me that you've been around this place for three years and haven't
run afoul of McReedy. Especially a man as – what's the word?
– inquisitive as you are. I believe McReedy would be referred
to in your parlance as a hit man.'

'He's a lunatic,' Philip whispered.

'He likes to kill people,' Mister Redhawk agreed. 'He would
do it for pleasure. But he gets paid for it, so I would imagine
the pleasure is double.'

I shook my head. 'I'd never figure Fry's Bay to be a place
that needed a full-time hit man.'

'You don't know the history of this part of Florida, Mr
Moscowitz.'

'In fact,' I said politely, 'I read a good bit about the goings-on
hereabout. I know, for instance, that you guys got screwed in the
worst way I ever heard of. The Seminoles, I mean. I compared
it to the treatment my family got in Russia in the old days at the
hands of the Cossacks. They would come swooping in and take
away everything you had.'

'Only the Cossacks, in this case, are your own government.'

'Hey,' I objected, 'not *my* government. Was I alive when you
guys got screwed? Did I arrest Osceola under a flag of truce?
Did a person like me elect *Nixon*, for God's sake? And P.S.: the
Cossacks *were* a part of our own government in the old days in
Russia.'

'Well,' he said briskly, 'we agree that this is a sore spot for
both our cultures.'

'We do.'

'But I'm trying to tell you that you are unaware of the more
socio-economic developments of this area in the decades since
WWII.'

'Oh.' I calmed down. 'That's probably true.'

'Land is money,' he said, somewhat enigmatically, at least to my mind.

'OK.' I was hoping he'd go on so I could follow the gist of his thinking.

'Land,' was all he said then.

'Land.' I repeated the word a third time, hoping that the magical qualities of the number three might reveal what the hell he was talking about.

'This is the way of the world, most of these powerful white men will stop at nothing to keep the power they have and to get the power they want. They are not guided by any moral compass. They are not human beings. They are, I believe, demons. Demons keep dogs to do their bidding, and this McReedy is one such underling. He is a sub-animal entity whose sole purpose in life is to eliminate any obstacle, however miniscule, that lies in the path of these non-human, power-drinking white men. Do you understand this?'

'I hear the words that you're saying,' I told him once again.

He gave me the droll eye. 'I'm well aware that you're using phrases that you know I want to hear. And I also know that the *way* you're using them is, to you, only a half-truth.'

'Yes,' I told him, not the least bit shy about it, 'that is entirely correct. On both counts. I want to show you respect, partly because you spook Fat, which doesn't seem that easy to do, partly because I really like Maggie, but mostly because I can sense that you're a person who doesn't take any guff, and not just because Philip is with you. Though that doesn't hurt. But even if you were here alone, I would know you had juice. It's all around you, like an aura.'

He seemed amused by my speech. 'An unexpected bit of mysticism from you, Mr Moscowitz.'

'You also confuse me with that *non-human*, *power-drinking* crap. I never heard it put that way before, but I know these guys, guys just like that. And I would agree, upon the slightest reflection, that they are, in fact, demons. Not men at all. I know this from experience.'

'So.' He stood up very suddenly. 'We have communicated.'

I stood too, because it seemed like the right thing to do. But I said, 'Maybe we have, and maybe we haven't. What is it that you hope I'm going to do now?'

'You're going to step back,' he said. 'You're going to let things happen. Stay out of sight for a while so that Philip can take care of your Mr McReedy, and then just go about your business. Go to work, eat at Yudda's, drink here; live your life. One day, you may return to New York. One day, your troubles there may have gone. One day, you may come to forgive yourself for your crimes and stop punishing your spirit with this odd and humid exile here in Florida. You say to Philip that you'd rather have the stones, and I see the truth of that. You prefer physical discomfort to the things that are torturing your soul. But what is pain? Often we learn that separation from home, from loved ones, from our people in general, that's the worst pain of all. I know. I know that pain all too well. So I hope that you will let Philip take care of McReedy, and I hope that you will let fate take care of everything else. I can see why my sister likes you. You are a very likeable man.'

'I'll give you a list sometime of all the people who would disagree with that sentence, Mister Redhawk,' I told him, 'but I am very glad to hear you say it.'

Without another word, Mister Redhawk turned and headed for the door. Philip looked at me like he wanted to say something else, but instead he just gave me the nod, a sort of brotherly exchange. I nodded right back and, just like that, they were gone.

FOURTEEN

I got absolutely nowhere with Fat when he reappeared behind his bar. He was agitated beyond imagination. I tried to ask him about Mister Redhawk and Philip, but all he could do was tell me to get out of his place and not come back until there was news that McReedy was dead. *Dead.*

I could see that the guy was about to have a heart attack, so I acquiesced to his demand. To wit, I split.

I headed back to the office, but I was a bit spooked and kept checking up and down the streets for the sight of a red Corvette or a mad killer. Neither appeared. I made it back to my place of so-called business, but I was barely in the front door to our suite when I heard Sharon bellow like a bull.

'What the *hell* are you doing here?' She was standing up and careening around her desk, headed right for me. 'Get out get out get out!'

I froze. This was the most animated I had ever seen her, and I found it alarming.

She motored up to me – two inches taller because, despite her height, she always wore heels – and looked down, right into my eyes.

'Do I want to get shot to death by a stray bullet from McReedy's forty-four?' she demanded to know.

I did not blink. 'I'm going to say that the answer is "no".'

'You're going to say more than that!' she barked. 'You're going to say that you're getting the hell out of here and hiding out somewhere until something happens to McReedy, or until he kills you and I come to your funeral sobbing and eyeing the buffet!'

'They'll have a buffet?'

'Get! Out!'

At that moment I was glad that no one else was in the office. There were only two other employees. One was part-time and I had yet to meet her – she was a kindergarten teacher most of the time. The other was a kid who was related to the mayor in some way or other, but I didn't talk to him because he was hardly ever there. I was the man of the house.

'I *will* get out,' I responded calmly. 'But I am past my daily quotient of "How the hell does Sharon know these things" and I would like to know what you've heard.'

She fumed. She breathed loudly. She started to speak several times. Then she closed her eyes. 'OK, that's fair.'

'So? Give.'

She opened her eyes. 'I would not ordinarily tell anyone what I'm about to tell you. But seeing as you're in the biggest trouble of your life, and you might not make it out alive and it might be partly my fault, I'm going to give you some information that you'll take to your grave or I won't say another word.'

I managed a smile. 'Take to my grave? I mean, how long is that really going to be, at this point? I'm sure I can keep your little secret for an hour or two, right?'

'I'm serious as a crutch, Foggy.'

'OK, OK. I'll never tell a soul. So let me in on the big secret.'

She stood swaying for a second, a little like a willow in a windstorm. I could see that she was thinking how to begin. Finally she settled on, 'How did I get to be the boss of this shindig, our little government work scam? It's the plumb gig of the county and you know it. How did I get appointed head of Child Protective Services not two months after the federal mandate and ahead of a hundred more qualified people?'

I shrugged.

'I'm the daughter of Pascal Henderson.'

A ton of bricks – a ton of concrete bricks – could not have hit me harder.

Pascal Henderson owned . . . well . . . everything. Not just everything in Fry's Bay – he owned controlling interest in IBM, Coca-Cola, Dow Chemical, Walt Disney, some new oil company, and even J.C. Penney. The guy was a monster. When the market crashed last year, because of Vietnam and Watergate, and every stock in America lost nearly half its value, this guy swooped in and bought, to review, *everything*.

All I could say to Sharon was, 'Pascal Henderson is a bachelor. The unmarried kind of bachelor.'

'Correct. So, that makes me a bastard,' she says right back, very defensively, 'or a bastardette or whatever you would call a girl child out of wedlock. My mother was a waitress. She's out of the picture. Henderson does not publicly acknowledge that I'm his bundle of joy but, every once in a while, he throws me a fish. Maybe he's guilty about what he did, maybe he's nervous about what I'll do. I don't care. I got educated at Western College for Women in Oxford, Ohio. I took a year abroad, in London. I spent the summer in Tuscany one time. And when a new federal job was created with a very nice salary for ten people, he somehow made it a fantastic salary for one boss and two other saps. I divide the leftovers amongst the three of you. Yours is the largest bundle.'

'Because I'm the most qualified?' I suggested.

'Because I like you,' she corrected sternly, 'or at least, I did until you came in just now obviously trying to get me killed. So when I say get out, I mean it.'

'But you were telling me how you know the things you know,' I insisted.

'Well, because of this tenuous association with one of the richest men in the world, I am sometimes privy to a smattering of his resource network.'

'Which means?'

'He knows all sorts of people, and they tell him anything he wants to know. I know some of them too, and they keep me informed concerning my little corner of paradise.'

I nodded. I was wise. 'Pascal Henderson. You don't get to be a guy that rich without having questionable and sometimes seamy associations. Thugs, crooks—'

'Hookers, perverts, and gymnasts,' she interrupted. 'Yes. All that, and more.'

'I'm familiar with the territory,' I explained.

'I know,' she said right back. 'I know practically all about you. I know you used to steal cars for a living. I know you were a good P.I. – I know everything. Including the real reason you took this job.'

That stopped me. I did not feel so very wise at all, suddenly. I felt like I didn't have any clothes on. I felt like I was being X-rayed, even.

'Look,' she told me right away, letting me off the hook, 'I know you don't want to talk about that, I'm only telling you this stuff for your own good. You have got to get out of here. Right now.'

'I'll go,' I told her, 'but I am not without recourse myself. As it happens, one Mister Redhawk has given the order to a moose named Philip that McReedy should leave me alone.'

It was her turn to reflect. 'Redhawk paid you a visit?'

'Yes. With Philip.'

'Why?'

I started to tell her, but for some reason, for the first time since I'd met Sharon, I decided not to reveal the entire matter. 'I'm friends with his sister, Maggie Redhawk. At the hospital.'

That was true, as far as it went. So I didn't lie to Sharon, I just didn't tell her everything.

She started pacing. 'OK, OK. That's good. That's why you were asking me about the Seminole Tribal Council?'

'Yes,' I faked it, remembering what Mister Redhawk said. 'He's the power behind the throne, but I'd like to know more.'

'I got you a file on the Tribal Council like you asked,' she said absently. 'Put it on your desk. Just before I got a call that McReedy wrecked his Corvette outside the donut shop. Understand?'

'Jesus, you get this information stuff fast,' I told her. 'And, thanks for the file.'

I headed for my desk to pick it up.

'Uh huh,' she mumbled, 'but look, that's it. That's all I can do for a while. I mean I can't help you with any of this. You get me? I'm just someone who gives you your paycheck in this particular carnival. Sorry.'

'OK,' I said.

'No,' she insisted. 'It's not OK. But it's the way it's got to be. I've got to figure out what's going on. I've got to figure it out good and right away.'

'Figure what out, exactly?'

'What's going on with you,' she told me.

'Because you like me,' I said.

'No,' she snapped, pacing faster. 'Because this McReedy? I know him.'

'You know him?'

She stopped moving and locked eyes with me. 'He works for my father, Foggy. McReedy works for dear old dad.'

FIFTEEN

I might actually have looked like a cartoon leaving the office. I was moving faster than my feet could carry me. I had the Tribal Council folder in one hand and my wallet in the other. I was checking to see what kind of dough I had on me. I didn't figure to go back to my own pad; I had to assume that McReedy knew where I lived. I also understood that he knew where I worked, and that he was probably waking up on the sidewalk in front of the donut shop with a headache and a gun. His first stop was going to be my office, because it was closer, and then he was going to ransack my tiny but tidy apartment.

There was no point in hopping into my car either. I figured he knew my ride. I drove a raven black 1957 Ford Thunderbird. It was the only one in town.

Oddly, it was not a stolen car. Not per se. I borrowed it from a guy. He is in the Joliet Correctional Center in Illinois. He's due to get out in 1995 so I figured to get some good use out of it until then, or until I got dead which, at this point, was very likely to come first.

In short, I eschewed the T-Bird. I wasn't really thinking. I was more just moving very fast and hoping to run into something that would hide me for a while. Other people referred to this sort of behavior as instinctual, but by me it was panic with a thin veil of improvisational jazz on top.

So no one could have been more surprised than I was, five minutes later, when I ended up in Lynette's apartment building. I knew that Lynette was sequestered somewhere deep in the swamp, and I didn't have the notion that her apartment would be the right place for me to hide, but there I was, on her floor, walking down the hall like I owned the place.

Without even giving it a thought, I knocked on the door that said D-10 on it. I was remembering that the landlady or concierge had told me that *Gerard* lived there, the guy who had called the hospital when Lynette had the baby. I soon discovered that my completely ridiculous plan was that Gerard would be home and that I would barge into his apartment. I would stay there under the guise of investigating the whole baby thing. I mean, I actually *did* work for the organization that conducted that kind of investigation.

So I knocked on the door.

Miraculously, someone opened it. A delicate face covered in a half a pound of make-up peered out.

'Yes?' the face asked.

'Gerard?' I asked right back.

'Who wants to know?' he snapped.

I produced my sort of badge. 'I'm with Child Protective Services. It's about—'

'Lynette!' Gerard flung the door wide. 'Come in. Jesus. I've been trying to find out what the hell happened to her, but you'd think I was asking about . . . I mean, I've been getting the biggest run-around, you can't imagine!'

He was dressed in a tube top and a mini-skirt. The tube top was loaded, so either it was a specially made garment for Gerard's work or Gerard had made some additions to his upper body real estate. As for the mini-skirt, he had the legs for it.

'Don't even start me on the run-around,' I commiserated calmly. 'I've been all over town, and I think I might know less than I did before. Plus I'm about to drop.'

'Well, come in and tell me about it, why don't you?' He stepped aside.

I sauntered, so as not to seem too anxious, but I couldn't wait for him to close the door behind us.

His place was the nicest looking hovel I had ever laid my eyes on. It was the exact layout that Lynette had, and even smaller than Jody the pusher's place. But it looked like the Taj Mahal.

Where to begin? There was a deep green oriental rug that covered most of the floor and looked like a million bucks. Instead of a sofa, he had what they call a fainting couch, like Sarah Bernhardt. It was gold, but not gaudy. There were studio photographs of Gerard on every wall. They were big; like, two by three feet, black and white, and looked like 1940s film star shots. In makeup and the right wig, Gerard looked a lot like a young Jane Russell, and just about as buxom.

By the window there was a nice little bentwood café table and chairs. The set was close to the kitchen, which was immaculate. I actually thought I saw sunlight sparkling off the faucet.

Nearly everywhere there were very healthy plants, some even flowering. Somewhere behind one of them he'd rigged up some sort of little waterfall. You could hear it gurgling over rocks or something.

'Nice digs,' I said. 'I've been across the hall and, as you probably know, Lynette does not have your flair.'

'Nobody does,' he said, but it was a little sad the way he said it. 'Look, do you have a card or something besides that junior

G-Man badge? I'm not the paranoid type, but you can never be too careful.'

I produced a snappy card from my inside coat pocket. He examined it. It seemed to satisfy.

'OK, shoot,' he said.

'They tell me that you were the one who called the hospital when Lynette went into labor.' I stood still, not remotely knowing where to sit down.

'You hear a lot of strange noises in this dump,' Gerard explained to me, 'and I work nights, so I'm just coming home most mornings at four. That's the time when all good boys and girls are in bed and the monsters come out to play.'

'You said it,' I agreed.

'Sit,' he commanded, pointing to a very comfortable looking overstuffed chair in one corner.

He collapsed on to the fainting couch and I slouched down low in the chair. Suddenly it felt very nice to sit in a comfortable chair in a nicely appointed environment.

'This is just fine,' I said, brushing the arm of the chair. 'This might be the most relaxed I've been in two days.'

'It's the plants,' he told me. 'They produce extra oxygen. Plus, can you hear my fountain? The water? It's incredibly soothing, don't you think?'

'I do think.'

'So tell all. Where the hell is Lynette, and baby?'

'Baby's safe in the hospital,' I said right away. 'She's got to kick a habit that her mother gave her, but she seems to be doing quite well in spite of it all. The whereabouts of Lynette Baker? That's a little more difficult to answer. I think she's being held captive in the swamp by the Seminole Tribal Council.'

Why lie? Plus, by telling the truth, I got to see his reaction.

It was worth it.

Gerard snapped up, nearly off the couch, eyes wide, then blinking, and his head was cocked just about as far right as it was going to get.

'What?' he demanded in no uncertain terms.

'You heard me,' I said. 'I don't know why, but the Tribal Council is interested in mother and baby, and they're trying to clean Lynette up.'

'Oh.' Gerard relaxed a little. 'Well, that's good, right?'

'I guess.'

'But, look, cowboy,' Gerard said, settling back, 'you do *not* want to mess with the Tribal Council. They will fry your testicles with *you* still attached.'

'Had a bad experience with the Seminoles, have we?' I asked.

He sighed. 'In my line of work – I'm a dancer – you meet all sorts.'

'I'd imagine,' I told him.

'And some of the Council members have, what they like to call, *investments* in all sorts of shady goings-on. And who's shadier than yours truly, would you think?'

'I wouldn't venture a guess,' I admitted.

'Right? So I'm working at the only strip club in the county and because of my, what should I say? *Attributes*? I get a lot of business.'

'Do you mean that some guys don't know that you have exterior plumbing, or some guys *want* it that way?' I asked, as respectfully as I could manage to.

'It's a little of both,' Gerard said casually, not the least offended. 'Baby, it's a wild world.'

'Like a stampede sometimes,' I commiserated. 'But, let me see if I have this right: sometimes you get patrons from the Seminole community who enjoy your wares?'

'Oh, God no,' he was quick to answer. 'They're all straight as an arrow, no Indian pun intended. No. They own land, which they don't sell but they don't mind who rents it. The shady characters who built my shady world are the kind of critter that can't get a decent howdy from the mainstream hoi polloi hereabouts in the way of cash backing or a place to exhibit, so they need people who don't care if the white man sinks in the mud and vanishes from the face of the earth.'

'In short,' I surmised, 'your employers can't get a bank loan or rent a decent building around here, except from the Seminole Tribal Council.'

'Bingo,' he assured me. 'They rent to my bosses, and they loan large sums of money for building, with large interest rates attached and large men to enforce the payment of the large interest on the large loans.'

'Yeah,' I told him, 'I actually met one of those guys today. A Goliath named Philip.'

Gerard swallowed. Like, visibly. 'You mean that gorilla who follows Mister Redhawk around?'

'Yes.'

'Well,' he said, standing again. 'Look at the time.' He did not even bother to glance at a watch or a clock. 'I have to get my beauty rest.'

I stood too, hoping to calm Gerard. 'Mister Redhawk spooks you.'

'Like I lived in a haunted *house* he spooks me. And if he's got his goon on your ass, then your ass is not worth a dime.'

'Agreed,' I said, 'but for the record: Philip is not after me. He's my protector.'

That gave Gerard pause. 'Say it again.'

'Philip is not looking to pop me,' I reiterated, 'he's looking to take care of my problems.'

'Which problems are those?'

'At the moment, in no particular order, my problems include that I am cold, I am tired, I want to know where Lynette Baker is and why Lou Yahola shot at me and, while I'm at it, why my boss just now told me that she's related to one of the richest men in the world. But, most pressing for Philip, I would have to assume, is the fact that someone called McReedy wants me dead.'

Gerard stayed frozen like a statue for a little too long.

When he thawed, he said, 'All right, if you're OK with Redhawk, you're OK with me. Plus, you're interesting.'

'Oh, I'm interesting,' I concurred.

'So McReedy – he's real?' Gerard fell back on to his fainting couch. 'I mean, one hears the name, but I thought it was like the bogeyman or, I don't know, evil Santa. Like, if you don't behave, McReedy's going to get you.'

'Evil Santa?'

'That bastard leaves lumps of coal in little children's shoes or something. You don't think that's right, do you?'

'I'm Jewish,' I said. 'This is the first I ever heard that Santa had an evil alter ego.'

'No,' Gerard said, 'it's not his alter ego. If you're good, Santa gives you presents and candy canes but, if you're bad, he leaves you a lump of coal.'

'Suddenly my childhood dradle seems OK,' I told him. 'It's unconditional. If I was good, if I was bad, didn't make a never mind, I got a dradle.'

'OK, I don't know what that is, but I guess the Jews are just lucky or something.'

'Chosen people,' I said. 'But we've strayed from the point.'

'Which was?'

'McReedy,' I said. 'You say you've heard the name?'

'I've heard rumors, that's all. But relax. When you've got Mister Redhawk and Philip on your team, you don't worry much about the rest of the underworld.'

'Fair enough,' I conceded. 'So how about this, how well do you actually know Lynette?'

He slumped down, then, rather primly, adjusted his hem. 'I have enough problems of my own without associating with known junkies. And Lynette was a known junkie. So I tried to steer clear. But sometimes she was just so trashed that I had to ask her to settle. She was always nice about it. I don't think she'd even know who I was she was so wasted when we talked.'

'But you called the ambulance when she had her baby.'

'I love babies,' he said softly, 'and I don't see how it's the baby's fault that the mother is a louse. I mean, right?'

'Right,' I agreed.

'Plus, as we have already discussed, I know which side my bread is buttered on, let me tell you.'

I blinked. 'Sorry?'

'I say, I know which side—'

'I heard what you said, I just don't know what you mean.'

'We already talked about it. I'm very wary of the Seminole brotherhood. For professional reasons.'

'And that involves Lynette?'

'Oh.' He raised his eyebrows nearly to his hairline. 'I thought you knew, Lynette is half Seminole.'

And there it was, a large and central piece of the puzzle. It hit me in the head like a lead pipe. Lynette Baker was half Seminole. And then I glanced down, realizing that I still had Sharon's file in my fist. And then I thought, *Maybe there's something in here about that, and about this famous Seminole*

Brotherhood. And *then* I put a pretty obvious two and two together; her last name was Baker, she left the baby with Lou Yahola at the old Baker building. Did that have anything to do with Seminoles, I had to wonder?

Suddenly, I was having a bit of vertigo.

'Whoa, cowpoke,' Gerard said, 'you OK? You look like you might pass out.'

'I might just do that,' I admitted. 'I'm having the funniest feeling.'

'Do you need to lie down?'

'No,' I said. 'I think I need a drink.'

'Can do.' He jumped up like he was on fire and dashed into the kitchen. 'I make a martini that causes the angels to weep.'

'Good,' I said to his back. 'Make mine a double. It feels like a two angel day.'

He turned to me and flashed a smile. 'Doesn't it, though?'

'So here's what is hitting me in the head,' I told him. 'Is everyone in this burg a Seminole Indian?'

'I'm not.' He shrugged, continuing to concoct the beverages.

'So that makes two of us.'

'There was a lot of intermarriage, they tell me, for a while. Why do you ask?'

'Lynette's part Seminole, Jody's part Seminole, Maggie and Philip and the mysterious Mister Redhawk are *all* Seminole.'

'Jody? Jody Boyd?'

'You know her?' I asked.

'She's . . . I don't want to tell tales out of school.' Gerard lowered his voice. 'But one of the strippers where I work? A female stripper? All girl? She's Jody's girlfriend.'

'Jody has a girlfriend?'

'Mum's the word,' he whispered.

'So you know Jody.'

'Jody is exactly the sort of person one avoids,' Gerard intoned. 'She has a lot of money, but she doesn't ever spend it. Plus, her chosen profession pisses me off.'

'She's a drug dealer.'

'So you know. Good. I don't have to, what's the expression? Pussy foot.'

'That may be the expression,' I told him, shifting in my chair, 'but please don't use it. Ever again.'

'Right. Anyway, Jody's a pusher and God Damn the Pusher Man, if you know what I mean.'

'I don't.'

'That song?' Gerard said. *'God Damn the Pusher Man.'*

'Don't know it.'

'Nina Simone, come on,' he said, 'I thought you people knew all about the entertainment world. Don't you own it or something? Like in New York? That's where you're from, right? I could tell by the accent. Hey! Martinis!'

He spun around with two cocktail glasses, one in each hand, and didn't spill a drop.

I made as to stand to receive this manna, but Gerard would not have it. He moved, well, like a gazelle, and handed me my beverage, which I sipped immediately.

'Dreamy, isn't it?' he said, standing over me.

'Angel tears indeed,' I concurred. 'So you were saying that you don't approve of Jody's profession.'

'I don't. I'm strictly clean and decent. And P.S.? Jody's as much of a Seminole as you and me. She tell you that baloney about a soldier father and a Seminole woman?'

'She did.' I sipped again.

'That's Lynette's story, not Jody's. I don't know if Jody is confused because of the junk or likes to think of herself as a half-breed or what. But she was born in Miami to all-American stock.'

'And you know this how?' I asked politely.

'Girl talk,' he said, retreating to his fainting sofa. 'Dressing room gossip. Jody's girlfriend and I used to be close.'

'Used to be?'

'Before she took up with Jody, naturally.'

'Naturally.' Another sip and I was beginning to feel much better.

'So,' Gerard said, in a very deliberate voice. 'You didn't really come here to ask me these questions because, if you actually are with this so-called Child Protective Services, your work is done. The child is protected. Right?'

'After a fashion,' I demurred.

'Meaning what?'

'Meaning,' I said, after yet another sip of the glorious martini, 'that Mister Redhawk is going to get the baby and spirit it away. Whence I do not know, but I don't like to save a kid from the clutches of junkies and donut cooks who have guns only to have said tyke be removed from the safe environ of the hospital.'

'Ah,' he said. 'A man with a mission.'

'Plus,' I was forced to admit – partly because I wanted to be honest, partly because the martini had really kicked in – 'I kind of have to hide out for a while to let Philip rid me of this McReedy pestilence, see?'

'There it is,' he said, saluting me with his drink. 'I'm your backstreet jelly roll.'

'OK,' I admitted to him, 'I don't know what that means either, but you certainly do have a colorful way of expressing yourself. If you mean that this apartment is maybe the last place in America that McReedy would go looking for me, then, as you say, *bingo.*'

'It means,' he explained, 'that thanks to me, you're going to be that rarest of birds, the good man that is hard to find.'

'Not only is your speech colorful,' I told him, polishing off my beverage, 'but it is also rife with innuendo.'

'Double entendre is my métier,' he sighed. 'And *you're* out of refreshment.'

He hopped up, setting his own glass on the floor, and without another word scooped the glass from my hand and retreated into the kitchen.

'You can stay here as long as you like,' he said from the kitchen, 'but in a bit I'm going to have to get ready for the club.'

'I don't want to interfere with the ordinary course of your day,' I told him.

He stopped for a second in his work with the shaker and said, a little softer, 'I kind of like the company.'

I didn't know why that made me sad, but it did. Not sad for Gerard, exactly, or even for myself, because I could probably have said the same thing to him.

The human condition, as I understood it, was primarily built out of loneliness, occasionally interspersed with brutality, terror, and meals.

SIXTEEN

By eight o'clock I'd taken a nap and Gerard was dressed for work.

'How do I look?' he asked.

I gave him the once-over from my sleeping chair. 'Pretty spectacular, actually.'

'Smooth talker.' He winked.

He was dressed in a tight black slinky number with sequins all over it. The heels were at least three inches tall and red as a fire engine. His wig was a kind of a Judy Garland thing, like toward the end of her life; black and tight around the head. The hose were black with a seam up the back like they used to have.

'Don't wait up,' he said at the door. 'I'll be very late.'

'OK, but chances are I'll be gone by the time you get back. Assuming I can wake up. I slept really hard.'

'You'll be gone.' He nodded. 'But look, you have to come back and give me the scoop, right? If you don't get killed by McReedy.'

'Will do.' I smiled. 'You know, you might be the nicest person I've met in this burg so far.'

'Well,' he shot right back, 'I'm certainly the nicest looking.'

'One hundred percent,' I agreed.

With that he was out the door.

I sat there a second trying to rouse myself and then looked around for a phone. I figured to call my apartment first, just to see if somebody would answer, but a second later that seemed silly. I nixed calling Sharon, least for the nonce, on account of her surprise father. Then I thought, maybe I would give Fat a call to see did he know anything. Then I tried to think who else might offer me information, if not solace.

And this question gave me pause, because I realized that I really had no friends to call. I'd been in Fry's Bay for three years, and I had plenty of friendly associates, but no pals. Back in Brooklyn I had Steady Pete, the shyster. He was always giving out with the jokes. And Pan-Pan Washington, an artist with a blowtorch. I once saw him change a Ford Falcon into a Jaguar sort of looking thing. It was a beautiful piece of work. I would have called Pan-Pan, if I'd been in Brooklyn. But I was not.

So I thought to myself, *Do I call the donut shop?* Cass was the one who'd hipped me to McReedy. Maybe she'd heard something by now. Even Yudda might know something, or Myrna his waitress. What to do, what to do?

I finally decided on Fat, because he'd been the most scared. That meant he had the most to lose, I thought. Sure, he'd told me not to come back for a while, but he hadn't told me not to call him.

So I found the phone in the kitchen and I dialed up Pete's Billiard Emporium.

The phone rang for a while, but finally Fat picked up.

'What?' he said, though not unpleasantly.

'Do not repeat my name but this is Foggy.'

'Foggy?'

'What did I *just* say?' I moaned.

'Oh, yeah. Jesus. Sorry. But it's OK. There ain't a soul around. The joint is like a morgue. It's like word got out that Redhawk and Philip were here or something, and suddenly my place got the stink.'

'Ah. Well, that's too bad, but I have some problems of my own right now.'

'You're telling me. Where are you?' His voice sounded very nervous, and suddenly I wondered if maybe he might not be telling me the truth about his place being empty.

'I'm Nowhere Special. It's just outside of Mind Your Own Business.'

'Look,' he said, 'don't get mad at me just because your playhouse fell down.'

'It did not fall,' I corrected him, 'it was pushed. I was doing my job. Someone else didn't like it.'

'That's the understatement of the year, brother.' He lowered his voice. 'McReedy was *in here*.'

'When?' I panicked a little, partly because there was a man who wanted to kill me abroad in the land, partly because Fat seemed to know all about it. I figured he overheard a lot, but the fact that he knew who McReedy was gave me pause. 'McReedy was in there when?'

'Like, a couple of hours ago.' He sniffed. 'He looked around, didn't say word one to me, and then he was gone. Like that.'

'Did he look mad?'

'He always looks mad.'

'You know him that well?'

'I know enough to be scared to death,' he said. 'And you can't own an establishment in this part of Florida without somehow owing something to the Seminoles, or to Pascal Henderson, who is actually the mortgage holder on my blue heaven. So over the years I've been warned about McReedy. It works – I'm never late with the payment.'

'And yet you say that the place is yours,' I said, unable to keep the suspicion out of my tones.

'You got any idea what happened to the economy last year?' he asked me, incensed. 'I'm lucky I still got half my ass, let alone this joint. I got a second mortgage that's eating my liver! You have no idea what the small businessman faces, my friend. You, with your carefree life of Riley. With that sum-bitch Nixon in the White House, I don't see it getting better anytime soon, either.'

'OK, OK. Times is tough all over.' I took a deep breath. 'So you haven't heard anything else about my particular situation, then.'

'Like what would I hear?'

'Like that Philip shoved McReedy down an elevator shaft or something.'

Fat made a noise like ice cracking. 'You should be so lucky, Foggy.'

'Please stop saying my name.'

'Right. Sorry. But, no news.'

'Nothing at all of interest?' I asked.

'I'm telling you, this joint is like it's closed on account of a death in the family.'

'Gee,' I said, a bit harshly perhaps, 'that's the phrase you decided to use?'

Before Fat could answer I heard scuffling over the phone, and then the distinctive, sickening pop of a handgun firing.

After that, there was nothing.

SEVENTEEN

I had just awakened from a martini-induced coma, so my judgment was cloudy. My reaction to the shock on the phone was to hang up, run out of Gerard's apartment, and run as fast as my wobbly legs could carry me to Pete's Billiard Emporium. Which is always the wrong decision; running *toward* the gunfire.

Nevertheless, within three or four minutes I was standing outside Pete's. To my surprise, the local constabulary was already in evidence. This was something of a shocker too. Under ordinary circumstances you couldn't get a cop to move past tortoise pace unless free food was involved.

The sun had gone, and I was able to hang back a bit, somewhat hidden in shadows. In front of Pete's, I saw two cop cars, several citizens, and a minor but vocal hubbub. There was no ambulance, and I didn't hear sirens. Just as I was trying to decide if this was a good thing or a bad thing, I felt the unmistakable sensation of a gun in the middle of my back – a feeling a person doesn't forget.

I reacted the way the person holding the gun always hopes you will. I held up my hands and said, very politely, 'OK.'

'OK?' said a very high-pitched voice behind me. 'You think this is OK? Because of you, you piece of crap, I got a scraped-up face, a raging headache, and I had to shoot up one of my favorite bars to get your attention. Turn around!'

I did. There before me was a short little guy in a seersucker suit. The right side of his face was a mess, the result of a side-walk surfing. He was sweating like a sweat factory, even though there was quite the chill in the air. He was pointing a very familiar looking pistol at my gut, a .44 Auto Mag Pistol, AMP for short. This was the exact kind of pistol I had taken off the kid at Pete's earlier, the pistol that was now unfortunately gone from my coat pocket.

'You would be McReedy,' I said, continuing my congenial tone.

'Shut up,' he growled.

I did. But not because he told me to. I shut up because of what was behind him. It was a mountain of Philip, just about to smite a mighty smote. I couldn't quite figure how the big guy was moving so quietly. He was like a dancer.

'Here's the thing,' McReedy began.

But he never got a chance to finish whatever it was he wanted to tell me. Philip bashed him in the head with a fist the size of a gumball machine. McReedy went down hard, and his pistol clattered on the sidewalk.

'Let's go,' Philip said and took off, away from Pete's.

I agreed, following in a likewise direction, but not before I scooped up McReedy's gun.

'How did you do that?' I asked Philip, catching up with him.

Philip was now dressed, for some reason, in a tux. For a man his size, he carried it off quite nicely.

'Well, you hit a fellow in the head like that,' Philip said calmly, 'he's going to drop. You have to come in at just the right angle or you'll only make him mad. That's no good, because then he's liable to shoot you. If he has a gun. Now, a man without a gun on the other hand—'

'I meant,' I interrupted, 'how did you move like that?'

'Like what?'

'Silent.'

'Oh.' He smiled, like it was a big joke. 'Old Indian trick.'

'Uh huh,' I said, because I didn't think it was that funny. 'So where are we going?'

'Well, I didn't want to have to kill McReedy. He's just doing his job. But I don't want him to kill you, because the tribe owes you a debt of honor. So after considering all my options, I have decided to take you with me. Besides, I want you to meet someone. So let's go.'

We made it around the corner of the next block to where a beat-up, rusted Army Jeep was parked.

'Where?' I asked.

'What?' he repeated, going to the driver's side of the Jeep.

'Where are we going?' I said.

'Ah,' he told me. 'Into the swamp. Get in.'

PART TWO
Seminole Swamp

EIGHTEEN

The swamp in that part of Florida, where the Seminoles lived, was very humid. Even in the cold part of the evening. We drove for maybe an hour and a half in silence, and I might as well have been on Pluto. I was sweating like the proverbial hooker in temple, and I had absolutely no frame of reference for what I could see by the light of the moon. Everything around me was mystery vegetation, including some trees that had stalagmite-looking things growing up out of their roots. So I had to ask Philip about them, breaking a perfectly peaceful evening drive, except for the bumping and the banging, because a Jeep was never a smooth ride.

'What the hell are those things?' I asked Philip.

'Which things?' He wanted me to be more specific.

'Those things,' I said, pointing, 'that look like stalagmites.'

He glanced. 'Oh. Part of the cypress trees. This swamp is named after those trees.'

'No,' I said, because I thought he didn't see what I was pointing at, 'those things there.'

'Yes, I know. You never saw a cypress tree before?'

'I never saw any of this stuff before. And I'm assuming, since there isn't a light anywhere except your headlights, that we're in the middle of nowhere.'

'No,' he corrected me, 'we're somewhere.'

'I mean, if I jumped out of the Jeep at this point, I would die.'

'Yes.'

'If I got lost in this swamp, you would never hear from me again.'

'Yes.'

'Because I would never find my way out. You're not even on a road as such, so there's nothing for me to follow back to Fry's Bay.'

'No, you're right,' he agreed. 'And besides, something would kill you – or kill you and eat you – within an hour out there.'

I didn't know if he said that to scare me or not, but it was a pretty good line.

'What would kill me? It's my first time in this part of Florida. Nobody around here is mad at me yet.'

'Alligators, water moccasins, diamondbacks, the occasional panther or black bear, and even the wild pigs are pretty mean. They don't have to be mad at you. They just have to be hungry. Any one of them would consider you a nice snack.'

'But your tribe lives in here?' I asked, a little shaken.

'We always have,' he said.

If I didn't think about the teeming wildlife that was, at least according to Philip, hungry for something kosher, I might have thought that the landscape had some wild kind of charm. The moon made everything look nice, I guess; the fan trees, the cypress, the tall grass, and something that smelled like gardenias. I started to think that the place was pretty nice.

'What's that smell?' I asked Philip after another short period of silence.

'Good or bad?' he asked me.

'Good,' I said.

'Mmm,' he told me, smiling and nodding. 'Magnolia. My favorite. Do you know that song? I like that song.'

'What song?'

'*Magnolia*, you sweet thing,' he sang. 'It's J.J. Cale – beautiful. Very sensitive.'

I turned sideways a little so I could get a good look at the big man. His profile was impressive.

'So now I have to ask why you're wearing a tux,' I said, settling back.

'This is Mister Redhawk's idea,' he informed me. 'He says that most people would not suspect that a man in a tuxedo was out to kill somebody, or was a tough guy sort of a person. If you wear a tuxedo, you're headed for some important affair in a hotel or a ballroom, not for bopping a guy in the head.'

'Unless you're James Bond,' I retorted.

He thought for a second. 'Good point. But who, in Fry's Bay, is going to mistake a big Indian for James Bond. He's British.'

'And you're not.'

'Not that I know of.' He smiled.

'Look,' I said, 'maybe I forgot to tell you thanks for stopping McReedy from shooting me. I mean, I can usually take care of myself in this regard, but apparently McReedy is something of a professional, and you never can tell about a thing like that. So. Thanks.'

'You're welcome,' he said right back. 'You certainly do like to talk.'

'You don't?'

'I'm actually enjoying the conversation,' he admitted, smiling bigger, 'but you can probably tell that I'm more the strong silent type.'

'Again with the clichés,' I whined good-naturedly. 'First your "old Indian trick" and now the stereotype of the big man.'

'I come from a simple family,' he explained.

'Fair enough,' I agreed. 'You want me to shut up?'

'Not necessarily.'

'OK so then I'm going to ask where you're taking me. You're taking me to the same place where you've got Lou Yahola and Lynette Baker, right?'

To this statement he did not respond and, just like that, our conversation was over.

So I gazed once again on the scenery. I had thought, in general, that a swamp would be a place with lots of water and bugs and, I don't know, sulfur-like smells. But as the moon luxuriated over the flora, I could see how people wouldn't mind calling this place home. There was a very nice clatter of frogs and owls filling up the air. Every once in a while, I saw a deer hopping around. Pine and cypress trees were everywhere. All in all, it was pretty fetching, as long as you didn't step on a diamondback snake and get poisoned to death.

Strangely, this got me to thinking about the way life was – all in one place you had beauty, nice smells, peaceful sounds, and certain death. All at the same time. In that way, I thought, the swamp was like my part of Brooklyn, minus, of course, the nice smells, and peaceful sounds. We just had beauty and death.

NINETEEN

I didn't have on a watch, but my guess was that it had to be just before midnight when we rolled into the Indian camp. I couldn't say what I had expected, but what I saw in the moonlight was not it. There were a dozen or so small concrete block houses, all with tin roofs. There were dogs, plenty of dogs, but they seemed to recognize Philip and his Jeep. They didn't raise much of a ruckus as we pulled into the compound.

Here and there a few lights were on. Some of the windows were open. I could barely make out the figure of a man sitting beside the front door of one of these hovels. He was smoking a cigarette and seemed to be watching the Jeep.

Philip waved as we came to a halt in front of that particular house. The man waved back. Philip got out. I stayed put, mostly because of the dogs.

Philip said something to the smoking man in what I assumed was the Seminole language. The man answered and they both looked in my direction.

The smoking man stood and took a step or two toward me. He was a fairly old geezer. Even his wrinkles had wrinkles. But his eyes caught the moon just right, and they looked very young. He was dressed in a flannel shirt and jeans – cowboy boots of some sort, no hat. His hair was white like smoke and pulled back behind his head.

He tossed the cigarette in the dirt, ground it out, and motioned for me to come his way.

'I'm a little afraid of the dogs,' I said, soft, so I wouldn't wake up the neighborhood.

The old guy turned to Philip, who repeated what I'd said in his language, I guess, and the geezer laughed. He whistled a couple of times, and the dogs vanished, like they had never been there.

'It's OK now,' Philip assured me.

I looked around and I was skeptical, because a dog can be a tricky animal. You never could tell. Sometimes they wait in the shadows and jump out at you, and make you have a stroke. So I was very cautious, because I figured I didn't need a stroke at that point.

The old man motioned impatiently. He apparently wanted me to walk faster.

I took a few wary steps, but no dogs appeared. I gained a little confidence and ambled a bit more expeditiously. Philip took off his tux jacket. I could see that he had a very clean .44 in a shoulder holster. The cleanliness meant he took care of his gun. Taking care of a gun meant you used it a lot. That told me a little more about Philip, and I began to understand what he said about not shooting McReedy – professional courtesy.

As I approached the old guy, Philip took one step closer to him, sort of protectively. I could see that this was a reflex, so I was not offended, but I wanted to make it clear that I meant the codger no harm, so I held out my hand as to shake his.

Philip said, very politely, 'He won't touch you. Not yet. He's not sure about you. He has to talk with you for a minute. You understand.'

'Who better than I?' I assured him.

'This is one of our older citizens,' Philip explained. 'He's been around for a while, and he knows a lot of stuff. He's not a chief or anything like that. He's maybe the village grandfather or something.'

'Can I ask his name?' I wondered.

'He won't tell anyone his boyhood name, and he has too many titles and adult accomplishments to go into, but sometimes he lets people call him John Horse, after another Seminole from a long time ago. The old John Horse was a great leader, and some of the old members of the community started calling him New John Horse, but since the Old John Horse has been dead for around a hundred years or something, we shortened it to John Horse.'

'Sure,' I agreed congenially, 'because there's really no danger of confusing the two.'

'Exactly.'

'So. I have to say both names? John Horse?'

At that the old geezer raised up his head and said, 'What?'

Philip explained something and the old guy nodded. Then Philip turned to me and said, 'Go on.'

'Go on?' I asked him. 'Where?'

'Into his house,' Philip said.

'By myself?' I held my ground.

'Yeah, and by the way, I have to ask you for McReedy's gun, OK?'

'Oh.' I looked down. 'You saw me take that.'

'Yes.' He held out his massive hand.

I gave out with a fairly hefty sigh, but I dug into my pocket and handed over the pistol.

'You're going to give it back to McReedy, aren't you?' I assumed.

'Maybe.' Philip shrugged. 'One day. If I think of it.'

'I see.'

The old guy was more impatient than ever and began to talk to me in his native tongue.

I glanced at Philip. 'So how am I supposed to understand him?' I asked. 'How are we supposed to communicate?'

'Go on,' Philip repeated. 'It'll all work out.'

I tried to register my doubts with a strenuously unhappy look, but what could I do? I headed toward the old man's door.

This made him smile, and he disappeared very quickly into his house. I moved a little slower, but I achieved the same end: through his front door and into his *shtub*.

My first impression was that it was depressing. It was poorly lit, one lamp. There was a beat-up old chair that a junk heap would have refused to take, a dining table that wasn't much better, a cot that looked like it had been tossed out of a chain-gang prison cell, and various spooky paraphernalia. There was something that looked like a bear skull in one corner next to a bunch of feathers all tied together with brown twine. Five or six cardboard boxes took up another corner. They looked to be filled with papers. On the floor next to the dining table was a two-burner hotplate. Something was simmering there, and it smelled like crap. There was nothing on any of the walls; it was all bare concrete block. There was one window in each wall except for the one with the door. That was it.

The old guy plopped down in the beat-up chair. I looked around, but there wasn't even a pillow I could use for a seat. Still, he motioned me down, using his right hand. It wasn't a command, more like a suggestion.

What the hell, I figured, the pants needed to go to the cleaners anyway. So I sat on the floor.

He smiled. 'Want some tea?' he asked me, with not even a hint of an accent.

I tried not to react too harshly. 'You speak English?'

'I do.'

'So why all the show outside?' I wanted to know.

'I don't know you yet, and I don't trust you,' he said. 'Best not to reveal too much at the start of any relationship. But I feel a little more comfortable inside my own house.'

'OK.'

'So. Tea?'

'Is that what I smell over there on your hot plate?' I asked him. He nods.

'Then I don't think so.'

'It stinks,' he agreed. 'But I think you might like it anyway. I'm going to have some. Give it a try. It's made from black nightshade.'

'I don't know what that is,' I admitted.

'It grows wild around here,' was all he would tell me. 'And you would be rude not to accept my generosity, don't you think?'

'As long as it doesn't taste like it smells, and you drink it first, I'm in, I guess.' I shifted around trying to get comfortable on the floor.

He arose, a little majestically, and motored toward the hotplate. He squatted there, which took all the majesty out of the moment. Somewhere in the shadows there were, apparently, a couple of big coffee mugs. He set them beside his hotplate and poured some of his so-called tea into each one. In a nonce, he was back in his chair, and I was holding a cup that was burning my hand.

'Set it down,' he advised. 'Let it cool.'

I did that. Then I said, 'Look, I appreciate that Philip saved my life, but did he have to lug me out here to your camp or whatever you'd call this compound?'

'I don't call it anything,' he said.

'Fine,' I told him, 'but the point is, I have about a dozen questions for you or for someone like you or for Mister Redhawk or, I don't know—,'

'Stop,' he interrupted. 'Let's just take our time. Let the tea cool. Drink the tea. Then we'll talk.'

'I'm nervous about the tea,' I confessed.

'You're nervous about the answers I might give you, the answers to your questions.'

'I'm nervous because I'm out in the middle of the swamp with rattlesnakes and dogs and people who don't trust me.'

'Well, that's a fair point. I guess anything could happen to you out here. No one would ever know.'

'Thanks,' I told him. 'Thanks very much. That sets me right at ease.'

He chuckled. It's been a long time since I'd heard anyone actually *chuckle*.

'You can relax,' he said. 'We take our debts very seriously, and you've done a pretty good thing. You saved a very important baby.'

'It's my job,' I said.

'There's more to it than that,' he told me quietly. 'For you and for me.'

The way he said it made me think he knew something about me. Then he leaned toward me and said, very seriously, 'Pick up your cup.'

'Do I really have to drink this tea?' I asked him.

'No,' he said, 'but it's bad manners not to. I offer you my hospitality, you're supposed to accept it. Wasn't it that way in your family?'

I had to nod. 'Well, you've got me there. My aunt Shayna would murder you if you didn't eat everything she gave you. And it didn't matter to her if you were stuffed and about to throw up, you still had to take it, like it, and tell her how wonderful she was.'

So I picked up the cup.

'Well, then.' He raised his cup up.

'OK,' I sighed. 'Here goes.'

I watched him take a sip, saw him swallow, and then blow on

the cup. I shrugged. Trying not to inhale, I took the most modest of sips myself.

'Hey,' I said, very surprised, 'it's sweet.'

'That's the orange blossom honey,' he told me. 'It's local.'

I took a bigger gulp.

'Better to sip it,' the old guy warned me.

He sipped again, as if to demonstrate.

So we sat and we sipped, like it was high tea at the Ritz. I had to admit that the drink was warming, and I began to feel a bit of a glow in my face.

'This stuff doesn't by any chance have booze in it, does it?' I asked.

He shook his head. 'No. But what it *does* have, you'll feel in a second.'

I didn't like the sound of that. I set the tea down in front of me. 'You poison me?' I tried to make it sound like a joke, but my voice came out a little unsteady.

He smiled. 'No. I'm drinking it myself. We're going to have a conversation in a few minutes, and when that conversation is done, we'll know each other better. I'll trust you. Or I won't. You'll know me. Or you won't. But there will be no doubt. No confusion of any kind. No one will be on the fence. We'll either be one or the other.'

'One or the other?' I asked him.

'Friends or enemies,' he told me calmly. 'Time will tell.'

I had no idea what he was talking about, but it didn't seem at all good to me, so I leaned forward and tried to stand up. That didn't work out. I couldn't, in fact, coordinate any of my muscles. My brain was disconnected from the rest of my body. I was pretty sure I'd been poisoned, no matter what the geezer had told me.

'Philip!' I called out, trying not to sound too desperate.

I figured it like this: Philip's job seemed to be to protect me from harm. And I was feeling pretty close to panic at that moment. So I thought maybe he'd want to give me a hand.

'He's gone to bed,' the old man said. 'Just settle in. Maybe you'd like to rest your back against the wall. And try not to clench your teeth. That can give you a headache the next day.'

'The next day,' I repeated, getting dizzier and dizzier. 'So I'm going to have a next day, then?'

'Of course.' He downed the rest of his tea and leaned back in his chair. 'This is a herbal medicine. It's very strong. If the mixture is wrong, yes, you could die. But I've been doing this for almost a hundred years, and nothing's gone wrong so far.'

Did he actually say a hundred years, or was I hearing things, I wondered?

'Boys take it at a certain age to show that they've become men – like a bar mitzvah,' he said, 'and, especially, we used to use it in the Green Corn Ceremony, before all of this Christian nonsense took our people.'

I found myself leaning against cold concrete blocks, and I confessed to him, 'I don't really understand what you're saying. I know that you're speaking English, but I can't seem to put the words together right. Personally? I never had a bar mitzvah, and I probably know less about Christian nonsense than you do.'

'Just breathe in and breathe out,' he said slowly.

I accepted his advice, and I realized that the sensation of breathing was very nice. I also realized that it was very loud. My breath sounded like thunder when I exhaled. My heart was pounding in my ears. My face was red hot. And I was having trouble seeing.

'What the hell is in that tea?' I asked him loudly.

'I told you. Black Nightshade. Belladonna. And some nice honey, and a few other ingredients to calm everything down from the nightshade. Why do you ask?'

'What?' I was starting to think I couldn't hear so good.

'In a minute or two I'm going to start asking you questions, OK?'

'What?' I yelled again.

'Just relax,' he said, and again, he chuckled.

I was beginning to hate that chuckle.

Suddenly, something was rustling over in the corner, in the shadows behind the codger's chair. I got it into my head that one of the dogs from outside was over there and about to menace me.

'Get the mutt out of the house, all right?' I asked as politely as I could.

'You see a dog?'

'Isn't that a dog?' I asked and I pointed to the corner.

But, as soon as I pointed in that direction, I saw what was

actually in the corner. It was a dwarf deer. I could tell it was a female deer, though I had absolutely no idea how I would know that.

'Is it a dog?' he asked me without turning around.

'No,' I said softly. 'It's a deer. A little, tiny female deer.'

He grinned ear to ear. 'That's great! What's it doing?'

I started to ask him why he didn't just turn around and see for himself, but the deer blinked. And it was a pretty cute number, so I lost my train of thought.

'What's the deer doing?' he repeated.

'It's looking at me.'

'Is it saying anything?'

I tore my eyes away from the deer and looked at the old man. 'Is it *saying* anything? Is that what you're asking me?'

'No, don't look away!' he snapped.

But it was too late. The deer was gone.

I looked around.

'Where did it go?' I asked him.

'Sh!' he snapped.

We sat there for a while, and I was feeling pretty weird.

'Wait,' he said after a minute, or maybe it was an hour, I had no idea. 'Did you have anything to drink today before you came here? Like alcohol?'

'Yes,' I said immediately. 'I had something very much like alcohol; a nice Hot Tom and Jerry and then two martinis.'

'Oh, hell,' he said to himself. 'I should have asked about that. That's getting in the way.'

'In the way of what? I don't think I could feel any more looped.'

'Just . . . OK, so just listen to the sound of my voice. Close your eyes, all right?'

I shrugged. I closed my eyes. What the hell. I expected to die any second anyway.

'Picture yourself down by the water. There's a nice lake just a few hundred feet from this house. We could walk there right now. The moon is full. The stars are out. The tree frogs are singing. The reflection of the night-time sky in the water is so lovely and so perfect, it's hard to tell the real sky from the mirror. Do you have that in your mind?'

'Sure,' I told him. 'Nice night, a little chilly, but it feels good because my face is hot. I like the tree frogs. That's nice. The moon is big.'

'And beautiful.'

I could see it in my mind's eye. Everything he said.

'And beautiful,' I agreed.

'What else do you see?' he asked gently.

'There's a woman.'

'Yes. A woman. What does she say?'

'Say? She doesn't say anything. But she is entirely without benefit of clothing, and I will tell you that she is not the least bit embarrassed about it.'

Just as I said that, and I was picturing this doll outside by the water, she sauntered over to me and said, 'We're going down into the water. Come with me.'

'It's a little cold for a skinny dip,' I told her.

'Skinny dip?' the old man said.

'You'll be fine,' the girl said and took my hand. Her hand was warm.

She pulled me to the water's edge. I went in. It wasn't so bad. The water wasn't too cold, and it was a lot clearer than I had expected. We sank to the bottom, and it was like we weren't in the water at all anymore. We were in a beautiful house made out of all the things I'd seen in the swamp: cypress stalagmites and pine trees and tall grass. There were other people there, too. Water people.

The doll holding my hand said, very sweetly, 'Have a seat.'

She pointed to a giant water turtle.

I said, 'I'm pretty tired. I'd rather lie down.'

'Oh,' she whispered. 'Good. There's the bed.'

She pointed to a giant yellow snake of some kind, but it looked like a pretty inviting place to take a nap, on the back of a friendly snake. The snake wasn't creepy at all. It seemed very nice.

One of the other water people, an old man – or maybe it was the old man in the chair right in front of me in the concrete house, I couldn't tell which – he said to me, 'Did you kill someone?'

'No,' I said right away. 'Kill someone? What are you asking me?'

'You didn't kill anyone?' he asked me again.

And before I could answer a second time, I realized that I am crying. This got me pretty scared, because I couldn't remember the last time I had cried.

'Why are you crying?' the beautiful doll asked me.

'I don't know,' I told her.

'You know,' the old geezer said.

I was silent for a moment, but then I admitted it. 'Yes. I know.'

And like that, I was back in Brooklyn, and it was three years earlier.

TWENTY

I was on the corner of 53rd and 12th, and it was way after midnight. It was only a few days after I'd found myself on a slab in the morgue, so I wasn't thinking too clearly. Also I had just come from Gravesend Park and was filled with artificial vim and vigor, even though it was around ten blocks from the park to where I was standing now.

It was a nice night. No one on the streets, and I experienced the kind of satisfaction I always had late at night in my neighborhood. It was quiet, for a change, and it was lit by a big yellow moon, and everything in the world seemed to be asleep.

I was thinking of calling it a night myself when, what did I see? Not half a block away there was a 1967 Ford Mustang Fastback, red on red, with silver wheel wells – it was glowing like coal in a fireplace.

I looked around to see if maybe someone was playing a joke on me. No one parked a car like that on the streets around there. Not with a guy like me around. I mean, I had a reputation.

Still, all was quiet, so I took a few casual steps in the direction of this delectable treat. Nothing happened. So I took a few more steps. By and by, I was standing next to the driver's side door. I pulled out my handy rod and hook toolkit and, in seconds, I was sitting behind the wheel of a very nice automobile.

In those days I could hotwire any vehicle in less than ten

seconds. That one took about seven. The car fired up. I eased
the wheel to the left and glided into the street. I turned on the
lights, like it was my own car, and proceeded at a very reasonable pace toward the end of the block.

All of a sudden from behind me I heard the kind of shouting
and yelling that people did when someone had been murdered.
I glanced in the rearview and saw two citizens running after me. I
floored the accelerator, and the Mustang took off like a rocket.

I flashed through three stop signs before I turned left on to
some street or other where the lighting wasn't so good.

It was then that I heard a noise from the back seat that scared
the hell out of me; a sort of inhuman shriek.

I stopped the car in the middle of the street and turned around,
and there, on a soft pallet, buckled in with two seat belts, was a
little kid who couldn't have been much more than a year old.
And it began to wail up a storm.

I didn't know what to do.

I panicked.

I left the car right there in the road and I took off. I beat it
out of the neighborhood, running like a maniac, and I ended up
in Prospect Park by the lake, where I crashed hard. I couldn't
help it. I bedded down under a convenient tree and started hoping
that I'd been dreaming.

It was a day or two later before I heard the news in the neighborhood. Some dame, cheating on her rich husband with a deli
clerk, had left her fourteen-month-old kid in the Mustang that
the aforementioned husband bought her for a present. She was
kissing the sandwich maker goodnight when she heard her car
start up. She and her paramour raced down the stairs just in time
to see the car take off. They hollered up a storm because there
was a baby in the car. They chased the car. They didn't catch it.

But the end of this story, it wasn't good.

Later that night, or early the next morning, the cops found the
car and the kid. The car was fine, the baby was asleep, and all
was well in that regard.

Here's the bad part—the really bad part.

The mother, the owner of the Mustang, she chased the car like
a bat out of hell, and she was screaming and crying, and then
something terrible happened. She felt a cramp in her chest, and

she fell down. Her boyfriend caught up with her. She was having a heart attack. The boyfriend started crying because he didn't know what else to do. And in the time it took for him to decide that maybe he should call an ambulance, the girl died. Just like that.

So I heard this story, and I didn't know what to do. I thought about turning myself in. I thought about visiting the baby in the hospital. I thought about a lot of things. What I actually did was go to Temple for the first time since I was a kid.

And it turned out that I didn't have to do thing one about my guilt or my sleeplessness, because the cops had already put two and two together and were waiting for me when I came home from Temple. As I said, I have a reputation. I didn't try to run. I just put out my hands and they took me into custody in handcuffs.

That was how I found myself in the back of a police car three years ago. That was when I heard the cops talking. One was saying that the charge would be involuntary manslaughter and the other one said that it would be felony theft added to the manslaughter charge, also reckless endangerment and child kidnapping and boom – I'm looking at twenty years. Minimum.

Then came the kicker.

I heard the first cop say, a little softer, that the rich husband was so mad about the fact that his wife had been cheating on him with a deli clerk that he was washing his hands of the whole mess. He was giving up the baby for adoption. The kid was in foster care. Meanwhile, there were also charges against the sandwich maker. I didn't know what they were, but it was a very bad situation all around.

I pondered this for several blocks.

I couldn't stand the idea that there was a little kid up for adoption who ought to have lived the life of Riley with a rich father and a carefree mother. Of course, I also didn't care for the possibility of a twenty-year stretch.

So I did what I thought was right. I slipped out of the handcuffs, got out of the cop car, and ran as fast as I could.

All the way to Florida.

I established myself as a private investigator in the State of Florida and got a license because I gave my real first name, not my nickname, and I spelled my last name a little differently. That was easy to explain. I just had to say the words 'Ellis Island' and everything was clear. No one crosschecked it with any other police files, so I was in the clear.

The thing was, I had become a PI solely in order to find out what had happened to the kid that was an orphan because of me – and I did. The kid got adopted by a very nice professional couple in Yonkers. The father was in advertising and the mother was a dental hygienist.

Then I started actually taking cases as a PI so that I could make a little money. First, I had to eat, and second, I wanted to send a little something every month to the kid anonymously. I did this through a series of beards and a shylock or three, and ended up with an untraceable bank account that only the kid could access. This went on for a few years and, surprisingly, I got pretty good at the job.

Then the State of Florida got federal money on account of the congressional passage of Public Law 93-247, the *Child Abuse Prevention and Treatment Act*. I finagled a job on the team almost instantly. I said it was because I needed the moolah. But maybe Dr Freud would have an alternate explanation.

'I mean,' I said out loud, 'I'm not an idiot.'

And it was at that point I realized that I was saying all of this out loud to the doll under the water in the lake. I was sitting on a turtle's back and all of the water people were staring at me. I had apparently been talking up quite a storm. The beautiful naked doll was crying.

'You certainly do like to talk,' the old man said.

I was a little embarrassed. 'Do you want me to shut up?'

'No,' the doll said.

'If you want to go back to the surface now,' the old man told me, 'you may.'

I looked around. 'OK. Yeah. I think I'd like to. But it's nice down here.'

'You can't stay here,' the girl said sweetly. 'You have to go back, to save children.'

'I know,' I told her. 'I'll go.'

TWENTY-ONE

The next thing I knew, I was opening my eyes. I was outside and the sun was coming up. I was soaking wet. I had two or three blankets over me, and there was a nice big roaring fire close by. I looked up. I was right at the edge of a lake, and the old geezer, John Horse, was sitting beside me, staring out at the water.

I groaned.

'There he is,' the old guy said very jovially.

'What . . . the hell . . . was *that*?' I squeaked out. My voice sounded very squeaky to me.

'That, my friend, was your Indian bar mitzvah.' He thought that was a very, very funny thing to say and laughed until he started coughing.

I sat up, but it wasn't easy.

I did notice that the day was very beautiful. The fact that I was alive at all was a little surprising to me, and the water and the sunrise and the roaring fire, it all worked hard to make me feel better than I could remember feeling in several years. For that, I had no explanation.

'Are you hungry,' John Horse asked me.

'Did you just say the words *my friend* to me a second ago?' I asked him.

'Yes.'

'So. We're not on the fence anymore.'

'I'm not,' he said plainly. 'I don't know how you feel.'

I yawned and stretched. 'I'm surprised to say that I feel, all in all, tip top.'

He nodded. 'Sometimes the medicine works like that. I'm glad.'

'Medicine?' I swallowed, which was also a little difficult. 'I can't begin to tell you how much that was not like medicine.'

He nodded. 'I think it's a matter of how we use the word *medicine*.'

'OK.' I looked back behind me and I saw the camp, or the gathering of concrete houses, or whatever they called the place where John Horse lived. It was about a hundred yards away. 'How did I get out here?'

'Not sure,' he said. 'I took the medicine too, remember.'

'I had the weirdest dreams.'

'They weren't dreams,' he said, but he wouldn't look at me when he said it. And he wasn't smiling.

'Have it your way,' I said, 'but I went underwater in that lake there, with a beautiful naked woman. I met her family and sat on a turtle. That kind of thing, it doesn't happen to me very often, you know.'

'It didn't *happen* to you either. It wasn't a dream, and it didn't happen.'

'I almost went to sleep on a snake.' I shivered at the thought.

'You also told the water people why you're in Florida.'

'Yeah,' I said slowly. 'I remember that.'

'You're in exile from your home. I know what that's like. I was forced to go to Oklahoma, once, when I was a teenager. I was made to go to school there. Oklahoma is a terrible place.'

'I wouldn't know,' I admitted. 'And also I don't know what you're talking about.'

'I've been told that guilt is something your people have more than my people,' he said, 'but we've got it too. I understand.'

'My people?' I asked, a little riled. 'What is it with that crap? I just had to explain to another person the way I'm about to explain to you: I'm not a Caucasian. I'm not the white man. *My* people were slaves to Pharaoh before *your* people even existed! My people invented the Ten Commandments, for God's sake!'

'But you didn't invent guilt,' he said, smiling. 'That was my point.'

'Oh.' I nodded. 'OK, then.'

'You don't want to talk about your past,' he said. 'I understand that too. Maybe you're hungry, though.'

'I am,' I told him. 'I'm famished.'

'I'm not surprised,' he said, standing up. 'You threw up six or seven times last night.'

'That's why you got me out here and tossed me into the lake?'

'I didn't bring you out here,' he said.

He moved to the fire and took something out of it. 'You need to let this cool a little, but it's good.'

He tossed an ear of corn, still in the husk, on to the blankets covering my legs. I could tell it was hot, but through the blankets it felt kind of good. Warming.

He got another ear in his hand and he was peeling back the husk very carefully. I could see the steam rising off the white kernels, and I could smell how sweet it was. He got all the husk back and used it as a sort of handle, waving the ear around in the cold morning air. After a while he took his first bite. I could hear the pop and crunch. Suddenly I was so hungry I felt like eating the whole thing, husk and all.

So I did exactly what he did: peel, wave, bite.

'God in Heaven,' I sighed once I swallowed. 'This is the best tasting thing I've ever eaten in my entire life.'

He nodded, still chewing, 'It's good.'

We ate in silence for a minute and I was praying there was more corn. Just as I finished my last bite, I saw him toss his decimated corncob into the lake and go to the fire. He pulled out two more.

I couldn't say how many pieces of corn we ate, but it was a lot. The sun was a little higher, and I was drying out nicely by the fire.

He sat down beside me and we stared into the lake. 'So. Are you mad at me?' he asked. 'Or are we friends?'

I looked at him sideways. 'Friends? I don't know.'

'All right,' he allowed, 'you can think about it for a while. You had a hard night.'

'If you say so,' I told him. 'I have no idea what went on. You gave me some kind of strange tea, I spill my guts both literally and figuratively – I don't know what to make of it. Can you blame me for not knowing how I feel about you?'

'Would it help if we went to see Lynette and her baby?' he asked. 'You can see that we're helping them. Might make you feel better. Might help you to decide how you feel.'

I tossed my final corncob into the lake. 'It might. But I think you're going to have to help me get to my feet. I'm still pretty zonked.'

*　　*　　*

I was assured that it would be a short drive from where the old guy lived to the hut where they were keeping Lynette and child. I was still a little wet and, despite the sun, the day seemed cold. The Jeep that Philip was driving did not have a top. Or heat. Luckily the old guy let me take the blankets with me, so I wasn't too freezing. I was sitting in the backseat by myself, and Philip and John Horse were up front.

I didn't pay much attention to my surroundings because I used the short drive to get my mind in the right place. I couldn't figure why these Seminole people had kidnapped Lynette and baby. I didn't understand why Sharon's father, the unbelievably rich Pascal Henderson, would send McReedy to kill me. What was the connection between those two circumstances, I had to ask myself? What, I wondered, was I missing? Whatever it was, it was a big piece of a very odd puzzle. Unfortunately, I was beginning to feel the effects of the morning after the night before, and my brain had fuzz on it.

'You should just sit back and relax,' John Horse told me, like he could read my mind. 'You'll feel better when you see that the girl and her child are doing well. And then I'll answer your questions. I'm sure you have questions.'

'OK,' I agreed and settled back.

Not three minutes later we came through a dense patch of forest into a clearing. There was only one building in the clearing, and it was a whole lot more like what I had been expecting from an Indian village. It was a kind of dome, maybe a hundred square feet, covered over with brush and twigs and fan palm. There was a hole in the top, and smoke was coming out of it. There was an opening in front covered by blankets, which were very much like the ones I had covering me. On either side of that opening there were two men, Seminoles obviously, both sitting down on folding chairs. They both had on denim jackets and jeans and construction work boots. They weren't wearing hats. And they both had rifles.

The Jeep slowed down. One of the riflemen waved. Philip waved back.

'Come on,' John Horse said gently. 'You can keep the blankets around you if you're cold. It's all right.'

I hauled myself out of the back of the Jeep, still wrapped in the blankets, and I managed not to look too stupid. The riflemen stood up. One of them said something softly, and John Horse smiled. Close up, I could see that both guards were fairly young, not much older than the teenaged toughs who tried to menace me at Pete's. Wet and wrapped in blankets, I began to feel a little old.

John Horse went into the thing and Philip indicated that I should follow, so I did. Then Philip came in after me.

The inside was like a different world. It was very warm. There was a fire in the center, and it gave off a very cheery glow. The floor and the wall areas were covered with blankets. There was no furniture, as such, but a little tree stump served as a table. It smelled very nice, like lavender and rosemary and something else I couldn't quite place – maybe cedar.

And seated in front of the fire with a lovely look on her face was, I presumed, Lynette Baker. She was holding a sleeping baby. She was dressed in a loose blue flannel nightgown. She had her hair back in a bun, and her face was pink and calm.

'Lynette,' John Horse said very softly, 'this is Foggy Moscowitz, the man who found your baby.'

She smiled and shook her head.

'She's cleansing,' John Horse said to me. 'She'd rather not talk.'

'OK by me,' I said.

'Have a seat,' he told me.

I sat down on the blankets on the opposite side of the fire from Lynette. She didn't look up. She was staring at the baby.

John Horse sat beside me. Philip was standing by the door.

'Now,' John Horse began, 'let me see if I can answer your questions. You have questions. I'd have questions if I were in your shoes.'

'I do,' I admitted.

'Go on, then.'

I looked around. 'Let's start with the immediate. What is this place? It's a lot more in keeping with the whole Indian gestalt than your concrete house, if you don't mind my saying so.'

He smiled. 'This is what some people call a sweat lodge. It's a healing place.'

'You have Lynette in here to get her off the junk,' I said bluntly.

He nodded. 'The baby too. But that isn't really your most pressing question.'

'I'm warming up,' I told him. 'My most pressing question is that I'm very confused about why you have these two people here at all. I got a call from my boss last night – just as I was getting off work, I might add – that there was a missing baby. That's our racket where I work; we take care of things like that. So I went to the hospital, and there was Maggie Redhawk, a fine person, and she was very concerned about the situation, as she should be. To make the story short, I found the kid, took it to the hospital, and then you stole the kid, Lynette disappeared, and my boss's illegitimate father sent this McReedy character to shoot me. Not to mention that someone sent Mister Redhawk, whose first name I do not know, with Philip, whose last name I do not know, to protect me from the evil McReedy. And then Philip kidnapped me, and here we are.'

John Horse nodded, staring into the fire. After a minute he said, without looking at me, but with a little too much amusement in his voice. 'That's not really a question.'

'Oh,' I said, 'then let me be more specific. What the hell is going on?'

He smiled, still not looking at me. 'That's not really more specific.'

I shook my head. 'What do you want from me?'

'I want a real question,' he said unequivocally.

I thought for a second, trying to get the fuzz off my brain from the previous night's escapade. I glanced over at the baby, and there was the question: the baby.

'What's so important about this newborn?' I said softly. 'Why the hubbub about this kid?'

'There,' he said, very satisfied. 'That's the question I'd ask if I were you. Good. I'll tell you that.'

And then he was absolutely silent.

The fire popped. The smoke went up. I watched it, looking up at the morning sky through the hole in the lodge. I smelled the rosemary, and it was very calming. After a minute, John Horse started to hum with his eyes closed. It wasn't even a melody. It was more like a bee, a very low bee buzzing. The sound was making me sleepy all of a sudden, but I didn't want to get sleepy, so I moved around.

Suddenly John Horse stopped humming, opened his eyes, and said this: 'The baby that Lynette Baker had is a water spirit. There hasn't been one born to the Seminoles since the white man came to us. It's a very good sign that we have one now, and probably means that better days are coming for the Seminole people, at least in this part of Florida. Because of this, we had to make sure that the baby was safe and healthy. Part of the wellbeing of any child is a loving mother, so we had to make sure that Lynette was healed. We had to bring them both here to make these things happen, because we had to cleanse them in the Seminole way. That's my answer. The baby is very important to the future wellbeing of our people. It's a water spirit.'

I blinked. 'A water spirit.'

'Yes,' he said. 'That's why, last night, you visited the water people. That confirms something that I already knew, but some of the others wanted proof.'

'What are you talking about?' I tried not to sound irritated, but that didn't work out.

'You're a part of this. Otherwise you would have just thrown up and gone to sleep last night. I knew you were an important part of this, but Mister Redhawk was uncertain. Now he knows.'

I bit my upper lip. Just when I thought that everything was going to make sense, or at least that everything was going to be a little bit more comprehensible, I got this run-around.

'Now Mister Redhawk knows that I'm a part of this Indian fairytale?' That came out even worse than my previous question.

John Horse did not seem the least disturbed. 'You might have heard from someone, the real name of Fry's Bay is *Owv Hokte*. It means *Water Woman*.'

'I am familiar with that,' I admitted, albeit hesitantly.

'Once, all of this was a sacred land, a place where spirits and human beings lived together in harmony. But then a water spirit fell in love with a Seminole boy. She took on the form of a woman, and these two copulated. Their union produced a race of shadow spirits who came and filled the woods and trees and rocks and water and air all around us. They're still here. They're waiting.'

'Waiting for what?' I had to ask.

'This.' He glanced in Lynette's direction. 'Waiting for this child to be born.'

TWENTY-TWO

B efore I could ask my next of about a hundred questions, I suddenly felt Philip grab my arm, and I was whisked out of the teepee or whatever that thing was, and I found myself out in the open once again. John Horse followed close behind.

'So, John Horse,' I said, glancing at the silent young men with rifles in their hands, 'you want me to believe this, what you just told me?'

Once again, he was not insulted. He seemed to find the whole thing very amusing. He headed for the Jeep and motioned me to come with him.

'Bye, Grandpa,' one of the young Seminole guards whispered to me.

John Horse didn't hear that, or ignored it. He was already halfway to the Jeep. 'So,' I said, deliberately ignoring the kid, 'this is it? You dragged me away from my nice warm fire and that delicious roasted corn just to show me Lynette and baby, and now you give me the bum's rush?'

'I had to show you that Lynette and her child were safe from harm. That's what you were concerned about. You said that's your job, and it is – for the moment.'

'Look, John Horse,' I said, climbing into the Jeep, 'I think maybe I talked too much last night – a little too much about my personal life – while I was hopped up on Indian tea. I mean, that tea you gave me was a little too, what's the word?'

'Liberating?' he suggested.

The Jeep engine started up.

'No,' I told John Horse. 'I mean I was a little too—'

'Honest?' he interrupted.

'Stop,' I told him, 'I'm trying to collect my thoughts.'

'No you're not,' he said.

The Jeep made a U-turn and headed away from the lodge. I couldn't tell for sure, but it looked like we were going somewhere besides back to John Horse's house.

'You spoke the truth last night,' John Horse said. 'You don't like that because you haven't been completely honest with anyone about why you came to Florida. But I can tell you, from what I understand of your story, you're doing the right thing.'

'I'm not exactly certain *what* I said last night,' I told him. 'That stuff . . . I mean, I was talking out of my head for a while there.'

'But you spoke the truth,' he repeated. 'And it seems to me that something picked you up and shook you around, and then set you down in Florida. Now, instead of being a car thief, you rescue children. That's something, wouldn't you say?'

'I'm not comfortable discussing my past,' I said sharply. 'Could we change the subject, do you mind?'

'Did you ever have turtle steak?' he asked me instantly.

I got a little whiplash from his sudden change of topic, but I also appreciated it. 'No,' I told him, 'I never had turtle steak.'

'I think you're going to like it,' he said.

'It's good,' Philip chimed in. 'I bread it in corn meal and fry it up.'

'You have to tenderize it, of course,' John Horse said, 'and marinate it. But Philip's way is very good.'

'I beat the hell out of it with the butt of my pistol,' he said, smiling, 'and then I marinate it in oil and brine. It melts in your mouth.'

John Horse only nodded. He was done talking.

The rest of this Jeep ride passed without further conversation, so I had another opportunity to settle down and gander at the scenery. Once we left the clearing, the woods got plenty dense. Pine and cedar and underbrush were all around us, and the road was barely two wheel ruts in the ground. There were all kinds of animal noises, but the animals themselves were hiding. We were definitely not headed back to John Horse's house. I got the impression, from the brief discussion of turtle steak, that we might have been going to Philip's place.

As we rounded a sudden turn in the road, we surprised a flock of birds and they took off flying like angels, white wings and all. They rose up in a kind of spiral, maybe fifty of them. And then they disappeared into the trees. The Jeep started to slow down. We were coming up to a house literally built into a grove of trees. It was the most unusual house I had ever seen.

The sides of the house were almost touching the bare trees around it, and some of the overhead branches were bent way over to help out with roof duty. It looked like somebody had built a strange little bungalow and then these trees had grown up around it. The door was red, the windows had no curtains, and the roof was made of wooden shingles.

'This is very unusual,' I muttered, somewhat to myself.

'This is my house,' Philip said, and you could hear how proud he was.

'I can say without fear of contradiction,' I told him, 'that I've never seen another house like this in the entire world.'

'I know,' he said, staring at it and smiling.

'How long have you lived here?' I asked.

'Since I was a kid,' he said. 'My father built it. I've lived here almost all my life, and I still can't believe how great it is.'

'It's pretty great,' I agreed, 'it's like . . . *nestled.*'

'It is,' Philip agreed.

'We're going in here so that you can take a bath,' John Horse said to me. 'You stink. Your sweat smells like liquor and dead animals.'

'That would be the brisket that I ate yesterday,' I said, not the least offended, 'and the martinis I had last night. I will admit that I do not recall the last time I had a shower.'

'No shower, sorry,' Philip said. 'But I got a really nice bathtub.'

'And then Philip will make you some fried turtle steaks,' John Horse assured me.

We all got out of the Jeep and headed for the little cabin in the woods. Picturesque as it was, it was also solid as a rock, watertight and heavy.

Philip opened the door. It wasn't locked. I followed him in. The inside was every bit as impressive as the outside. The ceilings were high, maybe twenty feet, and they were arched like a cathedral.

'Man,' I said, 'this is really nice.'

'Yes,' Philip said, continuing on into his home.

'And you say your father built this joint.'

'Yes.'

'At least, what? Twenty years ago?'

'Twenty-seven, in fact,' Philip answered.

'And these trees grew around it like this?'

'Ah,' Philip said, turning to face. 'I think I see what you're getting at. Am I worried that one day the house will bust apart as the trees grow?'

'Bingo,' I said.

'Easy. My father and John Horse put a spell on these trees. They don't grow anymore.'

I glanced at John Horse. He avoided eye contact.

The décor of the joint was simple, if completely strange. It was one big room. It looked like there was a small stream running through the house, parallel to the back wall. There was a very nice rock border. There was one window in one of the side walls. The wall opposite the window had a small stone fireplace. The floor looked like moss, and it was a little soft for my comfort. The walls were all wood. I couldn't tell what the ceiling was. There was a large bed toward the back of the room, a bench and several chairs in the middle, arranged the way a sofa and club chairs would have been if it were a different kind of home. There was a chest of some sort by the bed.

It wasn't warm inside the place, there was no fire in the fireplace, but it wasn't too bad. I was almost dry at that point anyway.

'Where can I put these blankets?' I asked.

'Just drop them on the floor by the door, there,' Philip answered.

'You like this house,' said John Horse.

'I am most intrigued by the furniture,' I told him. 'Especially that bench, and the bed.'

'Amish,' Philip said proudly. 'All of this furniture is made by the Amish. I like them, as a people. In general.'

Once again I turned to John Horse for explanation. 'The Amish?' I said. 'The guys from Pennsylvania that look like Hassids?'

'In Sarasota,' John Horse told me, 'there is a little neighborhood they call Pinecraft. Plenty of Amish, some Mennonites stay there. This may be a new occurrence, I don't know. But there they are.'

'Seriously?' I clearly did not believe him, though I could not understand why he'd lie about it. 'The Amish in Florida?'

'I was in Sarasota on business once,' Philip said, as if that would explain everything. 'That's how I found them.'

'Their ideas are very simple,' John Horse said. 'I like them too.'

'That's not the point,' I complained. 'I . . . look, you know what? I don't care. I don't care about the Amish or the spell you put on a tree, or that goddamned tea you gave me last night. I only want to know one thing.'

'Why are you here in Philip's house?' John Horse ventured.

'Exactly!' I said, a little too loudly. 'Or I can make it even more general. Why am I here on Indian land at all? Why am I not asleep in my bed?'

John Horse nodded very sagely. 'I see. This is a complex question, of course, if you refer to your bed in Brooklyn. I think that answer is very complex.'

'My bed in Fry's Bay!' I said impatiently.

'Only a little less complicated,' he told me.

Meanwhile, Philip sat down on the Amish bench and offered his two cents. 'If you were home in your bed in Fry's Bay right now, you'd be dead. McReedy would have shot you in the head at least twice.'

'Twice?' I glared at Philip.

'He's very thorough.'

'You brought me here to save me from McReedy?' I asked, my words dripping with skepticism.

'Yes,' said John Horse. 'Partly.'

'Why do you care?' I fired back.

'Because you saved the child that is going to save us all,' John Horse told me in no uncertain terms.

'Oy, this again,' I moaned.

Philip smiled. 'Did you actually just say the word *oy*?'

'It comes out under duress,' I admitted, and perhaps my voice was a bit shrill.

John Horse nodded again, folding his arms. 'Are you thirsty?' he asked me.

I thought for a second, swallowed, and answered, 'Now that you mention it, I am a bit dry.'

'It's the tea,' John Horse said.

'I'm not drinking any more of your tea,' I assured him.

'I've got Coca-Cola!' Philip jumped up and stepped over to the little stream running through the back of his home. He dipped a hand down into the water and came back with three bottles of Coke. With each one he used his thumb to flick off the top; no small feat. Although, his was no small thumb, so I was not completely amazed. He handed out the bottles and sat back down.

As it turned out, the cola was nice and cold, and it went down pretty good.

'You want to sit down?' Philip asked me.

I looked around at the Amish numbers, all wood and right angles, picked one out, and sat. Better than the ground. John Horse sat on the bench beside Philip, and we fell into a kind of comfortable silence for a second or two.

Alas, I would not leave well enough alone. 'How long do I have to stay here?'

John Horse downed the rest of his Coke, set the bottle in his lap, and belched. Then he said, 'Why don't you just stay here as long as you like?'

'OK, then,' I fired back, 'I'm about at the end of that period, the period where *I like*, and now I'm ready to go home.'

'No you're not,' John Horse said, and he was laughing. 'You're not nearly ready to leave here. You haven't finished telling me your story, you haven't heard what I have to say, you don't know what to do next, and you have to talk with Lynette again. All that? It could take days. Weeks.'

'Now, look!' I set my Coke down on the mossy floor. It immediately fell over. 'I'm not staying here for weeks. I'm leaving right now.'

'I hate to disagree,' said John Horse, 'but how do you think you're going to leave? You can't have Philip's Jeep, and even if you could, you wouldn't know where to drive it. You have no idea where you are. You'd be dead before sundown if you left right now.'

A brief consideration of the facts left me feeling a little tapped out. McReedy would certainly get me if I went back to Fry's Bay. The swamp would get me if I tried to leave Indian Town. And, if I was forced to look at the bigger picture, the cops would get me if I tried to do much of anything else. So I was beginning to think of myself as fairly well screwed.

John Horse seemed to read my face, and he said, 'It's not so bad. You'll talk with me, we'll arrive at some conclusions, you'll feel better. Maybe even good enough to consider going back to Brooklyn.'

And of all the things John Horse had said to me, that was the thing that set my neck hairs on end. I reached down to pick up my nearly empty Coke bottle so that he would not be able to read my face again, because I was suddenly very, very nervous about the old guy.

I was beginning to understand that he was only playing the part of the wise old Indian medicine man. I had to wonder why he was interested in sending me back to Brooklyn, why he wanted to keep me out of Fry's Bay, and why he really wanted to keep Lynette. Because I did not, for a second, buy the line about her baby being a water spirit.

I mean, at first I had thought of this so-called John Horse as a convenient and convivial movie character. He was Chief Dan George from *Little Big Man* – a film that I saw three times on account of Dustin Hoffman, who was one funny Jew.

But now I saw John Horse as a sinister figure who kidnapped me, drugged me, got my story, and then wanted to keep me out of Fry's Bay – *way* out, like, far-away-as-*Brooklyn* out. All his nice manners and mystical pronouncements were a pose, and I would have none of it.

'Well,' I said, looking down, 'since I really can't do anything else, I guess I'll content myself to stay here and chat a while. Have some of the aforementioned turtle steak. But I really do have to be getting back to my apartment in Fry's Bay eventually. I have a job there. I have half a pizza in the refrigerator that will turn into a science project if I don't return to it in several days. And then there is the little matter of my ongoing investigation into the disappearance of Lynette Baker's baby. See, I haven't filed my report yet, the paperwork that makes my boss get off my back. See, to her – and to everybody else in the United States Government – that file is still open. By and by, someone will begin to wonder why. And then the creaky wheels of bureaucracy will begin to scrape together, rust will fall away, and a big machine of useless power will be unleashed. Alas, it just may roll your way. And you don't want that.'

Philip turned to John Horse and said, 'I love the way he talks. It's like poetry.'

'But he's troubled.' John Horse lowered his voice. 'Foggy. You're uncomfortable that I know about your past. That's completely understandable. Would it help you to know . . . would you feel better if you knew why I was in jail?'

'You were in jail?'

'I was in jail because I killed a horse,' he said.

That sentence hung in the air for a moment.

'That's really how I got my name,' he went on. 'I know what Philip told you about my name, and there really was a Seminole a century ago called John Horse, a real hero. But, mainly, I got this name because I killed a horse.'

I stared.

'You actually killed a horse?' I finally asked.

'Wasn't mine,' he said. 'That was the problem.'

Against my better judgment, I was forced to say, 'OK. I'll bite. What happened?'

'I'll tell you.' John Horse settled into his seat, slumped down a little, and began. 'It was an army horse. Belonged to the United States Government. Back in 1957, the first real Tribal Council was formed. Had elected representatives and everything. That's when the white Congress officially recognized us, even though we never signed a peace treaty with them. The problem was, some of us wanted to be known as the Miccosukee Tribe, and some of us wanted to be Independent Seminoles. Unfortunately, the Independents weren't recognized by the Bureau of Indian Affairs. This was a problem for me, because I was one of the Independents. I am against any government interference in my life. I also claim this entire swamp, and most of the state of Florida. This land all belongs to us. But, every once in a while, someone in the white government disagrees with us, and they send in people to convince us that we're wrong. Most of them never leave the swamp. I'm not sure what happens to them.

'But one man, an Army captain named Brighton, visited me in my house. He came in on horseback. I think he did it to show that he understood something about me. But he didn't. We argued, he got mad, he shot me, so I shot him, but he used his army pistol and I used my hunting rifle and my bullet went through him, busted my front window, and killed his horse.'

'The captain didn't die,' Philip said to me, filling in an important detail that John Horse had omitted.

'Yes,' I said, 'that's an important thing to know about the story. So, John Horse, you did not really get arrested for killing a horse, you got arrested for screwing with the *man*.'

'No.' John Horse shook his head. 'The man was fine. The horse was dead. I went to jail. I know what I did.'

'John Horse was wounded in the leg, and they didn't take him to the hospital,' Philip said. 'They wrapped a bandage around it and took him right to jail. All the way to the Columbus stockade.'

'I was there for several months,' John Horse said. 'I almost died.'

'Our lawyers got him out,' Philip said. 'They even sued the Army. But they lost.'

'They got John Horse off, though,' I concluded.

'No,' said Philip.

'I skipped bail in 1965,' John Horse said. 'I don't know if there's still a warrant out for me or not. But I haven't seen any army around my house for years now, so I might be all right.'

'You never went to trial?' I asked. 'You just beat it into the swamp and stayed here?'

He nodded, and I suddenly saw why he told me this story.

'Kind of like you did,' he said to me, smiling like a fox, 'coming to Florida.'

'Look,' I admitted, 'I'm not certain what I said to you and what I just imagined last night under the influence of your funny tea. But I gather that you think you know my story.'

'Oh, I do,' he said. 'You stole a car, the mother chased you down, she had a heart attack and died. You think that's your fault. The mother had a baby who is now in foster care, and you feel responsible for that baby. That's why you're in exile. That's why you have the job that you have. That's why you're here in this room with Philip and me right now. Because you think if you save enough babies, eventually the end of your story will be different: the woman would not die, the baby would not be given away, and you'd be snorting coke in Gravesend Park with your petty criminal cronies.'

I had to admit, that was pretty much the story, and it disturbed me greatly that he knew it. So I realized what I had to do.

'I have to go to the bathroom,' I said, standing up. 'Where is it?'

'I got no bathroom,' Philip told me, grinning.

This I already knew because I cased the place when I walked in.

'Well, I really have to go,' I told him. 'Maybe it's this cola.'

'You just go outside,' Philip said, still amused, 'far away from my house, not too close to anything in the swamp that would eat you, and do your business.'

'Christ,' I said, deliberately grumbling all the way to the door, although this was exactly how I had hoped things would go.

'Watch your step if you get too far away,' John Horse said plainly. 'There's a lot of swamp mud. That's what happened to a lot of the soldiers, I think. They fell in the mud and never got out.'

Philip grinned bigger.

I shoved through the door, jamming my fists into my pants, hoping to appear very angry as I left the house.

TWENTY-THREE

Now, hotwiring an old Jeep was, for me, a cinch. Philip's model, as it happened, was an M715 from 1965, a product of Kaiser-Jeep. It had heavy full-floating axles and a foldable windshield. I wouldn't care to give away too many tricks of my trade, but the first thing to know about starting an M715 would be that it had an on/off switch. If you wanted to start the thing, you had to turn it on. Then it was really just a matter of tricking the wiring, either through the fuse or through the positive cable and starter wires, into thinking that you've turned a key, which gave the sparkplugs a jolt and exploded a bit of gasoline.

By the time I was backing the Jeep up to turn it around, Philip and John Horse were out the front door of the little cabin in the woods. But it was too late. I gunned the engine and took off like a rocket down the wheel-rut road, glancing only once into the rear view to see two Seminole Indians chasing after me – and fading, ever-so-slowly, into the distance.

I kept my eyes locked on the wheel ruts, and followed the only path back out of that particular part of the swamp. It wasn't hard. It wasn't like I had a lot of choices. There was only one road, and I'm not an idiot.

Eventually I saw a clearing, the place where the lodge Lynette and baby were. I slowed down the Jeep, but something in me said, *Don't be a big shot, don't think this out. Just follow your nose, and you'll do what you need to do.*

So I drove right up to the door, about where Philip had parked the Jeep before. I left it running, of course, and hopped out, waving at the teenaged guards and smiling.

'Hi!' I said. 'John Horse told me to come get Lynette and the baby. He wants to talk with them. I mean, he has some questions to ask. So he sent me.'

I motored ahead, right for the door, before the two kids could even rouse themselves. They didn't appear to understand what I was saying, but I found it hard to believe that they didn't speak English, so I said it again, only louder.

'John Horse told me to come get Lynette and the baby. He wants to talk with them!'

They were up with rifles pointed before I could get all the way to the door.

'Why didn't Philip come?' one asks.

'Have you seen his house? All those trees,' I said. 'One of the limbs got busted in the rain last . . . no, night before last. He's trying to save his roof.'

'Bullshit,' the other guy said and pointed his rifle right at me. 'That house is as solid as a rock.'

'Well, then,' I said, pretending to be as perturbed as I could be, 'why did John Horse send me, genius?'

Tough it out, that's what I always said. The best defense is a kiss-my-ass offence, and it generally works. At least, it worked sometimes in Brooklyn.

The genius looks at the other guy and you could see that they were both trying to figure it out, so I barreled ahead, right for the door.

'Hold on,' the first guy said. 'Not so fast.'

And he put the rifle right on my chest.

'Really?' I said. 'You think it's the best idea to put a hole in my chest when I came here to do what John Horse told me to do? Let's follow your logic all the way to the end. I'm dead, on the ground, with my heart shot out. John Horse shows up, wondering what's keeping me. He looks at my corpse, then he looks at you guys, and he says, "What the hell? What did you do?" And what will you say?'

'This doesn't seem right,' the genius said.

'Well,' I began, taking one step closer, 'let me see can I explain it to you in a way that you will understand.'

Fighting a guy who is bigger than you is always a question of leverage. It was actually better that he had a rifle instead of a pistol. I grabbed the genius's gun by the barrel, put my left foot behind his left foot, and I pushed really hard. He let go of his rifle, I bopped his head with the hard part of the gun barrel, and he went down backward.

Before goon number two could figure out what was going on, I had the rifle by the barrel and I used it like a club. I swung it upward, fast as I could, and landed it right on the guy's chin, at which point he didn't feel like standing anymore.

Honestly, I was wishing somebody had seen me do this. It was a thing of beauty. There I was, with a fistful of rifle and two unconscious goons at my feet.

'Who's the grandpa now?' I asked them, but they seemed disinclined to answer.

'What's going on out there?' said a plaintive little voice from inside the lodge.

'Lynette?' I called out, dropping the rifle and stepping over the Indians.

I pushed the door cover open, and there she was, all by herself, naked, nursing her baby and smiling very sweetly.

She looked up.

'Let's go,' I said, moving her way.

She looked back down at her baby. 'I don't think so,' she said.

I got closer to her, and I saw why she wasn't in the mood to go anywhere. In front of her, by her left knee, was a nice wooden bowl and I could smell what was in it—it was very strong, the same kind of tea that John Horse had given me that made me wacky.

Then I noticed that, also close by, there were vials of very official looking hospital-type medicine, and I surmised that this was the juice that Maggie Redhawk wanted to get to the baby. But I didn't linger.

I zipped back to the door, tore down the blankets there, and brought them back to Lynette. I draped the blankets around her and got her to her feet. She didn't protest because she didn't seem to understand what was happening. I figured she didn't know if she was in trouble or in Cleveland. I tried to reassure her.

'We're going for a little ride in a Jeep,' I said, like to a five-year-old. 'How would that be?'

She smiled. I took this to mean she was all right with the idea.

I maneuvered her around the fire and through the open door, stepping over the sleeping Seminoles, and moved as quickly as I could toward the Jeep. The engine was beginning to cough, because it was cold, and old, and maybe even low on gas. I got mother and baby into the passenger seat with only a modicum of trouble, and made it to the steering wheel just in time to hear the first rifle shot. One of the Seminole guards was awake.

The bullet whizzed past my left ear. The shooter aimed outside, instead of between me and Lynette, so as not to disturb mother and baby. I thought that was very considerate. Then I put the Jeep into reverse and floored the accelerator. We flew backwards, in the direction of the gun. It was my theory that when a guy had something as big as a Jeep coming right at him, he's going to panic, at least a little, and momentarily forget how to fire his gun.

In this particular case, the theory worked. I screeched on the brakes just in time so as not to hit the guy hard enough to kill him. But I did tap him pretty good. He went flying into the side of the lodge. Then I shoved the gearshift into some forward gear and the Jeep made a jump, spraying dirt and grass behind us. We shot forward on to the wheel-rut road.

As it happened, I have always had pretty good spatial memory. I could be on a street anywhere in any town just once, and I could always find my way back to it. I was hoping that the same talent applied to a ride in the swamp. And I had a couple of things still on my side. The day was still young, it wasn't too cold, and maybe the rain was all gone.

Lynette was serene, the baby was still nursing, and I had a very good feeling about myself, our chances, and the world in general.

TWENTY-FOUR

I have no idea how many hours went by, but the sun was sinking low by the time Lynette's tea wore off, and I had reversed my previous rosy assessment of our chances. We were about as lost as a person could get.

Lynette, meanwhile, was groggy and trying to get her bearings.

'Where the hell am I?' she asked, her voice harsh and gravelly.

'Swamp,' I answered, trying to concentrate, 'Seminole territory. Lost as hell.'

'And who are you?' She didn't sound alarmed – more like she was trying to remember something that she thought she ought to know.

'I am the man,' I told her, summoning all the pomp I could muster, 'who rescued your baby from Lou Yahola. By the way, you understand how crazy it was to leave the baby with that guy, right? This was a sorry choice that you made. The baby was very, very sick. What goes on in your head?'

'I was in the hospital.' She squeezed her eyes shut for a second, obviously trying to snap out of her stupor. 'I had a baby.'

'Yes,' I said, not bothering to hide my irritation. 'Welcome to your life.'

'I had to get the baby out of the hospital,' she said, lowering her voice. 'I couldn't let them get her. She's a very important baby.'

I nodded, but I was only humoring her, because, suffice it to say, I knew paranoia when I saw it.

So I told her, to soothe her, 'No, but, see – it's OK now. I'm taking you away from the bad Indians.'

'What?' She was trying, you could see, to rouse herself. 'You think . . . you're trying to . . . wait. Stop the Jeep.'

I didn't.

'Stop the goddamn Jeep or I'll jump!' And, to prove her point, she started to stand up.

I eased back off the accelerator. 'Whoa. What are you doing?'

'I *want* the Seminoles to . . . you have to take me back. I'm supposed to be there, with them, with John Horse. It . . . look, dumbass, I didn't hide my baby with Lou Yahola to keep her from the Seminoles, I was trying to hide her from her father! Did you come here to . . . wait – did you come here to take me back to him?'

'Who?'

'The baby's father.'

'I have no idea who the baby's father is,' I said, almost completely stopping the Jeep.

'The hell you don't!' she screamed.

I could see she was about to panic.

'No, see,' I scramble, 'I'm going to take you back to Fry's Bay.'

'Fuck!' she screeched.

'OK. OK. Let's unpack a little,' I said. 'I'm confused. You *want* to be with the Seminoles?'

'Yes. God! They . . . they saved my life, they're making me better, they're helping my baby. I'm safe with them. But if he gets the kid, he'll take her away!'

'*He who*?' I asked. 'The father?'

'Christ Almighty, yes!' She looked around, a little wildly. 'Where are we? Where are we now?'

'Couldn't say,' I admitted. 'Somewhere in the swamp.'

She shook her head hard, trying to clear out the cobwebs. 'OK, look, buddy. It seems like you're too stupid to work for him, the father. So what's your deal?'

'I work for Florida Child Protective Services,' I told her, somewhat weakly.

'I don't know what that is. But listen to me. You get me back to the . . . to that lodge. I gotta finish my purge. And God help us all if somehow the father of my kid finds us here.'

The Jeep slowed to a crawl. 'Let's be very clear,' I said, really trying to collect the old wits. 'There you are in the hospital. You wake up after having the baby, and you panic because you're afraid that the baby's father will come and take it away from you. *That's* why you stole the kid and beat it out of the nice clean room and over to Lou Yahola's?'

'Yes, genius,' she barked. 'Why else would I leave the hospital in my condition?'

'To get dope,' I said bluntly.

That slowed her down a little bit. 'Fair enough,' she said softly. 'But that's not what I did.'

'So, when you left the baby at Lou Yahola's,' I went on, 'where did you go?'

'I went looking for Mister Redhawk,' she said. 'I mean, I can't drag the kid around in the cold, and I can't go back to the hospital to talk to Maggie because someone might see me there. So I went to the place downtown, near Yudda's, you know, that new building with all the fake art deco details?'

'Art deco?' I asked. 'You know art deco?'

'Yes,' she snapped back, exasperated. 'Do you know the place or not?'

'I know the place.'

'I thought that's where Mister Redhawk had a condo. I mean, I've seen him go in there a lot. Only, he wasn't there. I asked the doorman and the concierge, but they didn't know who he was. So I went to Yudda's and sat in the corner and ordered a burger, man was I hungry.'

'And?' I encouraged.

'And, after a while, Philip showed up. You know Philip?'

'We're practically intimate,' I told her. 'How did he know you were there?'

'No idea,' she said. 'How does he know half the stuff he knows?'

'All right,' I said, deciding to let that go. 'So Philip came, and?'

'And he gathered me up and got me out of there,' she said, 'because, unfortunately, that art deco condo building, he told me, is where the father of my baby has a place. So we went back to Lou Yahola's, only, when we got there, there was blood in the hallway, and everybody was gone. Do you have any idea how crazy that made me? I thought I was going to have a heart attack because somebody took my baby!'

I tried not to have the shivers when she told me this. I tried to stay calm. I tried to get back to the facts of the story.

'So,' I managed to say. 'So.'

'I was so nuts at that point that Philip had to put me in the back of some slinky limo and give me a joint. He promised to find the baby. I gather that you got her from Lou, shot Lou for his trouble, and took my kid back to the one place where she shouldn't have been: the goddamn hospital!'

'Yes,' I said. 'I am responsible for that.'

'So, Mister Redhawk had to get over there, get with his sister, fake more records, and liberate my child – *again* – while I was passed out in the back of a stretch. The next thing I know, or I vaguely remember, I'm in a sweat lodge with John Horse and my baby. I was nice and warm and everything was fine. Until some idiot showed up and jerked me out of the *only* place on the planet where I'm *safe!*'

'Yes,' I repeated. 'I am responsible for that.'

'Well cut it out, goddamn it!' she fumed. 'You don't think I got troubles enough?'

'I am beginning to see that you do,' I confessed. 'And I also, maybe for the first time, am beginning to understand what's going on here. A little. You have, however inadvertently, and angrily, answered a lot of my questions about this entire affair, and now I wish to know more. For example – and I think this may be the crux of the proverbial biscuit – *who* is the father of your child? That seems to be a primary problem.'

'You're actually asking me questions?' She seemed outraged. 'You think *that's* the problem? We're lost in the swamp, the sun's going down, my kid is just about the size of an alligator appetizer, and you want to ask me questions? Get me back to the lodge, let me get back to my stuff, and then maybe I'll tell you something, or maybe somebody will hit you in the head long enough and hard enough for you to understand that *you're the problem!*'

'Well,' I said, 'I don't think that's fair. I genuinely believed that I was doing the right thing going after you and the kid. A: It's my job. B: Maggie told me to do it, because, apparently, she didn't know why you left the hospital. C: It's the law, and D:

Lou tried to shoot me and dosed me with Seconal. Oh, and by the way, E: Some mook named McReedy is out to kill me.'

'Stop!' she screamed. 'Stop, for God's sake. Stop with the letters and don't bring up McReedy. He's after me too, and I'd rather not mention his name. That guy is one scary mother.'

'Apparently.' I resisted the obvious temptation to ask her why McReedy was after her because I could see that she was upset.

'So how in the hell do you think you're going to keep all three of us from dying before sunrise?' she wanted to know.

'I'll tell you,' I said, getting out of the Jeep. 'Take it from me; it's a lot easier to get caught than it is to hide out. And I believe that I can employ a bit of an Indian cliché, here.'

'What are you talking about?' she whined.

'Smoke signals.'

With that I cast my eye about and quickly found appropriate underbrush. I plunked it all down about six or eight feet from the Jeep, and stacked it up log cabin style. This I learned from Pan-Pan Washington who, as a tyke, was a Boy Scout. I made much sport of him on account of this when we were together, because his chosen profession had so much to do with altering boosted wheels, but he often regaled me with stories of camping out in the Berkshires and eating a treat they called *s'mores*, which was a nauseating concoction of graham crackers and marshmallows and Hershey bars which I wouldn't have touched on a bet. Still, I was, at that moment, grateful to Pan-Pan because I knew how to start a fire in the woods. And let's face it, how else would a person like me know such a thing?

So I stacked.

But Lynette would not let it go.

'What are you doing?' she whined. 'That's wet wood. You'll never get it started, no matter how many matches you have.'

'In point of fact, I don't have any matches,' I told her, still stacking. 'Do you?'

'You don't have matches? How the hell are you going to start . . .'

'Just keep hollering like that,' I interrupted her, 'and I won't need to. They'll hear your voice and come running.'

'Bite me,' she grumbled. 'So how do you think you're starting this fire with *wet* wood? Spontaneous combustion?'

'Once again,' I said, 'if you know how to do that, it would come in really handy about now, but if you don't, please shut up while I concentrate, OK?'

'I gotta see this.' She shook her head. 'I gotta see your nine-teenth nervous breakdown. I mean, how many more things could you possibly get wrong?'

'Oh, I have a pretty mean record when it comes to getting the wrong thing.' I stood up and examined my stack. 'There.'

'There?'

'There is step one. Now, step two is a little tricky.' I took off my tie.

'You're getting undressed? What, are you going to do a fire dance?'

'You wouldn't by any chance have any Hebrew heritage in you, would you?' I asked her.

'No,' she said, momentarily taken aback. 'Why do you ask?'

'No reason, except you should know that you are a noodge,' I mumbled. 'I'm only removing my tie. Everything else stays intact.'

I slipped off said tie, stepped to the gas plug on the Jeep, unscrewed it, and slipped it down the chute. I was somewhat relieved that there was still a fair amount of gas there, so I doused my tie. Then I removed it and arranged it nicely around my log cabin stack.

'Now comes the tricky part,' I told her, ripping a piece of gas-soaked tie away from the rest. 'I have to turn off the Jeep for a second, which is not the best thing to do, because you never can tell if it will start up again.'

'What are you talking about?' she asked me.

I did not answer with words; I showed her what I was talking about. I came back to the Jeep and found the two wires I used to start the Jeep in the first place. I took a deep breath, and then turned off the on/off switch. The engine sputtered, and then was silent. I took two wires underneath the steering column and pulled them apart. There was a little snap, and it startled Lynette, which made the baby nervous and it began to cry.

'Yeah,' I muttered, 'you keep yelling and let the piker squall like that, the Seminoles will find us in no time.'

'You're going to blow us all up!' said Lynette, scrambling to get out of the Jeep.

The baby was screaming its head off at this point, and Lynette was in a panic to get away, and I was trying to concentrate so that I would not, in fact, blow us all up.

I held the gasoline tie scrap between my ring finger and pinky finger, and then I took hold of both wires with my thumbs and first fingers, and smacked a spark.

Nothing else happened because I was nervous and holding the tie too far away from the spark. I momentarily wished I was more religious and better inclined to pray.

I moved the tie shard right next to the bare wires, held my breath, and tried again.

Flash! The tie ignited.

It was already burning my fingers, but I managed to zip right over to the log cabin and drop the flaming cloth on to the rest of the tie, which caught with a whooshing sound.

In under three seconds some of the wood was smoking. I put my slightly singed fingers in my mouth, and they even tasted a little burnt.

But the wood was catching fire.

I gathered up more and waited until the stack was going pretty good, then added to the flame. In a couple of minutes there was a very nice fire, and lots of wet wood smoke.

I turned to Lynette, who was standing by the Jeep. The baby was quieting down, and Lynette was shaking her head.

'What?' I said. 'I get no credit?'

'You want a medal?' she retorted, renewing my suspicions about her heritage. 'Even a broken clock is right twice a day.'

She got back into the Jeep and began nursing the tyke. I discretely turned my back, stared at the fire, and then upward at the column of smoke it was making, which was thick and black, forty feet high and climbing.

After a minute or two, I moseyed back over to the Jeep.

'I don't like to disturb mother and baby,' I announced, 'but I'm going to have to start the Jeep again and then lay on the horn. It's the icing on the rescue cake, you understand.'

Lynette only nodded, and I could see that the wind was out of her sails. She was getting sleepy. And the sun was just about gone.

So, I started up the Jeep and revved the engine a bit.

'OK,' I said as gently as possible, 'are you ready? It's going to be very irritating.'

'OK,' she said and started petting her baby's head.

I laid on the horn. Lynette jumped again. The kid started in to wailing like before, except only louder, if such a thing was possible.

Then I started pumping the horn in the only code I knew. Here, also, I benefited from Pan-Pan's scouting days. He taught me a little Morse code, and I began to bang out the old S.O.S. It didn't really matter to me if John Horse or Philip or anyone knew the code. Someone, I figured, was bound to hear the noise and wonder what the hell was going on.

The sun disappeared really quickly. There was still a little light left in the sky, but also the fire was beginning to wane. I could feel Lynette getting nervous, and, to tell the truth, she might have been getting some of that from me. She looked at me and, for the first time, she looked her age. She was a scared little kid with a scared little baby. I tried to think of something to say that would make her feel better, but nothing came to me, because I frankly did not give us much of a chance.

And then night, as it will, descended.

TWENTY-FIVE

I couldn't say how long it took, because time was different in a swamp, but maybe a half an hour after the sun went down, I decided to take a break from the honking. I was a little concerned that the battery would run down, and I was certain we were about out of gas. I considered maybe shutting off the engine, but the thought of sitting there in the dark and quiet was very disconcerting.

Then, I heard something in the darkness over to the right of the Jeep, maybe four hundred yards away. I really started wishing, then, that I had taken a gun off the goons at the lodge, because I imagined some god-awful swamp thing slithering up out of the ooze toward us. But when I listened closer, I heard something more rhythmic. Like, a train. But I knew it couldn't be a train. Then I heard something even odder. I heard Benny Goodman. I heard him playing 'Memories of You.'

Swear to God.

I was just about to turn to Lynette and ask her if I was dreaming when, out of the darkness just down the road, I saw flashlights bobbing up and down. And right after that I saw four guys on horses carrying those flashlights.

Benny Goodman was not, in fact, on one of the horses. Not in person anyway. Philip had an old-style transistor radio slung over a part of his saddle and the radio was playing the tune.

John Horse was beside him on a fat chestnut pony. The two young kids that I had clocked at the lodge were in the parade too. And everybody had a gun.

'Oh, thank God,' Lynette sighed.

I turned to her. 'Know much about General Custer?' I asked her, because I thought she might find the question amusing.

'What do you mean *we*, white man?' she mumbled, using the punch line from a different joke.

By that time, John Horse and Philip were nearly up to the side of the Jeep.

'Nice smoke signals,' John Horse said. 'And Morse Code on top of that. You really wanted us to find you.'

'I did,' I confirmed.

'Confusing,' he said right back, 'in light of your escape from Philip's house and the kidnapping of these two children. Are you all right, Lynette?'

'I am now,' she sniffed.

The baby had settled down nicely at that point.

John Horse turned his attention back to me. 'Did you think someone from Fry's Bay would hear you?'

'No,' I said. 'I thought you'd hear me. I wanted you to hear me.'

'Again, confusing.'

'Not really,' I said calmly. 'I've come to realize that, until very recently, I've been working for the wrong side.'

'Is that so?' he asked me.

'It is so.'

'Whose side are you on now?'

'Your side,' I said. I glanced at one of the goons from the lodge. 'His side.' Then I said to the kid, 'I'm very sorry that I wonked you in the head.'

The kid took it in stride. 'I just didn't expect it. You were lucky, but . . . I'm sorry that I called you grandpa.'

'Tell me in words that I can believe,' said John Horse, apparently impatient with my gentlemanly behavior, 'why you're on my side all of a sudden.'

'Lynette explained a few things to me,' I said. 'Turns out I did not rescue her from anything at all. In fact, I made things worse for her. You, on the other hand, were trying to help her. You wanted her off the dope, you wanted to keep her safe, but, most of all and to the point, you tried to protect the baby. Which, after all, is my raisin tetra – as the French say. So, in conclusion, upon further examination of the facts, I'm on your side. Not to mention, P.S.: the other side has a guy trying to kill me. So.'

'Just like that?' John Horse said.

'Just like that,' I answered cautiously, 'with a caveat.'

'And what would that be?'

'I have all kinds of respect for your native culture and everything,' I said quickly, 'but, look, John Horse, you don't really impress me as the kind of person who truly endorses quaint fairytales when the fate of his entire *people* hangs in the balance.'

'Meaning?' he asked, but I could see a glimmer that he might be coming around to believing me.

'This isn't about some holy child come to save the Seminoles with a wave of his chubby little messiah hand,' I said. 'That crap's for the rubes – of which I am not one. Do you understand me?'

For a moment things were still. I tried not to be overwhelmed by the surreal nature of the scene. I was sitting in a Jeep with a nearly naked girl wrapped in a blanket, and she was nursing a baby while we were in the middle of a swamp surrounded by Seminoles on horseback listening to Benny Goodman. Seriously, if it got any stranger, I'd have to consider just jumping in the swamp and getting it all over with right then and there.

Finally, John Horse cracked a smile. 'OK, you're right. All that was bullshit.'

The other men on horses started to laugh quite heartily and, it seemed, a little at my expense.

Benny Goodman came to the end of his song and the announcer said, in a very soothing voice, 'It's exactly eight in the evening, and that was Benny Goodman's touring combo, on WUSF-FM, listener supported radio. In just a second: *Central Park West*, Coltrane, of course, and featuring McCoy Tyner, Elvin Jones, and Steve Davis on the bass.'

'Nice tunes,' I said to Philip.

He was still laughing, but he managed to tell me, 'I can't always get this station, not out here, but they play jazz most every night, so it's worth a try. Nice.'

'Nice,' I agreed.

'Can we please go back to the lodge,' Lynette insisted. 'I'm cold, I'm really straightening out, and I'm starting to get some muscle cramps, so, OK?'

Philip got down off his horse immediately, transistor radio in hand. 'Get out,' he said to me, but not in a rude way. 'You're going to ride my horse. I'm going to drive my Jeep.'

'Me?' I said, not moving. 'On a horse. Seriously?'

The Coltrane tune started up, soothing and peaceful, like a rainy Sunday afternoon in a really nice apartment in Manhattan.

'Yes, you, on a horse,' he said. 'I assume you can't ride, so there's not as much chance of you getting away.'

'Because I don't know how to hotwire a horse, so I can't steal it, right?' I smiled at John Horse.

'Don't make me change my mind about you,' he said. 'Get out of the Jeep.'

'OK, but it's a little low on gas,' I told everybody. 'Plus, I'm going to need some help getting up on that horse.'

'You never watched a Western?' Philip said. 'On television?'

'We didn't have television when I was growing up,' I told him. 'We had radio. My mother and my aunt didn't believe in television. It was hard to tell how the Lone Ranger got on his horse over the radio.'

'OK but get out,' Philip said again.

I crawled out of the Jeep. John Coltrane's ballad was making me feel very calm until I realized that my right arm was sore from all the honking, and I ached in general from all the rough-housing with the Seminole kids.

'So, what?' I asked, staring at the horse. 'Does it bend down a little, even?'

The kid that I chopped in the noggin spoke up, very sweetly

under the circumstances. 'You put your foot in the stirrup, hoist
yourself up, then fling your leg over, and there you are.'

'Easy for you to say,' I muttered.

Without offering the embarrassing details, suffice it to say that
after a few tries and some very uncomfortable physical comedy,
I found myself atop a horse for the first time in my life. And I
hoped to my soul it would be the last.

'I'm Joseph,' said the kid who offered me the horse-mounting
advice. 'This is Taft.'

'The Indian Taft?' I rejoined.

'They call you Foggy,' said John Horse, 'and you're worried
about a Seminole named Taft?'

'Good point,' I admitted, 'and stated, if I may say so, in a
very Jewish manner.'

'Let's go,' he said.

All the horses started moving, including mine, like they understood what the old guy had said. I decided that it was best for
me to let the horse do the work, since it obviously knew more
about what was going on than I did.

Philip started up the Jeep, turned on the headlights, gunned
the engine, and we were off.

'How far away from the lodge are we?' I asked Joseph.

'We're closer to John Horse's house,' he said.

'So I was going in the right direction to get out of the swamp.'

'Yeah,' he admitted. 'That's pretty good, really. When I first
came here? I got lost a lot.'

'You weren't born here?'

'God, no. I was born in Oklahoma, where a lot of the Seminoles
were taken – boys especially. We were supposed to go to school
there to learn how to be more white.'

'Ah,' I said. 'How'd that work out?'

'Apparently better than you might imagine,' John Horse spoke
up. 'He let his ass get kicked by a Yankee Hebrew twice his age.'

The kid looked down, and you could see that he was genuinely
embarrassed.

'Look, it's not your fault,' I told him, trying to help, 'I was
raised in the streets by criminals and miscreants all my life. None
other than Red Levine, you know, who *retired* from the
Combination in the late '40s, actually took me under his wing

in 1962, when I was just a teenager. And although I did not wish to zotz anybody, I was nevertheless versed in that particular vernacular, because I learned a lot about it from him. This is *the* Red Levine we're talking about.'

Joseph raised his head. 'I don't know what most of the words you just said mean. I don't know what a Red Levine is, or *the Combination*, or the word *zotz*. I can kind of tell that you're trying to make me feel better, but you have to speak English, OK?'

'He's trying to say,' John Horse interrupted, 'that if you had been raised by your own people, people who know ways to help you survive, who could teach you things you *really* needed to know, you would have been a lot better off.'

'Exactly,' I said. 'That's exactly my point. God knows what would have happened to me if *I'd* been born in *Oklahoma*. I mean, what can a person learn to steal there? What do they *have* in Oklahoma?'

'Dust,' said Joseph right away. 'There's a lot of dust.'

'Stop talking, please,' John Horse said gently. 'I would like to enjoy the night air and the music and the sounds of the swamp for a moment.'

So I shut up. And, to tell the truth, the sounds of the swamp were very nice. The moon came up, and there was that magic that happens when certain black skies turn almost lavender with moonlight and the humid air from the swamp. Tree frogs and night insects and birds and the wind, they all worked together, and it was just like a soft palate of strings or something behind Coltrane's solo, which, all of a sudden, was making me so lonesome for New York that I almost cried.

TWENTY-SIX

Back at John Horse's house I said goodbye to Lynette, baby, and Philip and the rest. John Horse and I hunkered down in his bungalow. The only light was from an oil lamp and the only sound was the monstrous noise of the local fauna. It was very loud.

'How do you sleep with all this noise?' I asked John Horse.

He was sitting in his chair, and he'd found me a pillow to sit on, back against the wall, slumping down.

'When I was in prison,' he said, 'there was a lot of noise from other men. Talking, yelling, crying, cursing – *that* was hard to sleep through. When I went to Chicago, once, for a convention, the traffic and the street noise almost made me lose my mind. This? I don't really hear the frogs and the insects. What do they call it, when you have a sound that can mask other sounds?'

'White noise, I think,' I told him.

'White noise.' He seemed to find this amusing.

The sounds of nature were, indeed, a kind of mask. There might have been people talking in other houses close by, but I couldn't hear them. There might have been other cars or Jeeps or trucks out in the swamp, but all I knew was that tree frogs were very loud individuals.

'Are you going to tell me,' I began, 'why you fed me such a line of crap about Lynette and her baby?'

'It usually works with most white people.' He shrugged.

'Maybe,' I said, 'but that wasn't what I asked. I asked why you said that the baby was a water spirit and Lynette was like the Virgin Mary.'

'Virgin Mary,' he repeated. 'It's a very funny religion, this Jesus religion, don't you think?'

'It's a scream.'

'You don't get a holy creature in any other culture on the planet, that I know of, without some sort of copulation.'

'This was not really my point either, John Horse. You are something of a master at changing the subject. I want to know why you made up such a story.'

'Oh, I didn't make it up. There really are water spirits, if you care to look at it that way. And there really is something special about the baby Lynette had. But I can tell that you're not a fan, exactly, of metaphorical language, or not properly educated in the—'

'*I'm* not a fan of metaphorical language?' I asked, ire dripping from every syllable.

'You are, then?'

'Plenty,' I assured him. 'Metaphorical language is my middle name.'

'Crap,' he suggested. 'I don't believe you.'

'You think I'm a jerk? Just because I'm not college educated doesn't mean I'm not smarter than most other people I meet.'

He lifted his eyebrows. 'Easy to say. Maybe if you gave me an example.'

'Leonard Cohen's *Story of Isaac*,' I said right away. 'The entire song is a metaphor, a beautiful metaphor.'

John Horse stared at me for a minute. Then he said, 'You aren't exactly what you seem to be – or you're more complex than you let on. I would imagine that you surprise people all the time.'

'I don't mean to,' I told him, 'but there you are changing the subject again. You're really good at it.'

He nodded. 'It's something you learn in my line of work.'

'And what, exactly, is that, your line of work?'

'I'm a real estate agent,' he said, but he had a grin on his face that, once again, told me that he was throwing around the old horse manure.

'Am I going to get anywhere with you,' I asked him honestly, 'or are we just going to call it a day? I'm beat and I don't much feel like going around the metaphorical mulberry bush.'

'I don't know the song,' he said in another of his whiplash-inducing left turns. 'The song you just mentioned. Tell me about it.'

'Why do you want to know about a Leonard Cohen song?'

'Indulge me.' He leaned forward. 'It might lead somewhere.'

'OK, but I'm not drinking any more of your damned tea.'

'The song,' he insisted.

'It's about . . . it starts with Abraham and Isaac. From the Bible. You know the story?'

'No.'

'God tells Abraham to kill his son, name of Isaac.'

'Why?' John Horse interrupted. 'What had the son done wrong?'

'Nothing,' I said, 'God was testing Abraham, to see how far he'd go in the service of the Lord, see?'

'This is a Hebrew story?'

'Yes. So Abraham takes his son high up on a mountain and he's about to kill the kid when all of a sudden God says, "It's OK. Stop. I just wanted to see if you'd do it." And he let Abraham off the hook.'

'And Isaac.'

'Right.'

'And that's the song?'

'The song goes on,' I told him, 'to talk about men of power who are willing to sacrifice children on golden altars, but these are men, Leonard Cohen says, who have not spoken with God. These are millionaires and billionaires who rule the world, men with power, who only know how to scheme. He says, "a scheme is not a vision," this is what Leonard Cohen says.'

'Yes,' said John Horse, sitting back in his chair. 'A scheme is not a vision.'

'And it's a pretty great song. Maybe not my favorite one of his, but a great song nevertheless.'

'What is your favorite?' he asked.

I started to think about it until I realized that, for the third time in a couple of minutes, he'd done it again: thrown me off the subject.

'My favorite Leonard Cohen song is kiss my ass,' I said, in no uncertain terms. 'Why are we talking about it?'

'Calm down,' he told me. 'You don't realize what you've just said. My telling you about the water spirit baby may have been a little contrived, but when I said that you were directly involved in all this business? That turns out to be right on the money.'

'What?' My voice was nearly as loud as the tree frogs.

'I don't know how,' said John Horse, 'but you have some sort of connection with all this. And you know more about it than you think you do – more than your conscious mind is aware of.'

'My conscious mind?' I asked. 'Did you study Freud when you were in prison too?'

'Look,' he said, trying as hard as he could to sound reasonable. 'We may have gotten started on the wrong foot. You don't trust me because you think I kidnapped you. I don't trust you because you escaped from Philip's house and stole Lynette. But, from what I can tell, objectively, we're on the same side. I see that now.'

'This is what I was trying to tell you back at the bonfire,' I said. 'I realize now that Lynette is much better off here than in Fry's Bay, what with the baby's father . . . wait.'

John Horse folded his arms. 'What is it?'

'I'm thinking, all of a sudden, that I don't know who to trust,'

I said. 'Maybe you've just convinced Lynette that the baby's father is out to get her. That's what she thinks. And she made me feel like a bonehead for rescuing the baby from Lou Yahola. And for rescuing her from you. But I am, just now, getting another uncomfortable feeling. What if that's more bullshit from you guys? What if you're not telling the truth and just making up more baloney about the father so that you can keep Lynette and the baby here?'

'You're tired,' the old guy said. 'You probably need some sleep.'

'Why are you keeping Lynette Baker here?' I demanded. 'Why did you steal her from Fry's Bay? What the hell is so important that you have to keep the baby away from hospital care?'

'You're getting all wound up,' he said.

I scrambled to my feet. 'Yes I'm wound up and with good reason.' I took a step in his direction.

And out of nowhere, John Horse produced the very significant handgun that Philip had taken off of that McReedy character. It was pointed right at my gut.

'Please sit down,' he said very calmly.

I didn't. I was judging things. Things like, how far I was from the man with the gun and how good was the old man's coordination. How dark would it get in the room if I kicked over the oil lamp, which was only a few feet away?

Then John Horse said, a little louder than before, 'Taft?'

The door to the house opened slowly and in stepped the Indian Taft. He was holding his rifle very tightly.

'Yes?' he said.

'Do you happen to know,' John Horse began, not bothering to hide his gun, 'what your mother made for dinner?'

'Turtle,' said Taft.

'Mmm,' said John Horse right back. 'Your mother's turtle is very good. Is there any left? I think Mr Moscowitz would enjoy it.'

'I'll check,' he said, and he was gone.

'Please sit down, Mr Moscowitz,' John Horse told me. 'I don't want to shoot you. Not even a little bit.'

'Look,' I said, about to begin a tirade.

'The millionaires who run this world, like in your song.'

That was all he said. But it was enough to give me pause.

'How, exactly, do you mean?' I asked, still standing.

'Of all the things you could have said to me, under the circumstances here in my home, you picked a quote from a song about the rich men who make most of the world's decisions. Politicians are their stooges, of course, and other people sometimes have the illusion that they run something, but they don't.'

'Are you changing the subject again?' I asked, confused.

'I've been talking about the same thing the entire time you've been with me. I don't know what you've been talking about.'

At that point I had to sit.

'You want to know about the father of Lynette's baby,' he said. 'You want to know why we're keeping Lynette here. You think that you want to know these things because you were given a job to do and you want to finish that job to your satisfaction. You also have a strong subconscious motive for protecting the baby because of something that happened to you in Brooklyn when you were, let's face it, a different person. You want to know why these things are happening to you. And I'm trying, in the only way I know how, to tell you the answers to all these questions. It's just that, sometimes you think you're asking a question about, say, a hired killer in a small town in Florida, and the answer is actually *turtle*.'

And, swear to God, at that exact moment the Indian Taft came barging into John Horse's house with a steaming bowl in his right hand and said, directly to me, 'Turtle!'

'It's a stew,' said John Horse. 'That's how she gets it so tender. It cooks for a long time. It's not the turtle steak we were going to have at Philip's house. I think it's better.'

'It has little potatoes in it,' said Taft, smiling down at the bowl. 'Be careful. It's hot.'

And, as it turned out, I was suddenly famished.

I took the bowl, grabbed the spoon that was in it, and began to devour the turtle stew. It burned my tongue and the roof of my mouth, but that didn't seem to stop me.

For a while, the only sounds in the cinder block cabin were the ones I was making with my spoon and my bowl, plus the occasional, embarrassing sounds of my enjoyment.

At length, I was finished and I set the bowl down. I saw that the floor was nothing but dirt, and I was a little surprised I hadn't noticed that before. I was usually better with details.

I looked up at Taft, about to express my undying gratitude for the stew, but he beat me to it.

'I'll tell my mother that you enjoyed it,' he said, still grinning.

'This would be an understatement,' I told him. 'Could you please say to her that it's better than my aunt Shayna's brisket, which, until tonight, was the best thing that I'd ever eaten. And then, if you don't mind, please tell her not to mention anything about what I just said if she ever finds herself in Brooklyn.'

'Sure,' he said.

He swooped over and picked up the bowl, and he was gone.

'God in heaven that was good.' I leaned back.

'The secret is slow cooking. A lot of white people today are interested in how fast something can get done. Instant food. Fast food. It's one of the main things wrong with them; their food.'

I nodded, but I was wise to him at last, I thought. I didn't entirely trust him, and it was still possible that he was a bad guy, but I was confused by turtle stew. Can anything truly evil come from a people who make food that good, I asked myself.

'You're trying to tell me something,' I said. 'You've been trying to tell me something since I came here yesterday, although it seems like about a week ago to me at this point. But now, I get it. I get, from your little speech before my dinner, and then again from your little speech about the food itself – you, John Horse, you cook things slow.'

'Ah, that's how it happens sometimes,' he said, nodding. 'You take a second to reflect, sometimes over a meal, and the light dawns.'

'It does,' I admitted. 'So now let me see if I can piece together the loose fabric of the past couple of days and come up with some kind of cloth we can use. I'm supposed to be pretty good at this.'

'You have so many talents, really,' he said, almost like a grandpa. 'Why did you ever take to stealing cars, of all things?'

'Well,' I said, 'it was a trick I learned from Red Levine. Perhaps you heard me tell Joseph about Red Levine.'

'I did, but I have no idea who or what that is.'

'Jeez, you guys never read a newspaper? Red Levine was only the foremost member of the Combination who never got caught by the New York constabulary.'

'I,' he began, then shook his head. 'No. That didn't help. Explain it better.'

'To tell you the story of my life would take more time than we have,' I said, 'so I'll give you the high points. My father, apparently, was a minor figure in the Combination.'

'Stop,' he said. 'What is that, "the Combination"?'

'Ah. The Combination. Sometimes it was called *Murder Incorporated* by the ignorant gentile press, but it was essentially an organization of hitmen who were Jews and very good at their trade.'

'Like McReedy.'

'So I'm told,' I went on, 'although Philip certainly seemed to be pretty good at thwarting that particular guy, in my experience, so I'm not sure how good he actually is.'

'But to return to your father,' he said.

'My father was a driver for Red Levine in the younger days,' I said. 'This was all I ever knew, except that something went wrong one night on a hit, and my father got shot. They left him behind and called an ambulance for him, thinking the cops would take him to the hospital. The ambulance and the cops arrive. The cops assume that my poppa was the shooter in the hit. They wouldn't let the ambulance take him until he confessed or gave up the name of the actual shooter, which he did not do. So as a result he died on the spot, and the ambulance became a hearse.'

'I'm sorry.'

I shrugged. 'I never knew the guy. This happened when I was, I think, two. My mother and my aunt raised me as good as they could, considering that they both worked twelve hours a day and then came home to do more work there.'

'So this man, Red Levine, he felt responsible for your loss, and he wanted to help.'

'Something like it, I suppose, or maybe he just watched out for me to see was I irked enough with him to rat him out to the cops or try and zotz him myself.'

'What is that word, *zotz*? I heard you say that to Joseph, too.'

'Ah,' I said, 'this is a word which means to ice someone.'

'Ice?'

'To bump off, to burn, to pop.'

'What are you talking about?'

'What McReedy tried to do to me!'

'Oh,' he said, rearing back his head, 'you're talking about *killing*.'

'Please,' I said, uncomfortably, 'we don't like to use this word. It's too . . . obvious. And, if I may say so, a little disrespectful.'

'So,' he said, folding his hands in front of his face, 'this is the male figure in your life: a man who was responsible for the death of your father, a man who might have killed you, or whom you might have killed. And he taught you to steal cars? Why?'

'That's where it gets a little parental,' I admitted. 'As it turned out, Red liked me, and I liked him. He got me into boosting wheels because it was the only safe racket he knew. I mean, he was a career criminal. So he introduced me to Pan-Pan Washington, who became, in some fashion, my best friend, and who is a genius with a blowtorch, by the way. That was important, of course, because Pan-Pan could make Philip's Jeep look like a Chevy station wagon if you wanted him to. He converted the merchandise I brought him into something so unrecognizable that we actually, twice, sold back said stolen merchandise to its original owner, and they never knew.'

'And you were *how* old when you began this enterprise?'

'I must have been about twelve, I think. The years run together. I also did my fair share of coke at that time in my life. My fair share and the fair share of several others, truth be told. So, in addition to running together, the years themselves are fuzzy.'

'I see. You did drugs as a teenage boy.'

'Doesn't everybody?' I asked him. 'But coke can be a good support system when you're boosting cars. It makes a person alert. Now, for recreation I prefer mescaline, if you can get it pure. But I'll tell you that I have never gotten as wacked as I was after I drank that damned tea you made me. It was the serious delirious.'

'But it's not a recreation. It's . . . it's something like a holy encounter.'

'I don't know what that means.' I settled back and closed my eyes.

The day's activities, the stress of being lost in a swamp, and my suddenly satisfied stomach were all combining to make me sleepy.

'You were going to tell me,' I heard John Horse say, 'before you had your dinner, what conclusions you had come to about the events of the past several days.'

My eyes snapped open. 'How do you do this?' I hollered. 'You made me forget the subject altogether, by saying the magic word *turtle*! How do you do it?'

'I tried to tell you,' he said, 'that it isn't something I'm doing. I think I'm just talking with you, and answering your questions, and leading you to answer mine. I'm not doing anything. We just have very different ways of talking, you and I.'

'Oh, really,' I said, but it wasn't a question.

'Well,' he said to me, 'you were about to fall asleep just now, I think. If I had actually been trying to throw you off the track, would I have reminded you that you were about to piece together a puzzle?'

This took me aback. 'You do have a point there.'

'OK.' He folded his arms. 'I'm listening.'

'OK,' I said, right back to him. 'Let me see. I was about to get off work a couple of nights ago when my boss called and said I had to find a baby.'

'Is that unusual?'

'A little,' I said. 'Most things wait until the morning. Government hours. But it seemed urgent because the little tyke was going to die if I didn't find it right away, because its mother was an addict. So, off to the hospital I went, where I encountered my acquaintance Maggie Redhawk, only one of several Seminoles I was soon to run into on that particular night. With some effort, I found the baby, shot Lou Yahola – who I need to ask you about in a second – and took the tyke back to the hospital. So all was supposed to be well that ended well, until suddenly there was a hit out on me, and the hitman, this McReedy character, was hired, for some unknown reason, by Pascal Henderson, one of the richest men in the world and the father of my boss. Wait.'

I stopped in mid-thought, because something very strange was occurring to me. Again, I was nearly overwhelmed by the gigantic noise of the tree frogs. The oil lamp sputtered. John Horse was nodding, eyes closed.

'Go on,' said John Horse, as if he was talking to himself. 'You're just about to figure this out.'

'No,' I said, 'but it can't be what I've got in my mind at this moment.'

'What have you got in your mind?'

'I've got in my mind that Pascal Henderson put a hit out on me, and is chasing Lynette, and got my boss to make me find the baby because . . . but, seriously, it can't be what I'm thinking.'

'What are you thinking?'

'I am thinking,' I began, with a voice that didn't remotely sound like my own, 'that Pascal Henderson, who owns a quarter of the world, is the father of Lynette's little baby.'

'Your insight is remarkable,' said John Horse, opening his eyes. 'Really amazing.'

'He's the father?' I repeated, leaning forward.

'And that's only the beginning. How far do you think you can take that line of thought?'

'Well, I don't know,' I said, trying to focus. 'This is huge. I guess, first, I have to ask myself why a gazillionaire like Henderson is anywhere near Fry's Bay. And my conclusion is that there is money to be made here, because what else does a guy like that live for – besides, apparently, schtupping young girls out of wedlock.'

'Go on.'

'And the Seminoles are involved, so it has to do with whatever it is that is important to you guys, which, my guess would be land. Stolen land.'

'You really do have a gift for this sort of thing,' he told me. 'What a waste that the first third of your life was spent in something so mundane as stealing cars.'

'So the Henderson guy,' I said, at least in part only to myself, 'is the father of Lynette's baby, and also the father of my boss, which means he is something of an old guy at this point, and it also means that Lynette's baby and my boss are sisters.'

'Interesting,' he said, 'but not a part of the story, not for us, at least.'

'And by *us* you mean the Seminoles, so it must be true to some extent that Lynette is at least part Seminole.'

'She is.'

'And, let me guess, like the Jews, heritage is passed through the mother, not the father.'

'This is the way for the Jews too?'

'Yes,' I said. 'If your mother was a Jew, you're a Jew all the way. If your father was a Jew, but not your mother? You can cop a walk. No hope for me, though. Both parents: Russian Hebrews, on the lam from Stalin and his Cossacks.'

'Well, that is an interesting fact. And you are correct, most tribes are, at least to some extent, matriarchal – or were before Christian missionaries taught us that it was wrong.'

'So, the point is that, somehow, this little baby you're hiding here in the swamp, it's got something to do with land. Seminole land that Henderson wants, or has and might lose, or something along those lines. That's not the whole story, of course, but how am I doing?'

'Almost perfect.'

'I'm not finished. The fact that Henderson has a place, a condo, in Fry's Bay, that says something about the importance of the land or the holdings or whatever. Maybe he just wants to be close to the scene for some reason, or maybe he has to establish some sort of residency requirement.'

'Right again.'

I folded my arms. 'Gee. I really did almost screw this whole thing up, didn't I?'

'You were misled.'

'Yes. I have to figure this out too: why are people misleading me? Is my boss, for whom I have had, until now, the utmost respect, in fact a demon in disguise; a devil in a blue dress?'

'Meaning, is she on her father's side in this matter.'

'Or at least this: is she trying to get me killed?'

'Well.'

'There are,' I told him, 'plenty of missing steps in this little story, but I believe I have hit enough of the high points for you to tell me . . . for you to fill me in on the rest, right?'

'That seems fair.'

'OK, so go.' I pinched my lips together.

'The Seminole tribes are the only so-called Indians that never signed a peace treaty with the United States. This is due, in part, to an intense distrust of the American government and military. In October of 1837, Osceola was captured by General Jessup under a flag of truce, a complete violation of the white man's rules.

Osceola died in captivity the following January, of malaria, they say. He lived in these swamps all his life and never caught malaria, but three months in the Ft. Moultrie prison killed him off.'

'Tragic,' I said, 'but this I already knew about, and I was looking for a little more recent history.'

'You're wondering about the land,' he said. 'That's what I'm telling you. The government tried to confiscate our land, scatter our people, take us to Oklahoma, rub us out. Some of us stayed here, in the swamp, and, as it turns out, we still have a legal claim to all this land.'

'Which land are we talking about, exactly? This swamp?'

He shook his head. 'All this land.'

'All what land?'

'I told you once before. Florida.'

'What?' I jumped a little. 'You were serious? You think you guys own all of Florida?'

'It would be difficult to prove,' he said, 'but yes. We own all of Florida. You can keep Miami and the Keys, if you want to. We'll take the rest.'

I had to laugh. 'OK, you realize that this is never going to fly.'

'Probably not, but if we start there, we can bargain down to what we really want.'

'Which is?' I asked.

'The part that Pascal Henderson wants.'

'And which part is that?'

'The part,' he told me, 'where all the oil is.'

TWENTY-SEVEN

John Horse told me that something called *Exxon* had recently replaced the Esso, Enco, and Humble oil company brand names, but it only consolidated what had been going on for some time. Back in 1901, people started with the oil drilling on Seminole land, but they didn't hit anything until Humble produced oil in the early 1940s amongst the cypress trees. The cypress trees themselves were also valuable, and there was a sizeable timber industry on the land, but the oil would have been more profitable.

Pascal Henderson bought up a lot of this new *Exxon* corporation when the market dropped last year, in '73, and was very concerned that some Seminoles were saying that the land was not his, the profits were not his, the oil was not his, and, in general, he's out. All of which were things that might make a rich man mad enough to hire a hitman like McReedy.

My guess was that Henderson figured I stole the baby, or allowed the baby to be stolen, because I was in cahoots with the Seminoles, which, by that point, I guess I was.

John Horse spent most of the night explaining these things to me, and I would have to say that I got more and more upset as he talked.

Morning came a little too early for me on this particular occasion, and I was stiff from not sleeping and sitting all night on a cold, hard, dirt floor. John Horse got up eventually, sat next to his hot plate, and began to make breakfast.

The sun was up, but barely. It did make for a nice slant of sunlight through the eastern window of the crappy concrete cabin.

'Eggs,' he said.

'OK,' I answered.

'Here.' He held up a plate.

I managed to get up and take the plate. There was no fork or spoon or anything. I saw that John Horse was eating with his fingers. The eggs were hard scrambled, easy to eat with your hands. I hesitated, but not for long, and then I followed his example. And the eggs were pretty good.

'I have coffee,' he said between bites.

'I would kill for a cup of coffee,' I responded, somewhat dramatically.

'No need for that,' he said, laughing. 'I'll give you a cup for nothing.'

He set down his plate, still sitting cross-legged on the floor, and reached over for a big clay pitcher.

'I don't have a modern percolator,' he said. 'I grind the beans by hand and then steep them in water, like tea. It's kind of strong. Sorry.'

He put a sieve on top of a coffee mug – the same one he

gave me for the poison tea – and poured. The biggest coffee grounds got trapped in the sieve, and the coffee smelled pretty terrific.

He handed me the mug. The coffee was warm, really strong, and really good. I downed the entire mug.

'Good,' he said. 'Good. Now. What shall we do today?'

'Well,' I told him, resuming my work on the eggs with my fingers, 'I think I have some business to take care of in Fry's Bay. But I'm going to finish breakfast first, then pee, and then, if I may, I'd like to visit Lou Yahola for a second. I assume you have him around here somewhere.'

'We do.'

'So I'd like to see he is OK, and apologize for shooting him in the knee.'

'I think he'd like that,' said John Horse, 'but we should wait until the time is right, in a few days, maybe. He's having a little trouble healing. And he probably wants to apologize to you, too. He gave you some sort of sleeping drug and also shot at you.'

'Well, when you look at it the right way,' I said, finishing my eggs, 'we were both doing what we thought was right.'

'Good way to look at it.' He took my empty plate. 'You seem to be a little tense.'

'I didn't sleep,' I said, 'and I'm trying to control a major problem with Pascal Henderson.'

'What sort of problem?'

'He's behind my current dilemma, i.e. being shot, beat up, dosed, chased, and, in general, screwing things up for the past forty-eight hours or so.'

'So, we'll visit Lou another day,' John Horse suggested. 'Now, after you pee, then what?'

'Then what?' I repeated. 'Then I'd like to go back to Fry's Bay and see what I can do to mess up this Pascal Henderson bastard.'

'Not really your job,' he told me.

'Actually,' I said to him, 'it is. My job is to protect the child, and this guy is about as big a threat to the child as you can get. And incidentally, I just remembered a conversation I had with Maggie Redhawk. It was about how every baby lives in water before it's born, so I guess you could argue, if you wanted to, that we're all water spirits. I don't know why I thought of that just now, but there it is.'

'Interesting,' he said. 'Maybe you're turning into a Seminole, just a little.'

I shook my head. 'I don't think so. I don't think I could cook things as slowly as you do.'

'Meaning?' he asked me, cagey.

'Meaning I want to get back to Fry's Bay right away and really screw with this Henderson guy the way he's screwed with us.'

'Us?'

'Us,' I confirmed. 'You know, me, you, Lynette, the baby, the Seminole nation, and probably the entire American economy, when you come right down to it.'

'You seem to be fairly agitated about it,' John Horse allowed.

'Agitated!' I snapped back. 'The guy doesn't even know me, and he sent McReedy to kill me. He took advantage of . . . he takes advantage of everybody and gets away with. It's my opinion that he's a much bigger crook than Red Levine, or any of the wise guys I know in Brooklyn. He's . . . he's the main thing that's wrong.'

'Wrong with what?'

'Everything!' I snarled. 'Damn. Look at what he and his tribe did to you and yours, for God's sake! Plus, I've figured a few things out that I haven't told you about yet, about him and his older daughter Sharon, my boss. But he's behind it all, that's what I think.'

'I don't know what you're talking about,' he said to me, 'But what is it that you think you can do?'

'I'd rather not say,' I told him firmly, 'but let me ask you this. Could I borrow your gun?'

PART THREE
Fry's Bay

TWENTY-EIGHT

I t was raining in Fry's Bay by the time the Jeep pulled on to the side street, close to Yudda's Crab Palace. Philip was driving, I was in the passenger seat, and Joseph was wedged in behind us. We'd stopped at a gas station earlier, along the way, and Philip had made a call. When we got into town, there was Mister Redhawk waiting for us outside Yudda's. Mister Redhawk stood under a very large black umbrella and told everyone else what part they were to play in our master plan to mess with Pascal Henderson.

First, Philip was to go with Mister Redhawk directly to Rich Man Henderson. They were going to lay down the law, to wit. Not only would they make a claim on the swamp land with the oil on it because they're Seminoles and the actual rightful owners, but they would also make legal claim on behalf of Mr Henderson's new infant daughter by Lynette, who deserved her fair share, infant though she may have been. When that failed, which they were pretty sure it would, they intended to use the baby as some kind of ransom or blackmail or something. That particular part of the plan needed work, in my opinion. My opinion, loudly voiced, was that I would rather just walk into Henderson's penthouse and pop the guy.

Now, I probably didn't really mean that. I was probably just blowing off steam from being kidnapped and shot at and drugged and etcetera.

First, I never popped a guy in my life, and second, *my* first thing should have been to come to an arrangement with this McReedy character, which is why I got McReedy's gun from John Horse. My feeling was that if he saw his own gun pointed at his own head, he might listen before he killed me, at least a little.

So, while Philip and Mister Redhawk went to muscle old man Henderson, Joseph and I returned to my office. We all planned to meet back at Yudda's shortly.

Joseph and I went to my office so that McReedy would know I was back, because it was a good bet that either he had the office staked out or that my boss and so-called friend Sharon would tell him where I was the minute I set foot through the door. This was better than going to my apartment, which he might also be watching. My place was a little secluded. I believed that, if you wanted to avoid being killed, it was better to have people around. No matter how hardened a criminal is, he would always rather do his work in private. Nobody wants witnesses. So we went to my office under the theory that we could get the drop on McReedy and eliminate him from our list of worries. This part of the plan was also half-baked, obviously, but by that time I had figured a few more things out, and I had to confront my so-called friend Sharon with these newfound ideas.

So we walked, Joseph and I, as quickly as we could, keeping to the sides of the buildings so that we wouldn't get too wet. It only helped a little. By the time we reached the building where I worked, we were pretty much soaked. Joseph's denim jacket was like a sponge, and the blanket that I had wrapped around me to keep out the cold and rain was wet as a lake.

I had McReedy's pistol in my belt, safety on. Joseph wore a shoulder holster, just like a real gangster, under his jacket. We both looked a little like drowned rats when we marched through the door of the office suite which said, in bold and relatively new letters, CHILD PROTECTIVE SERVICES.

The lights were on. Sharon was in her office, at her desk. I addressed her thusly: 'I have it all figured out.'

I shrugged off my wet blanket by the side of the door.

She looked up, startled. 'Jesus!'

'No,' I corrected her. 'Foggy.'

'You can't be here.' She stood.

'I can and I am,' I told her. 'Sit down.'

'Look, Foggy,' she said, starting to come around her desk. 'I understand that you're upset, and I know that there are a few things we have to discuss.'

I pulled out McReedy's gun. I didn't point it at her because I still liked her, I guess. But the sight of the gun stopped her in her tracks.

I held up the gun so she could see it really clearly, and a .44 Auto Mag Pistol, made a nice show. It was a handsome sidearm, with magnum power and short recoil, semi-automatic. It looked like it could stop an elephant, which it probably could. It certainly got Sharon's attention.

'This pistol belongs to McReedy. I think you should know that.' I let that sink in, then waved it around a little and put it back in my belt. 'But where are my manners. Sharon, this is Joseph. Joseph, Sharon.'

Neither acknowledged the introduction.

'So, as I say,' I resumed, 'I finally figured things out. Please have a seat and let's talk it over until McReedy gets here.'

'Why would he come here?' she asked, and you could see that she was genuinely panicked. 'Did you tell him to meet you *here*?'

'Did *I* tell him?' I actually laughed. 'That's a good one. You don't think he's got this place staked out in some way or another? And besides, I thought *you* would tell him.'

'Me?' She seemed stunned. 'Why would *I* tell him where you were?'

'This is all part and parcel of what I have figured out. Now would you please sit down? You're making Joseph nervous.'

She glanced at him.

Joseph also made a nice appearance. He was tall and stern and chiseled looking, like he was made out of granite. He looked like the kind of thug who would just as soon shoot you as look at you.

The truth was much different, as I had learned on our long drive back from the swamp. Joseph was studying at FSU to be an accountant. He had a head for numbers. He was the one who came up with the particulars of how you could make money off of the oil and the timber in the swamp where John Horse lived. He was, apparently, something of a genius at this. So, while going to school in Oklahoma did him little good, going to college in Florida did him and his whole tribe a big favor. I learned that he was going for his doctorate. By the end of next year, he'd be Dr Joseph Yahola. Seriously. He was Lou Yahola's little brother. That's what he told me on the ride back into town. Lou Yahola had put the kid through school – on the salary he made from the donut shop. At least, this is what the kid thought. I thought Lou Yahola might have made a little extra on the side with Jody the pusher, but who was I, of all people, to consider that a problem?

The point was, Joseph *looked* tough. So Sharon sat down behind her desk.

'Good,' I said, taking a chair in front of her desk.

Joseph went to the entrance to the office suite, grabbed a handy chair, and positioned himself in the shadows so as not to be immediately seen by anyone who might come in unexpectedly.

'This is what I've figured out,' I announced. 'You set me up from the start.'

'Foggy,' she began, clearly nervous.

'I mean when I first started working here,' I went on, 'not just the past few days. I figure I'm a dope for not wondering why I got this job so easily in the first place, given my background, outstanding warrant and all. I thought that just because I gave my real first name instead of *Foggy*, and a different spelling of my last name, I figured I'd foiled the system – because the system is that stupid. But now I figure that your rich and powerful father not only pulled strings to get you this cushy government gig, but he also did the same for me so that I would be working here for a little while before his daughter – his newly arrived baby daughter – was born. You needed a fall guy, as they say in the Bogart movies. You needed me to snatch the baby from the hospital when you told me to, when you said that that baby was in danger from a junkie mother. I'd turn it over to you. That way, the father could do whatever he wanted with the tyke. Only Lynette, despite being drugged to the gills, knew she was in trouble and scrammed. That meant you had to get me to find the baby, bring it back to the hospital where, let me guess, your father is on the board, or owns it, or is the major contributor, or something. How am I doing?'

She stared down at her desk. 'Look,' she began again.

But I was on a roll. 'Anyway, you didn't reckon on the Seminole network being as good as it is. They wanted the baby too. I suppose you know why.'

She did not respond.

'Lynette Baker is half Seminole,' I explained, 'and they want the kid for all kinds of reasons, maybe even some of the reasons your father wants it, I don't know.'

Sharon looked up then. Her face was pale. 'I think I'm going to be sick, Foggy,' she said, and it didn't seem like a lie. 'I think I'm going to throw up, honest to God.'

I wasn't certain what was going on, but my sympathy quotient for her was fairly low at this point, so I said, 'This is what a wastebasket is for. Throw up if you have to.'

Without hesitation, she bent over and, indeed, tossed up into the garbage can she had by her desk.

'God,' she muttered to herself, straightening back up.

'What the hell?' I asked.

'You have no idea what you're into, man,' she said, wiping her mouth with the back of her hand. 'This guy, my so-called father, Pascal Henderson? He's nobody to mess with. I mean it. You have to understand. He does what he wants. There's nobody to tell him otherwise. I've got a reason to be nice to him because he's done right by me every once in a while, but that doesn't keep me from realizing that he's Satan.'

'He's not Satan,' I told her. 'Satan lives in New York. Trust me. Central Park West. Throws a nice party. But your father? He can be Satan's cousin if he wants. That's up for grabs.'

'You don't know what he's capable of.'

'He's capable of getting some young junkie pregnant when he's at an advanced age – though exactly how he met Lynette is a puzzler. He's capable of figuring out how I might be a sap. He figured that out pretty good. And he knows how to steal large. Very large. So I'll give him that. But, in general, the bigger they come, the harder they fall. I have always believed this.'

'You don't know what the hell you're talking about, Foggy.' She leaned forward. 'Look. I like you. I've grown to like you. Sure, I hired you at first just because my father told me to. He found you. He knows all about you. He knows your motivations. And he knew at some point that he'd want to get . . . look. By the time I hired you, Lynette was already pregnant and causing trouble. It was only a matter of time before something went wrong, see? So, yes, you were supposed to be a kind of a fall guy, if that's how you want to put it. You were supposed to get the baby from the hospital, bring it to me, and I'd give it to him. No questions asked. Or answered. But then Lynette freaked out and skipped with the kid, so we went to plan B. Only plan B was screwed up too because of the goddamned Indians! Which, after a second, I figured out all my own. I don't have any idea what my father plans to do with this baby, but it won't be good, I can tell you that. It won't be good for anyone. Except him.'

I nodded. 'Nice speech. Did you write it down and memorize it, or was that improvised?'

She closed her eyes for a second. 'I did kind of get it together in my head last night, just in case. But that doesn't make it any less true.'

'So, just for my own amusement,' I said, 'can you give me any idea how a guy like Henderson met a kid like Lynette?'

'I'd rather not.' She looked away.

'Come on. We have to talk about something 'til McReedy gets here.'

'Seriously, Foggy, I don't want to talk about it.'

'Because it's a family thing,' I surmised.

'No,' she said.

And then she threw up again.

'Do you have some kind of a bug or something?' I asked.

'No,' she told me, still all bent over.

'Then what the hell is going on? Why do you keep doing that?'

She shot up, red in the face. 'Because it makes me sick! What he does makes me sick enough to die!'

'What he does?' I repeated, a little startled by her vehemence. 'What does he do?'

'I told you. He's Satan. What does Satan do? He wants to be God. That's what my father wants. He wants to be God in people's lives. He likes to pick a subject, usually a girl, and warp her life all out of shape, just to see what she'll do. Just because he can. It's his hobby. He picked out Lynette when she was a toddler. There was an escapee from the Columbus Stockade, a solider in the army, a deserter from Korea.'

'I've heard this story,' I began.

'No you haven't,' she snapped. 'This deserter got as far as Fry's Bay. He came to my father for money.'

'The deserter? Why did he . . . how in the world did he even know . . .' but I did not get a chance to get my question or my thoughts together.

'My father thought a person like that would be useful here in a little town like this. But the guy didn't want to stay here; he only wanted a little travelling money. So my father had him sedated, shot the guy up with some God-awful flu bug, and had him dropped off in the swamp close to where the main Seminole hideout is. He thought that he could give all the Seminoles influenza, see, like germ warfare – kill them off, or some of them, anyway. Because that's what white people brought the Indians when they first came to America – syphilis and the plague. They don't have the tolerance or the medicine for it, usually. Because, see, if the Seminoles found someone sick near their camp, they would take care of him. And if they found a dead body, they would give it a proper ceremony. Because that's the way they are. That's why Henderson thought they would all get the flu, see? But everybody got lucky, if you want to call it that. The guy was found by some Seminole woman who was a nurse. She took him in, nursed him back to health, saved his life. The short of it is this: they had a baby. Right away. That baby was Lynette.'

'I told you I heard this story several times already in the past couple of days,' I insisted.

'The story doesn't end there,' she snarled. 'The little family had no peace. My father got wind that his plan didn't work. So he sent in the army. Seriously, the U.S. Army went into the Seminole camp, arrested the deserter, confiscated the baby. There was a fracas, and some army major got shot. They took in one of the tribal elders, too, and put him in prison.'

I looked over at Joseph. 'Are you hearing this? She's talking about John Horse!'

'Meanwhile, Lynette went to an orphanage.' Sharon's voice was growing shrill and more than a little hysterical. I could tell that she was starting to lose it. She was also speeding up, talking faster and faster. 'But my father had her released when she was fourteen, thrown out on the streets. He sent Jody – I think you know Jody – to get Lynette hooked on junk.'

'Why?' I was having a very difficult time believing what she was telling me.

'You'll see. Then, after a while, Lynette was messed up, naturally, and needed money for dope, right? So Lynette partied with an older guy to get the money. Then the older guy . . . my father . . .'

But she stopped right there so that she could throw up again.

'Wait,' I said, ignoring the heinous behavior of the vicious rich and continuing to add things up. 'Wait just a minute. Are you telling me that the Seminole woman we're talking about was a nurse?' I looked to Joseph again. 'Damn it! Is Maggie Redhawk Lynette's mother?'

'I think so,' he said.

He didn't seem as amazed by this concept as I was.

'Christ!' I said to Sharon. 'Your father really does wreak his fair share of havoc around here, doesn't he?'

'And he doesn't even stay here most of the time,' she said, weakly. 'He likes to come when the tourists are gone and everything's kind of sleepy. But I'm not finished. I got one more boom to lower. Are you ready?'

'Am I ready?' I asked. 'For more? You've given me in five minutes more information than I've gotten out of you in the previous year. You're seriously messing with my head. If you're about to tell me anything whatsoever about the party between your father and Lynette, I'd just as soon not hear it.'

'No, it's not about that,' she said, holding her head in her hands, 'and it's not about Lynette's baby either. Did you ask yourself, yet, who Lynette's father is?'

'Lynette's father?' I hesitated. 'I thought we were talking about—'

But Sharon didn't give me time to finish.

'McReedy,' she hissed. 'McReedy is the deserter, the army man, and *he's* the father of little lost Lynette. McReedy is his first name, see? It's an old family name. His complete name is McReedy Henderson Baker.'

'Wait, wait,' I stammered.

'See?' She grinned like a vampire. 'Welcome to my family.'

TWENTY-NINE

t became clear that Pascal Henderson, aside from being one of the sickest human beings I had ever heard about, had a way with motivational management. He kept his distant cousin McReedy in line, a little crazy, and angry enough to do anything, mostly by carefully screwing with McReedy's daughter beyond all recognition. Apparently McReedy wanted out of the relationship so bad he tried to kill himself less than a year ago. That's when Henderson took Lynette to bed, just so he could say to McReedy, 'Look what happens if you're not around to watch out for your daughter. You think it couldn't get worse? It could always get worse.'

By the time Sharon finished telling me everything, I felt a little like throwing up myself.

Joseph had a different take. 'Malcolm X was right,' he told me. 'White people *are* the devil.'

And at that moment I couldn't figure out a way to disagree with him.

No one expected Lynette to get pregnant. And when she did, no one expected Lynette to keep the baby. And when she did *that,* no one expected her to be smart enough to hide it from Henderson.

But all of that was in the past. In the present, there was a baby.

'Let me ask you this,' I said to Sharon, after I settled my stomach a little, 'why is it that your father wants this baby so bad, really?'

'I don't know.' She was all out of steam.

I turned to Joseph. 'Is it really plausible,' I asked, 'that a guy like this Henderson is really going to care about this baby one way or another without some weird ulterior motive?'

'Maybe you should know something,' Joseph piped up. 'We – that is, the Seminole tribe here in this town – we're about to have our whole area of the swamp, about five hundred and seventy thousand acres, declared a national preserve. That has something to do with all this.'

'Like a park?' I asked. 'They're going to make John Horse's house a national park.'

He shook his head. 'A preserve is different. This will be the first one.'

'The first one what?'

'This will be the first national preserve in America,' he told me. 'It's different from a park.'

'How different?'

'Well, for one thing,' he said, 'we'll be allowed, the Seminoles will be allowed, to keep our traditional hunting and grazing rights. You can't do that in a national park.'

And at this point, Joseph smiled a little.

'There's more,' I said, seeing that smile.

'Yes,' he told me. 'In a national park you can't drill for oil. But in a national preserve, we can.'

'Oh my God,' I said.

'John Horse and Mister Redhawk have been working on the deal, like, with *Congress* – for a while. You know Mister Redhawk is a lawyer, right?'

'A lawyer?'

'University of North Dakota. Started the Indian Association there, sometime in the 1960s. Last year he helped to start the National Native American Bar Association. He's a big deal. And, as a lawyer, he will kick your ass.'

'I have to admit,' I said, 'he looks the part, now that you mention it. But here is something I have wondered: am I ever going to know his first name, or is that something disrespectful or wrong?'

'His first name?' Joseph seemed momentarily confused. Then he smiled that smile again. 'Oh. I see. You don't get it, but you already know his first name.'

'No, I don't,' I said in no uncertain terms.

'Yes, you do,' he insisted. 'You say it all the time. It's *Mister*.'

This cracked me up. 'The guy's first name is *Mister*? This is excellent. Excellent. He'll always get respect from anyone who has to use his name.'

Joseph nodded, smiling even bigger.

We might have gone on for a while, admiring the genius of Mister Redhawk's parents, but instead the door of the office suite exploded inward and a raving lunatic in the person of one McReedy appeared in the room, a gun in each hand.

I thought we all reacted well under the circumstances. Sharon screamed and took a dive under her desk. My startled response kicked in so dramatically that I dropped the pistol I was holding, and it made a really loud noise on the floor. Joseph fell backward in his chair and landed like a turtle on his back, flailing for his own sidearm.

McReedy had an insane look in his eye. He was dressed very dramatically in a full-length trench coat, one pistol trained on me and the other pointed at Joseph's crotch. In my experience, there was no better way to get a man's attention than to point a pistol at his crotch. Joseph was very still. So was Sharon, who was trying to be silent underneath her desk, but she kept making little squeaking noises. Fear hiccups, I called them.

So it fell to me to be the spokesman.

'I can see that you're upset,' I said to McReedy in my most soothing voice. 'But there's really no need for you to be. I've seen Lynette and her baby. They're fine. Everybody's healthy and pink. Lynette is even straightened out from the junk, so there's that too.'

I was banking on a lot. I was banking on a fatherly sentiment that, for all I knew at this point, McReedy did not possess. But I figured, if Henderson had used Lynette to manipulate McReedy, maybe it was worth a shot for me to try the same thing.

Alas, McReedy only said, 'Shut up.'

'It's true, man,' Joseph said from where he was lying on the floor. 'I've been watching out for her. John Horse got her off the dope, and healed the baby too. Everybody's OK. They're in the swamp.'

It was hard to tell, but I thought I saw a few of the black clouds clear away from McReedy's eyeballs. It was obvious to me that he was loaded. My guess would have been coke, based on the takes-one-to-know-one school of observation, but his eyes were so vacant I thought maybe he'd been shooting speedballs.

A speedball was a dangerous thing to run into, because when you mixed coke and heroin in the same syringe, you got a person who was really messed up and who was also wide awake. It was a good combination for McReedy, because it kept him alert, but it also prevented him from giving a damn about almost anything on this earth. So he could aim and fire with clarity but his conscience wouldn't even wake up, not for a second.

So I just continued with the program, hoping for the best. 'It's true what Joseph, here, says. Your daughter Lynette is safe in the swamp.'

McReedy laughed. It was not a happy sound. 'Crap!' he said. 'She's not safe there. She wasn't safe there when she was three, and she's not safe there now.'

'You are referring to the fact that your employer, Mr Henderson, sent in the U.S. Army to get you back in fifty-seven,' I said calmly, 'when you and Maggie were living there, happy as the proverbial clams.'

Sometimes this worked – you could make a junkie think that you knew him, and that he knew you. It could confuse him, or it could make him think, or it could even encourage him to assume that you were his friend. Anything along those lines would have been good. It would keep him from pulling the trigger. Or, in this case, *triggers*.

'Shut up,' he told me again, but with less conviction than before.

So I kept it up. 'Then, when you got out of the joint from the desertion rap, Henderson got your kid addicted to drugs because you wouldn't do what he told you to do.'

That was mostly based on what Sharon had told me.

'You.' That's all McReedy could come up with. Then he shook his head, trying to clear it. 'You found Lynette and took her to the hospital.'

'And then we came to get her to hide her from Henderson,' Joseph chimed in.

'And, frankly, from you,' I said to McReedy. 'If I may say so, you're kind of a terrible father.'

That was obviously a risk, because it could have made him mad all over again. But I had seen many times in Brooklyn what could happen to a guy on the edge of a speedball, and very often he would get sad and sentimental. This was the heroin. Or some-times the oldsters used morphine in a speedball, but McReedy looked more like the skag type to me, and I knew from recent experience that skag was readily available in Fry's Bay.

I kept my mouth shut, giving McReedy time to think about what I'd said. But I was also eyeing the gun I'd dropped on the floor beside my foot, and I could see that Joseph was edging his hand toward his shoulder holster.

McReedy did, indeed, have a faraway look in his eye. And he was beginning to lower his guns.

Unfortunately, it was very dusty in our office, especially under the desks, and dust wreaks havoc on a person's nose. In short, Sharon sneezed.

McReedy didn't mean to fire. He just did. A bullet barely missed me and went into Sharon's desk. She screamed. A bullet from the other gun hit Joseph in the fleshy inner part of his right thigh, but missed anything important, as luck would have it.

Joseph moved faster than any human being I had ever seen. He rolled, he pulled out his gun, and he popped three direct hits right into McReedy.

McReedy grunted.

For a second, that was all that happened. We were all frozen, trying to assess the damage.

Then McReedy dropped both his guns.

'Shit!' he said, and he zoomed past me to Sharon's desk.

Sharon crawled out from under the desk, but she didn't look so good. She had a lot of blood on her face.

Joseph was on his feet, and blood was soaking his jeans.

I finally managed to motivate, and I scooped up the gun that I had dropped, stood, and kicked McReedy's pistols toward Joseph.

'Jesus, Sharon.' McReedy was pulling her up into her seat. 'I didn't mean . . . I really didn't mean to shoot you. Please don't be shot.'

He said it like maybe he could make time go backwards.

You couldn't see Sharon's face because of the blood, but she was moving and waving her arms, so you could see she wasn't dead yet.

'Damn it,' she swore. 'Damn it.'

She was trying to wipe the blood out of her eyes.

I couldn't figure why McReedy hadn't gone down yet. Joseph's bullets really had hit him fair and square.

'Sharon.' McReedy took off his trench coat and wrapped it around Sharon. Then he used the arms to mop at her brow.

'I'm OK, I'm OK,' she snapped, sounding anything *but* OK. 'I hit my head on the metal under the drawer. Twice. Once when I sneezed and then again when you *shot* at me.'

He stopped mopping. 'You bumped your head?'

'I sneezed,' she repeated, a little defensively.

McReedy was still for a second, and then he busted out laughing, like it was the best joke he had ever heard.

'I didn't shoot you? You hit your head?'

'Yes, damn it,' she confirmed.

It was about then that I registered McReedy's vest, the good old-fashioned bulletproof kind. It was a little ruffled where Joseph's bullets had hit, but otherwise very dapper.

'That's a lot of blood from a sneeze,' I said.

Again McReedy laughed.

Joseph was a little less jolly. 'You shot me in the leg, you son of a bitch,' he said to McReedy.

This is when we noticed that Joseph had his pistol pointed right at McReedy's head. I took a step back, to give Joseph a clear shot.

McReedy dropped the sleeve of his coat that he'd been using to clean up Sharon's face.

'Sorry,' he said. 'You want me to look at it?'

'I'd rather you just stay right there by Sharon,' I said, waving around my gun.

I moved over to Joseph, who kept his pistol trained on McReedy.

'It actually doesn't hurt that much,' Joseph told me softly. 'But, I'm pretty stoned.'

'So, it might hurt more later,' I said to him. 'But you're lucky in part; the bullet went right through the flesh. Clean. Let me see can I stop the bleeding a little.'

I went to my desk because I had, in my bottom drawer, a package of industrial size bandages. I pulled them out.

'I got these from Maggie Redhawk a while back,' I said to Sharon, 'when we went over and got that Tolliver kid whose father was roughing her up, remember?'

Sharon nodded.

I moved back to Joseph. 'Do you want to take your pants off or do you want to rip them up? I have to put one of these bandages on your wound, right next to the skin, you understand. Not over jeans.'

He lowered his voice. 'I don't have on any underwear.'

'Ah.' I nodded. 'Maybe you can un-tuck your shirt and it'll hang down—,'

But he didn't let me finish. 'Not far enough. It won't hang down far enough.'

'Oh,' I said, a little louder, 'look who's got a big opinion of himself. But, OK. Take off your jacket and use it like a skirt or a kilt or something.'

This, he went for. He was out of the jacket in two seconds, eyes always on McReedy.

But McReedy was, it would seem, more amused by the situation than anything else. This, also, was partly the speedball. The heroin was giving the guy a very nice sense of well-being. I figured McReedy was relieved that he didn't shoot the daughter of his employer and so was having a little flood of jollity. Plus, the ballet with Joseph was amusing, even under the circumstances.

'When you're done there,' McReedy said, smiling, 'maybe you would toss me a bandage to put on Sharon's head.'

'Absolutely,' I said, taking out a sealed pad about three inches square and tossing it to him.

In short order, I had bandages stuck on Joseph's thigh, and Sharon had one on her forehead.

I was standing by Joseph holding two pistols, and he was holding two pistols, and McReedy was beginning to look a little disoriented.

'What just happened?' he mumbled, to no one in particular. 'Wow.'

'Let's take this one step at a time,' I said to him. 'Let's back up to why you want to kill me, which you have failed to do three times now.'

He nodded. He sighed. He sat himself down on Sharon's desktop. 'Maybe my heart's not in it. I'm usually good at this.'

'Your heart's not in it?' I asked.

'You were trying to help Lynette,' he said, like it was the answer to everything. 'I could see that.'

'Yes,' I said. 'Yes that is exactly what I was doing. And she really is safe now. You should see her. And the baby: cute as a bug's ear.'

'Hey,' Joseph lit up. 'This guy really *is* a grandpa!'

I nodded. 'Joseph says this because earlier he called me "grandpa", but he meant it in a derogatory manner. In this case, he means it in a more familial way. Correct me, Joseph, if I am wrong.'

'McReedy has a little granddaughter.' Joseph seemed to be trying to figure that out.

'You need to think about your life,' I said to McReedy, using my mother's best scolding voice. 'You need to take stock.'

'John Horse got your daughter off heroin,' Joseph said, very sweetly, 'and he could do the same for you.'

And it was about then that I realized Joseph was kind of amazing, because he had been with me every step of the way as I attempted to get all psychological with McReedy.

'Joseph,' I said to him, 'you are a very perceptive young person.'

'Thank you,' he said.

'But, if I may return to a more pressing matter,' I told McReedy, 'you attempted to kill me a lot. Are you going to keep that up? Because I have in my hand the very gun which you tried to use on me only a short while ago.'

I held up the gun again for all to see.

'Henderson tells me what to do,' McReedy said, despondently. 'I do it.'

'But why?' I asked. I thought this a reasonable question. 'I mean, really, why?'

'Where should I begin?' McReedy was getting vague, which meant that the coke was slowing down and the junk was taking over. McReedy, theoretically, could have been about to nod off.

'Why don't you start when you deserted the American Army in Korea,' I suggested.

'I was never in Korea,' he said, but his voice had gone all hollow. 'I didn't make it out of boot camp in Columbus, Georgia. I smacked a sergeant and took off. They caught me. I got court marshaled as a deserter.'

'Why would that be?' I asked. 'Seems a harsh sentence just for smacking a guy.'

'I was in the Airborne School on Main Post. I was going to be an Airborne Ranger. They have these big free towers that they use to train paratroopers. There used to be four. Then, on March fourteenth in 1954, there was a tornado. A big tornado. The sergeant wanted us up on the towers anyway. He said that we had to get used to a little wind. I took three jumps and almost died. He probably didn't know it was building into a tornado, but when it hit, it took down one of the towers. With two guys on it. They both died. I told the sergeant that I was going to report the incident, and he went nuts. We got into it. He lost. I left. Went to a bar in Columbus to cool off. Next thing I knew, I was hauled into the stockade. I have no idea how the two dead guys were handled. I don't even remember their names. All I know is that I was given the world's fastest court marshal and shoved into the Columbus stockade for good.'

'But you escaped fairly quickly,' I said.

'You don't know anything.' He was getting dark, which was not a good sign. 'Six months in that place was like a lifetime in hell. You know how I got out? I ate rat poison. I thought it would kill me. Instead it got me to the infirmary. My guts were on fire for a week, but I got out. I got out at night. I stole a Jeep. I made it as far as Fry's Bay.'

'You came here on purpose,' I said. 'You thought you might have a relative here. A cousin or something named Pascal Henderson.'

'I knew that Pascal had a place here, for some reason,' he told me. 'I'd never been here before that. I knew it had something to do with establishing a residence in a state that didn't collect income tax, and something to do with Humble Oil. I didn't care. I just wanted traveling money. I had no idea if he'd be here or not. I was desperate.'

'But he was here, and I think I know the rest of the story from Sharon.' I stretched. 'Well, this is certainly a day for the surprises.'

'My leg is starting to hurt,' Joseph mumbled.

I looked around the room. All of a sudden I had the same sensation I had previously experienced in the swamp, to wit; I was having another surreal moment. Previously, it had to do with being surrounded by Seminoles and hearing Benny Goodman. This time, it had to do with a wounded accountant, a sympathetic hit man, and my evil boss. I thought to myself, *You're the one who needs to take stock, pal – at least as much as McReedy does.*

'All right, look,' I began slowly. 'Let's just think about this for a moment. I would like to start by putting away all guns.'

To verify my veracity, I set McReedy's Magnum on the floor, and the other pistol I had, which was a Smith and Wesson number. I looked at Joseph. He mumbled something which I didn't hear, and then put his guns on the desk closest to him.

'There,' I announced, 'this makes it much nicer. Does anyone else have any guns?'

After a moment's hesitation, Sharon sighed and tossed the cutest little concealed weapon on to her desktop, right next to McReedy. I thought it was a Model 210 Sig, which, in addition to being very accurate, was also remarkably expensive—and Swiss.

'McReedy,' I said, 'I would take it as a sign of good faith if you would please brush that little pistol of Sharon's on to the floor so that you won't be tempted by it. OK?'

He nodded. He brushed. The gun clattered to the floor.

Then, after another second, McReedy leaned over, really slowly, with his eyes on mine, and said, 'This is the last one.'

Turned out he had another gun taped to his left ankle. I couldn't tell what it was because of the duct tape and the bad lighting, but he ripped the tape and tossed the gun carelessly behind him, into a corner.

'Good,' I declared. 'Now, here is my thinking with regard to our situation. I am not the problem, because I am apparently too stupid to be the problem. Joseph certainly isn't the problem because he's a college graduate and an accountant. Plus, he's shot. The funny thing is, McReedy, I currently don't think that you're the problem either. While I don't care for the fact that you've tried to kill me every chance you got, I can see that it wasn't your idea. Which leads us to the one person who actually is the problem.'

'Pascal Henderson,' Joseph and McReedy said at the same time.

'Dad,' Sharon chimed in, somewhat haplessly.

'Good,' I nodded. 'We're in agreement. My suggestion is that we form some kind of short-term alliance whose first order of business would be to go to Yudda's and get something to eat. Food always makes you feel better. And we're supposed to go back there pretty soon anyway, to meet people. So who likes this idea?'

'I could eat,' Joseph allowed.

'I'd really go for some flapjacks,' McReedy said dreamily.

We all looked to Sharon.

'Far be it from me to throw a monkey wrench into these works,' she answered, 'but are we certain that the four of us don't make the most obvious group target in the southeastern United States? A wounded Indian, a soggy Jew, a known hitman, and a tall, bleeding woman? All we need is Sidney Greenstreet and we have the makings of some lost Bogart movie.'

'I'm getting used to that kind of weirdness,' I told her happily. 'And you only thought to say that about Bogart because I brought up his movies earlier in the conversation.'

'No,' she disagreed. 'I brought it up because if my father is anywhere around, he will recognize me and McReedy right away, of course, and then he'll see that we're dining with two other people who might mean to do him harm. And we're proposing to do this less than a block away from his sumptuous condo, a place where he actually is quite liable to see us. This isn't completely nuts to anyone else?'

'I see what the problem is,' I told her. 'I've forgotten to mention that Mister Redhawk and Philip are probably at Yudda's right now. They've had a conversation with your father, and are meeting us at Yudda's to tell us that this whole thing is over with.'

'What?' Sharon's mouth was open about as far as it was going to get.

'So I think we should gather up all these idle weapons, lock them in your desk, and adjourn to Yudda's. Right?'

Sharon and McReedy sat, stunned. But Joseph and I began to collect guns.

'Can we hustle it up a little?' Joseph asked me 'My leg is starting to hurt bad. I could really use a beer.'

THIRTY

Yudda was all by himself on that particular evening. No help, no customers. The sun was probably going down, but there was no way to tell because it was raining so hard. The rain was like little bullets of ice, very hard, very cold.

Yudda didn't make a peep when we walked in, even though we were a very strange assemblage. Maybe we looked so strange that keeping his mouth shut was a good idea.

Mister Redhawk and Philip were not in evidence, so we took the fourth booth, the last one at the far end of the diner. This would give us room and also a nice view of whoever came in the door. We jockeyed a bit for position, but it was finally decided that McReedy would go in first and I would sit beside him, both of us facing the door. Sharon went in first on the other side and Joseph sat kind of sideways so that he could face the door a little, too, but also he could stretch out his shot-up leg.

All this happened in a matter of around ninety seconds, and then we settled in. Still, Yudda did not move.

'Are there any specials?' I asked, looking right at him.

His eyebrows lifted. 'Other than the four of you? No. I got nothing on the menu half so special as that.'

'But you still serve food here, right?' I asked.

'The monkfish is good,' he shot right back.

'Yeah, sometimes,' I allowed, 'but the crab cakes are safer, right?'

'Crab cakes all around,' he said. 'They come with French fried potatoes and a provocative sauce.'

'Mine comes with three beers,' Joseph said, somewhat insistently.

'Yudda does not serve alcohol,' I told Joseph.

'I need beer!' Joseph roared, and in such a manner as to assure us all that he was serious.

'Let's put everybody down for beer,' Yudda said. 'I may have a few in my personal cooler. And I assume, since you're all looking at the door every three seconds, that we are expecting others?'

'Yes,' I said to Yudda. 'And thank you for your generous offer of personal beer.'

He went about his business.

I leaned forward and made my voice soft as I could. 'What do we think is the deal with Mister Redhawk? Why isn't he here?'

'He's very thorough,' Joseph answered. 'He's a little like John Horse in that way – they both take a long time to do what they do. I get kind of frustrated with it, but it usually comes out pretty good in the end.'

'Slow cooking,' I said.

Joseph understood why I said that, because of his mother's turtle stew. The other two seemed mildly puzzled, but not enough to ask about it.

A few seconds later, Yudda waddled over and plunked down an undetermined number of beers. I say *undetermined* because I didn't bother to count them. Joseph got more than one, and I got one for me, so what did I care?

Joseph's first one was gone in sixty seconds. So was mine. Sharon decided to nurse. McReedy did not touch his. His eyes were locked on the front door of the joint.

'You're nervous,' I said to him.

'Yes.' And he sounded nervous.

'Why, exactly?'

'Why?' He seemed to think this a stupid question. 'Why am I nervous that one of the most powerful men in the world, a man who has ruined my life and my daughter, is about to walk in here and see me sitting beside a man I was supposed to kill? Twice, or was it three times? And currently I am completely unarmed? Why am I nervous? Is that what you're asking?'

'OK, OK,' I told him. 'I can see your point. But what's he going to do in a place like this, with all these witnesses? I think you can relax.'

And at exactly that moment, two cops barreled into Yudda's, pistols drawn, and started yelling at us to put our hands behind our heads and shut up.

'Is it OK if I don't relax just yet?' he whispered to me.

'Shut up!' one of the cops screamed. 'Hands behind your heads!'

We complied, all four of us.

'What's going on, officers?' Yudda wanted to know.

'Shut up,' the other cop said to Yudda, but a lot more politely than the screamer had said it to McReedy.

Outside of Yudda's I could see the flashing lights of a cop car. Maybe there were more guys outside. Maybe it was just these two. I started weighing the options.

But before I could get very far, Sharon threw up again. This time on the table between us.

That seemed to confuse the cops, and they lost their concentration.

I stood up fairly quickly, so as not to get my best suit any more messed up than it already was. When I did that, McReedy launched himself out of the booth and into the midsection of the nearest cop. That cop went flying back, and into the other cop. They both knocked into the bar stools and thudded on to the floor. Before I knew it, McReedy had their guns. He pocketed one and pointed the other right at one cop's eye. Inches away from it.

'I work for Mr Henderson,' he said through clenched teeth. 'I assume Mr Henderson sent you here. Right?'

The gun was almost touching the cop's eyeball.

'Yes,' that cop said. 'Mr Henderson.'

'Then we're on the same side, right?' McReedy went on.

Yudda added his two cents to the cop. 'You know that you're talking to McReedy, don't you, Rodney?'

The cop swallowed loudly. We could all hear it. 'McReedy?'

'That's me,' said McReedy.

'Yes,' Rodney said, 'we are definitely on the same side, Mr McReedy.'

'Good,' McReedy muttered.

McReedy stepped back and offered Rodney a hand. Rodney hesitated but took it and was standing up in seconds. The other cop staggered to his feet.

'I'm going to leave now,' McReedy announced. 'You do whatever you want with these three.'

With that, he handed the cops back their guns, muscled past them to the door, and out on to the rain-wet streets.

The cops pointed their guns at us, but some of the stuffing was out of them.

'My leg really hurts,' Joseph said to one of the cops. 'McReedy shot me. I think I should go to the hospital.'

'Yes,' I chimed in. 'And this woman is obviously very sick. She should go to the hospital too. Which leaves you with me.'

I smiled.

The officers did not respond. I could read their faces, and it was easy to see that they had no idea what they were doing.

'Hospital would be the right thing,' Yudda grunted.

'Yeah, OK,' Rodney said. 'Hospital.'

'For the Indian and the woman,' the other cop said, tossing an uncalled-for look in my direction. 'He stays.'

'Oh, yeah,' Rodney agreed. 'He stays. I still think he's the one who stabbed that poor teenager over at Pete's the other night.'

'Oh, I get it, you're *Rodney*' I said. 'They told me that you were the constable who investigated that mêlée at Pete's.'

'What?' Rodney asked. And the look on his face was proof enough that the rumors around town were true: he was a moron.

The other cop went to the cop car and called for an ambulance, although it would actually have been quicker just to walk to the hospital.

After a second, I sat down at the bar and Yudda, as if nothing else was going on, brought me my crab cakes. I ate them instantly. They were delicious. The secret was in the remoulade.

The ambulance came. Joseph and Sharon went. Rodney sat down next to me. The other cop was nowhere to be seen.

'Yudda?' Rodney said with his eyes on me.

'What?' Yudda grunted.

'Take a walk.'

'It's raining,' Yudda protested.

'Take an umbrella,' Rodney snapped, 'and beat it before I find enough code violations to shut you down 'til next Christmas.'

Yudda mumbled something. I thought it might be some kind of Cajun curse. But he stepped outside.

'Look, wise guy,' Rodney began, his voice lowered, 'you don't know who you're dealing with.'

'Yes I do,' I told him politely. 'I'm dealing with Pascal Henderson.'

'OK,' he responded, only slightly thrown, 'but you don't have any idea who *he* is.'

'I apologize for disagreeing again, Officer,' I said, 'but, in fact, I know that Pascal Henderson is one of the richest men in the world, he has a condo in Fry's Bay for tax and oil purposes, the woman who just left here with her head in a bandage is his daughter, and he is also the father of a little baby whose exact location is unknown at the present time. And that particular baby is, currently, the crux of the biscuit.'

'What?' he said, proving that it was, in fact, Rodney who did not know who he was dealing with.

'It's true,' I assured him.

'That woman who threw up just now, that was Mr Henderson's daughter?' he said, looking at the door.

'One of them, anyway,' I told him, 'but not the one currently in contention. The aforementioned crux of the biscuit.'

He turned back to me, his face all contorted. 'I know that you're speaking English because I recognize some of the words, but I don't understand what you're saying. Who knows what you people are saying, ever?'

'*You people*?' I asked, hackles rising.

'Yankees,' he explained, as if it was obvious.

'Oh.'

'All I know is this,' he said, sounding seven years old, 'Mr Henderson wants you. So I'm taking you to him. Now.'

He stood up.

I kept my seat.

'I'd rather not,' I told him.

I figured this way: something had happened to Philip and Mister Redhawk. I did not wish to have the same thing happen to me.

'Get up!' he insisted.

Then he pointed his pistol at me to back up his insistence.

'Look,' I explained, 'Rodney. You understand that when you work for Satan, bad things happen.'

'Satan?' And there was that contorted face again.

'That's what Sharon calls Henderson,' I told him. 'And if his own daughter calls him that, who am I to disagree? So I'm just saying that when you work for Satan, bad things will happen to you.'

'Get up!' he shouted.

I put my hands on the tabletop. 'OK,' I told him. 'But I did warn you.'

As I was standing, I palmed the fork with which I had eaten my crab cakes. I stepped off my barstool, and poor Rodney did not even have the sense to take a step back. I kind of felt sorry for him, but it didn't keep me from going after him.

I slapped his gun away, kneed him really hard in the nuts, and jabbed the fork as hard as I could right into his trachea. This made it easier for me to take the gun out of his hand before he hit the floor.

Rodney started gurgling. I kneeled beside him.

'This is what you call a bit of irony, this fork in the throat treatment, wouldn't you say? I mean, considering your investigation the other night at Pete's. I never used a move twice in a row like that before, but I'm too tired to think up something new. I hope you understand.'

He flailed.

'That's right, Rodney. You're in trouble. If I do nothing, and you can't get the fork out of your throat in a minute, you're dead. Dead. Is that what you want?'

Rodney got a look in his eye like a wild animal – terrified, not quite comprehending what was happening to him. It brought out my sympathy.

'OK,' I told him, 'but you have to behave.'

I put my palm over his throat, two fingers on either side of the fork, and pulled it out with my other hand, really fast. Rodney had a serious convulsion, but it subsided.

Meanwhile, Yudda had come back in and was standing in the doorway.

I looked up at him. He looked down at me.

'Sorry to mess up the place,' I said. 'I seem to be doing this all over town lately.'

'Rodney deserves this,' Yudda said calmly. 'He's taking three different payoffs from guys, and he's about as useful a cop as I am.'

'Yes,' I said, 'I gather that Rodney is in the employ of Pascal Henderson.'

'At least,' Yudda said.

'So who do I call if I want an honest cop around here?' I asked. 'Or is there such a thing?'

'Baxter and Gordon,' Yudda told me right away. 'Both born here. Baxter's father is a commercial fisherman in this town since I don't know when. I buy all my stuff from him.'

'Baxter and Gordon,' I repeated. 'These are familiar names. I think they're guys my boss told me to steer clear of.'

'Why would that be?' he asked me, but he said it like he already knew the answer.

'Yeah,' I said, brain on overdrive, 'why *would* that be.'

'Your boy Rodney,' Yudda said, 'he don't look too good.'

I glanced down. Rodney seemed to have passed out.

'Do you have something like a clean bar towel in this joint?' I asked Yudda.

He moved. He got a white towel out of some drawer. I concentrated on keeping the holes in Rodney's throat kind of closed. There wasn't as much blood as you might think, but a nice big towel was called for, which was just what Yudda tossed. I wrapped it around Rodney's throat all the way. Then I woke Rodney up. He blinked. I took his hands and I put them on the towel.

'You hold your hands right here and don't pass out again, OK, Rodney?' I said to him. 'That will keep you from bleeding to death and it will help you to breathe. Yudda is going to call the hospital for you now.'

Yudda went to the phone.

'And don't worry,' I told Rodney. 'I'm going to go meet Mr Henderson, so you've done your job just fine.'

I patted his shoulder, stood, picked up his gun, and stepped over him.

Yudda was speaking into the telephone. 'It's the damndest thing I ever saw,' he was saying. 'The guy was eating so fast, and I think he was kind of drunk or something, and he actually stabbed himself in his own throat with his fork. I am not kidding.'

I nodded to Yudda. He nodded back, listening into the phone.

Then he said, 'Crab cakes. He was having the crab cakes.'

THIRTY-ONE

Of course, I had no idea which condo belonged to Henderson, but I headed out of Yudda's and toward the art deco building where he made his Fry's Bay home. If I was lucky, there wouldn't be a security guard or concierge to give me trouble.

The building itself was beautiful, and there were some things about it that reminded me of the Chrysler Building, only shorter. The rain was now an icy drizzle, and I was still not dried out from previous forays into the weather, so I was shivering pretty good.

Rodney's gun was a little disappointing. He carried a Colt Official Police revolver, which, in its day, was something of a big deal but had become something of a joke. I had it tucked away in the right outside pocket of my very wet suit coat.

I drew near to the front door of the building. It was a strange looking revolving number in glass and copper. I saw, to my dismay, that there was, indeed, a security guard. He appeared to be asleep in his chair, but it was a good bet that the revolving door would wake him up.

I took a deep breath and shoved through the door. There was a whooshing sound, and I was in the lobby, which was small but choice. There were paintings on the walls of women in blue dresses playing musical instruments. There was a kind of angular sunburst design on the floor. The ceiling was mostly hidden by a huge chandelier.

And the security guard woke up.

'No, no, no,' he began, before he was even on his feet. 'Turn right around and go out. This ain't a public building.'

I zipped out my wallet and flashed my so-called badge. 'Florida Child Protective Services,' I said, in my official voice. 'We've had a complaint that somebody is beating a young person somewhere on the premises. I'm going to need to see a roster of current residents. Now.'

'I . . . you're what? Florida child what?' He squinted at my badge.

'You actually want to go on record as a guy who'd protect a child beater?' I asked him.

'Child beater? What?'

'What's your name?' I demanded.

'My name?'

'That's right, just keep repeating everything I say. You may be able to tell that I'm wet and cold. This has put me in a really bad mood. In a bad mood, I might cite you for obstruction. If you keep stalling, I'll get into a terrible mood. That will get you a charge of collusion. Do you want to be known as a person who colludes with a child beater? What kind of a job do you think you could get after that? Once you're out of prison, I mean.'

'Prison?' He was beginning to wake up.

'Show me the damned residents list *now*.'

'Yes. Right. I got it right here.' He scrambled.

There was a kind of podium thing behind him. He reached into some inner recess and pulled out a clipboard, which he offered me.

'Here,' he said. 'That's the list.'

'How many floors you got here,' I asked, looking at the list. 'Three?'

'Yeah. Three. That's all. Just three.' He was shifting his weight form side-to-side – very nervous.

I took a good look at him. He was sixty or so and about that many pounds overweight. He was wearing a uniform, but it wasn't from any company. It came from an army surplus store, was my guess. He had a name badge that said *Ralph*. His head was almost completely bald, and beads of sweat were beginning to form there.

There were only three names on the list, including *Redhawk,* but I found that *Henderson* was not one of them.

'Penthouse?' I asked.

'Excuse me?' he replied.

'Does this place have a penthouse?'

'Oh. Sure. Yes. That's Mr Henderson, of course. He owns the building. The other tenants are, you know, mostly summer types – except Mister Redhawk, of course. I live in the basement. Mr Henderson lives on the top. He owns the building.'

'You said that,' I told him. 'Is this Mr Henderson in?'

'In?' The sweat on the guy's head got thicker.

'Yes. As the owner of the building, I think he'd like to know what's going on under his roof, don't you?'

He hesitated. 'I don't know.'

'You don't know if he's in?'

'No, he's in all right. It's just that he never . . . I get the impression that he doesn't want to be disturbed. Ever. So, I don't know if he wants to know what goes on in this building or not. I mean, nothing goes on, but I don't think he wants to bother with . . . Jesus. Are you going to arrest me?'

'Well, you did obstruct my investigation. Just a little.'

'I didn't mean to,' he said.

'Yeah, I get that. Look, I'm probably just tired and wet and all. How about this: how about if you were at Yudda's – you know Yudda's?'

'Of course,' he said. 'I eat there every night.'

'So, what if you were there, like on a coffee break. How could I arrest you then?'

'If I wasn't here? When you came in, I wasn't here?'

'Right.'

He nodded. 'Thanks. Thanks. I could use some coffee.'

He shot out through the revolving door like he was blown out of a cannon. Didn't even bother to put on a coat. I watched him go, and then I saw flashing lights and I figured Rodney's ambulance had arrived at Yudda's. Good. Maybe Henderson would see that; flashing lights can make people nervous.

A quick glance around the lobby told me that one of the elevators was for the hoi polloi and the other required a key, which meant that it was for the penthouse. So I began to worry about how I was going to get to Henderson's Shangri-La. I wondered if Ralph had the key, and I thought about skittering after him to fetch it. Then I thought to myself that maybe I could hotwire the elevator the way I hotwired a car. How different could it be?

I motored over to the Otis doors and took a second to glare at the lock. Turned out to be one of those big, loose jobs that was as much a button as a keyhole. That being the case, I fished in my pants pockets for a few small items that I always kept there for such occasions. Suffice it to say that a few slips and clicks and a little gentle pressure did the trick. Within thirty seconds, I heard the elevator gliding my way.

I took out the pistol I had in my suit coat and I stepped to one side, just in case. But the elevator doors opened up and the car was empty. So, just like Daniel into the lion's den, I stepped inside. The doors closed very genteelly. I felt a tug and, in no time at all, the doors opened again on to a stately pleasure dome like I had never seen before in my life.

In keeping with the exterior of the building, the penthouse was a very extravagant version of the same art deco style. Just from inside the elevator I could see the living room was something out of a movie set – it even had a beautiful 1930s Phillips radio, wood polished to the hilt, shaped like the top of a bullet, sitting under a poster of Greta Garbo in *Grand Hotel*. I knew this particular radio because my aunt Shayna had one just like it, only not in such good shape. And I knew Greta Garbo because my aunt Shayna wanted to *be* Greta Garbo.

What with the plush carpets here and the lush sofas there and the mood lighting and the silence and all, I was a little nervous to step off the elevator. But then I heard a noise and I decided I did not wish to be trapped in a moveable box roughly the size of two coffins. So I stepped out, into the foyer.

Even the foyer was fine. It had the same kind of sunburst pattern on its floor as the lobby. The columns that pretended to hold up the entrance into the apartment were Greek goddesses or some such, resting the arched doorway on their curvy shoulders.

I was on tiptoe, even thought I was certain that the noise of the elevator had alerted anyone in the apartment to my presence. But I tried for stealth. I peered into the living room. It was huge – more than twice the size of my entire apartment. One wall was windows that looked out on to the ocean. The opposite wall was mostly a mirror, which made the place disconcertingly gigantic. Straight ahead there was a dining room, which was half the size of the living room. Beyond that I thought was maybe the kitchen.

I continued to tiptoe into the living room, and then I heard something that sounded like the world's tiniest washing machine. Then it hits me: martinis!

I made it through the living room and peered around the wall to my left, opposite the window wall, and saw yet another in a series of surreal enclaves. Seated quite comfortably in a nice-sized den, with a fire going in the fireplace, I saw Mister Redhawk, Philip, Jody the drug pusher, and Ronald Colman – the older incarnation, graying at the temples.

I realized right away that Ronald Colman had died nearly twenty years previous to that particular night, so the fourth of the strange quartet would most likely be Pascal Henderson. At any rate, they were all holding martini glasses.

I put away my gun – it seemed rude at that point – and I stepped boldly into the den. The actual den, not the lion's den, although it was probably an equally risky enterprise.

'I apologize for busting in like this,' I said cordially, 'but I waited at Yudda's for a while, and when the police came, I had to kill them, so naturally I didn't want to wait there anymore. Ralph the security guy downstairs is dead too. I'm in a really bad mood. I'm wet and cold and I'm the only one in the place without a martini in my hand. So.'

Enter bold, that is one of the lessons I learned from Red Levine. Just saying a phrase like, 'I had to kill them' with a straight face, it can get you a long way in the respect department.

Oddly, Mister Redhawk and Philip seemed the most startled.

Philip sat forward so fast that he almost spilled his drink. 'You killed a cop?' He could hardly believe it.

'Two,' I corrected him. 'Rodney and some other goon. Can I have a martini or not?'

Ronald Colman smiled. 'Jody?' That's all he said.

Jody nodded, not smiling, and got up from the leather sofa where she and Ronald had been sitting. She stepped very quickly to a convenient bar close to the fireplace, where she began to make me a drink.

Philip and Mister Redhawk were stunned, it seemed. They said exactly nothing.

I circled around the furniture, making an obvious show of not turning my back on anyone, and ended up in front of the fireplace. The heat felt so good I considered jumping in.

Nobody said a word. Jody finished her concoction and brought me a glass.

'Thanks,' I said.

She did not rejoin. She merely returned to the sofa and sat beside Henderson

I sipped. 'Nice.'

Still no response from anyone. I decided to continue my modest onslaught.

'McReedy also paid me a visit,' I said casually, 'over at my office. Sharon's office, actually. Sharon's in the hospital. McReedy? He's switched sides. I mean, obviously he did not kill me because, as you can see, I'm not dead.'

I held out both arms.

Ronald Colman set down his drink. He did not use a coaster.

'Sharon's in the hospital?' he asked, trying to sound calm, but not completely succeeding.

'And you are?' I asked, mostly to irritate him.

'My name is Pascal Henderson,' he said, 'but you already know that, I'm sure. Now about Sharon.'

'McReedy shoots people,' I said, 'but you already know that, I'm sure. Sharon's alive but was bleeding very badly when last I saw her. So is Mister Redhawk's friend Joseph – bleeding, I mean. They're both over at the hospital.'

'Meanwhile,' Henderson said, 'McReedy is where?'

'Don't know.' I sipped.

'And you have gone on a sort of killing spree,' he said to me, all the while still smiling. 'Somewhat uncharacteristic of your usual behavior.'

'Desperate times, pal.' I sipped a third time, and my martini was almost gone. 'It was them or me. I prefer me.'

'McReedy shot Joseph?' Philip finally managed to say.

'In the leg,' I told him. 'He'll be fine. He could use a joint, he says, but otherwise all is well. Sharon, on the other hand, has a head wound.'

'Why would McReedy shoot Sharon?' Henderson wanted to know.

'He was going for me,' I answered.

Henderson folded his hands in his lap. He was dressed in a killer black pinstripe suit and a perfectly pressed pale blue shirt, no tie, unbuttoned at the collar. He sported a little gold chain around his neck.

Jody was still wearing her giant grey sweatshirt, only now she also had on jeans and pink rubber boots.

After another bit of silence, which you could slice with a knife, Henderson spoke.

'Mr Moscowitz,' he said, 'you may not be the person I thought you were.'

I finished my martini in one last gulp, set the glass on the mantle, also sans coaster, and said, 'Who do you think I am?'

'I thought you were an inconsequential criminal and an accidental murderer,' he told me crisply. 'A person who could be used and then tossed away, a little like a paper towel. Now I see that you may be more valuable than that.'

'*Like a paper towel*?' I asked. 'That's the best you can come up with? A man with your kind of money ought to have the sophistication to go with it. Only yesterday, John Horse and I were speaking about metaphorical language. Now there's a guy, John Horse, who has no formal education, no money, even was in prison for a while, but *he* is something of a genius in metaphorical conversation. And you give me *paper towel*. Well, that just shows to go you.'

I was deliberately trying to provoke the guy because I wanted to see what kind of a person he really was.

'Look, Foggy,' Philip began.

'And you guys!' I turned my attention to the Seminole faction. 'What the hell are you doing?'

'We're working out an arrangement,' Mister Redhawk said, straining to be patient. 'Or we were trying to before you came in.'

'Yeah, here's what I figure,' I said to Mister Redhawk. 'You talked me into going to my office, Sharon's office, in the hope that McReedy would show up and ice me. I let you talk me into it because I was confused about who's on what side in this little fracas. Although, I'm slowly coming to the conclusion that sides don't matter, and maybe there are no sides. But be that as it may, you can see that McReedy did not pop me, I am not dead, so I am still a problem for all concerned.'

'You don't know what you're talking about,' Mister Redhawk said confidently.

'I'm not finished,' I told him. 'Then, just in case McReedy didn't do his job, you told Mr Henderson, here, that you're supposed to meet me at Yudda's. Mr Henderson then called on the police force in Fry's Bay, a group that he has bought and paid for, and two of their finest came to menace me. What you don't get is that they're idiots, and I'm not. What you don't get is that McReedy is no match for me. I'm King Kong.'

Keep up the bravado, that's what you were supposed to do, especially when you had very little to lose.

'Are you finished?' Henderson asked me.

'Let me think.' I thought. 'Yes, I'm finished.'

'Good,' he said, 'then we can move right along. As Mister Redhawk was just saying, he and I are on the verge of an understanding. He had nothing to do with McReedy showing up at your office or with the police bothering you at Yudda's. McReedy was staking out your apartment and your office, because those are the main two places you might go. The police have kept their eyes on the pool hall bar, the donut shop, and Yudda's, because those are the other places in Fry's Bay that see you very often. It wasn't exactly the riddle of the ages. You are in some ways a very predictable man.'

'Yes,' I said, 'but you didn't figure on me to deal with McReedy, kill some cops, show up here, and drink your martinis. Not all in one night, you didn't.'

Henderson leaned back and crossed his legs, chin up. 'I don't believe you've killed anyone . . . tonight. I can't imagine what's happened to McReedy. But as to your being here, that is a surprise.'

The other three people seated on nice leather sofas, they didn't move – like they were frozen.

'And yet,' I said, 'here I am.'

'Yes, here you are.' He smiled, an expression that reminded me of the alligators I imagined in the swamp. 'So. What can I do for you?'

I nodded. 'Right, well, I haven't quite got that worked out.'

'I generally find that when people visit me like this,' he said, very comfortably, 'they end up asking for money in one way or another. That's why Mister Redhawk is here, certainly. And Jody, of course.'

'Yeah, that's a puzzler,' I admitted. 'Why exactly *is* Jody here?'

'Luck of the draw, actually,' he said. 'She was here on a personal matter.'

'What, you're her counselor?' I asked.

Jody blew up out of her seat. 'Can I go?'

'No,' said Henderson.

Jody fumed, arms crossed, moving away from the rest of the group. It was easy to see that part of her problem was that she hadn't had a shot in a while, and she was getting itchy.

'It's all your fault,' she hissed in my direction.

I leaned a little on the mantle. The martini had hit me in a very nice way.

'You'll have to be more specific than that,' I told Jody. 'A lot of things are my fault – but not *everything*.'

'I mean,' she snapped, 'how do you even know that greasy little spoon, Gerard? You're a queer?'

'Me?' I said. 'I try not to affiliate myself with any political party.'

'No,' she said, confused by what I'd told her.

'What happened? Why are you here talking to Mr Henderson about Gerard, who is a great guy, by the way. He's not greasy at all, and he is by no means shaped like a spoon.'

'He got Belinda fired!' she shouted, nearly over the edge.

'Wait.' I cranked the gears in my brain about two clicks. 'Belinda is your girlfriend. Gerard said something about the club where they both work. Belinda got fired?'

'You know good and well,' she said, beginning to grind her teeth. 'You told Gerard all about Lynette. He told everyone at the club. And Belinda got fired!'

I looked over at Mr Henderson. 'There's got to be more to the story than that.'

He rolled his eyes. 'You know how these people are.'

I paused to reflect, for a second, on what his definition of *these people* might be. Before I got finished with that thought, Mister Redhawk piped up.

'Listen, Mr Moscowitz,' he said, trying to sound smooth, 'we were in the middle of some rather sensitive negotiations when Jody, here, showed up. We were just trying to placate her when you showed up. I'm hoping to conclude matters and be on my way. But . . .'

'What are the odds?' I interrupted, kind of amazed. 'Who would have imagined that Jody and I would show up on the same night? Along with two Seminoles? Seriously, how did a thing like that happen?'

Suddenly, I saw Mr Henderson's face change. I couldn't tell why or what was going on, but something had shifted in his comfort level.

'Yes,' he began, very slowly, 'Mr Moscowitz brings up a very interesting point. Why would such a diverse array of people show up at my little home here in Fry's Bay at the same time on the same night?'

My mind clicked, and I saw an advantage.

'Almost like we planned it this way,' I told him casually.

My thinking was that a man like Henderson would have a fair degree of paranoia. I thought it was probably a trait of all rich people. They're always thinking that someone's out to get their money. They hoard gold and join the ranks of the misanthropic. Like *Silas Marner*, which was the last book I read in school before I graduated to car theft. I had no idea why this book came to my mind, but it did. Education is funny like that.

I could see that uncomfortable thoughts were playing around in Henderson's mind. What those thoughts might have been was anybody's guess, but, whatever they were, they were wrong. I knew that because they were based on a false assumption. The false assumption was that the Seminoles and Jody and me were all in cahoots, to somehow get his gold.

Henderson stood quickly enough to make Philip jump. He went to a wall console close to the bar and turned a knob of some sort. A grey light appeared. My guess was that he was looking at some sort of closed circuit television. He studied for a moment, the dim glow making his face look about a hundred years old, and then he looked at me.

'Ralph is not in the lobby,' he says.

'Ralph's body is in the lobby,' I insisted, 'only dragged out of sight so that no one can see it from the street. Or on the closed circuit either, I guess.'

'You killed Ralph.'

'He was in the way,' I said. 'I'm having a really bad couple of days, mostly thanks to you. So you can imagine how much more I feel like popping *you*.'

At that, I took out the police revolver and showed it to everyone.

Henderson did his best not to flinch. Jody took a couple of steps away from everyone pretty quickly. Philip stared, clearly wondering what I was doing. Mister Redhawk was the first to speak.

'All right,' he said to me, settling back. 'You're probably right. Go ahead and kill him. He's not being very cooperative, and we can just take the body to the swamp. As we agreed.'

In fact I had agreed no such thing. He was ad libbing as much as I was. But for the second or third time in the past couple of days, I was impressed with the ability of certain Seminole people to play along with a line of crap. Because it was clear to me that Mister Redhawk understood that I was messing with Henderson, and he saw an advantage too.

Henderson, meanwhile, looked uncomfortable for the first time since I walked in.

'You know,' Jody said, 'this is getting a little too heavy for me. Maybe I should just go.'

'You're not going anywhere,' I said, doing my best to sound mean. She deserved it for calling Gerard a greasy spoon – I didn't even know what that meant, but I didn't like it.

Jody sulked.

Philip, without making any noticeable moves, somehow managed to have his own gun in his hand all of a sudden. He wasn't pointing it anywhere, but it was clearly in evidence.

For a second everything threatened to come apart because nobody knew what to say next.

Then we all heard the elevator door.

Philip moved faster and more silently than a sudden breeze. I moved away from the fireplace. Everybody else stayed put.

'Pascal?' a voice shouted.

The next second, McReedy appeared in the doorway to the den, gun in hand.

There was another second or two of uneasy silence.

Then, quite unexpectedly, McReedy grinned ear to ear.

'Well,' he said, 'the gang's all here.'

I got a better look at his face as he stepped into the room's light, at which point I understand why his mood was better. He'd shot up and he was back on top, eyes wide, hands lively, heart glad. This made him dangerous again, in my book, because there's no telling what a hopped-up junkie might do.

'Look,' Henderson said finally, his voice cracking, 'I don't know what you all think you're going to do here tonight, but you must know that you can't just—'

'We can do anything,' McReedy interrupted. 'We can do anything we want to.'

His grin got bigger.

'I understand that you're upset about Lynette,' Henderson began.

That was the wrong play.

'No!' McReedy barked. 'I'm upset about *you.*'

McReedy pointed his pistol with a very firm hand directly at Henderson's chest.

'McReedy,' I said, trying to sound like a soothing ocean wave, 'you have to try and think this through. You have to stick to our plan. We take Henderson into the swamp, where you and Maggie once lived, right? You show him your home; you make him understand what it was he took away from you; and *then* you pop him. He'll go into the muck and the alligators will get a little extra fat in their diet. Like we planned.'

And in keeping with our improvisational connection, Mister Redhawk nodded, like it was something we'd all talked about.

McReedy's head twitched. He was clearly having a conversation with himself, asking what the hell was happening.

As luck would have it, before he could figure anything out, Henderson spoke up.

'Wait,' he said to McReedy. 'Wait. Who's going to take care of you? Who's going to take care of Lynette?'

'Take care of us? You mean, like you've taken care of us so far?' McReedy's hand was also twitching a little at this point.

'I really have to go!' Jody said suddenly, really panicked.

'Shut up!' McReedy shouted. 'Everybody shut up!'

This was a situation you truly did not want: two junkies vying for who's worse off, the one who just shot up and might have been peaking, or the one who's run out of steam and needs another shot.

I could see that chaos was about to ensue.

Just then, Mister Redhawk spoke softly.

'I have a proposal,' he said, like we were in a business meeting. 'Let's let Jody leave. She's obviously distressed. Then let's invite McReedy and Moscowitz to have a seat and include them in our previous negotiations, tabling, at least for the moment, the idea of shooting anyone.'

I instantly put away my gun. 'I second this motion,' I said heartily.

Jody was already heading for the elevator.

Henderson wasn't certain what to think. McReedy looked confused. Philip didn't move a muscle.

'What previous negotiations?' McReedy wanted to know, proving that he was not completely zonked.

'May we all sit down?' Mister Redhawk suggested.

I went for a cushy club chair. Philip returned to his place beside Mister Redhawk. Henderson and McReedy, only a little hesitantly, went to the leather sofa where Henderson had been sitting before.

Jody was gone.

The fire crackled, my martini was doing me a favor, and a general air of relative civility descended over our little group – like a shroud.

'Let's start from the top,' I suggested, 'so that everybody's in the same ball park.'

'Agreed,' said Mister Redhawk. 'The short version is this: our Seminole tribe is about to consolidate an agreement with the United States government to make our area of the swamp a national preserve. We, the Seminoles, will retain all hunting, fishing, logging, and oil rights to the land. Mr Henderson can, of course, oppose this idea, and he certainly has powerful resources at his command to do so. But, if he does, we have, in our possession, proof that he has a biological daughter and we will, with our own considerable resources, make a claim on her behalf, through our legally verifiable right of matrilineal descent, to much more than the meager swamp land here in Florida. Court battles will ensue which could last for years, and, as luck would have it, we have already secured the immediate rights to everything on the land in question for the Seminole people until all disputes are settled.'

'Meaning that John Horse and Joseph and Philip and all,' I

chimed in, 'they get the oil money for as long as these court battles go on.'

'Exactly,' Mister Redhawk said.

'I mean, it seems obvious to me now,' I said, to no one in particular, 'but this is why you wanted me to get the baby, why you got Sharon to hire me in the first place. You wanted to take care of the baby so that there would be no question of Seminole inheritance. And you figured that my own psychology would muddle my thinking somehow. How you knew anything about me at all is a mystery, but I figure a guy like you can always find out whatever you need to find out to get what you want. That's the way your world is. There's a possibility, of course, that you didn't want to be reminded of the terrible things you've done to Lynette, and McReedy, and Maggie Redhawk. You ruined their lives – and for what? Of course, this would imply that you're human, and even your other daughter doesn't think you are, so.'

Henderson didn't respond.

'All right,' I went on, 'then let me ask Mister Redhawk a question. If you're about to have a deal with the United States government to make your land a national preserve, why do you need to deal with Henderson and his baby at all?'

'Insurance, as I said,' he responded impatiently. 'I'm certain that when you spent time with John Horse you got a dose of his *slow cooking* philosophy.'

'I did.'

'He takes the long view of history in general,' Mister Redhawk continued. 'And in the long view, white people are not to be trusted. You understand that one of our great Seminole leaders, Osceola . . .'

'Yes,' I interrupted, 'I know all about how he was tricked by the evil General Lying Bastard or whatever his name was. You and yours can't hold a candle to me and mine when it comes to the *never forget* philosophy. So, you don't trust Caucasians. Cool. I don't either. Who does? Because they are, in general, an untrustworthy lot. So you think, what? That the government might nix your arrangement about the preserve in favor of big business and big money? Upon the slightest reflection, I'd say that's not a bad bet.'

'We need to prepare for every contingency,' he said, a little more animated than before.

'Yeah,' I fired back, 'if you actually could prepare for every contingency, this would be a perfect world. But things pop up – things that you can't prepare for.'

'Look!' Henderson interjected, 'I'd love to listen to the two of you go on and on, but, as it happens, I have to get to my plane. I have pressing business elsewhere. So let me condense this for everyone. The search for oil in these swamps began in 1901, and the first producing well came to Humble Oil in 1943. That's my version of the long view of history. It has nothing to do with Indian squatters on land legally purchased by Humble Oil, which is now a part of a new company called *Exxon*, in which I hold a controlling interest. You can embarrass me with this baby, and with Lynette, but that's about all. I can fight off this matrilineal inheritance nonsense in my sleep. And, in truth, find a man in my position in the global economic world who *doesn't* have an illegitimate child or five, and *that* would be news. It would have been easier, and cleaner, if I could have obtained the child, but I've already wasted enough time here in this back-water sewer. So let's take care of the final details, shall we? And then I'll be off.'

He turned to McReedy.

'I'll provide for Lynette for the rest of her life,' he said. 'Shall we say a yearly stipend of ten thousand dollars, with a cost of living increase every two years?'

Before McReedy had time to answer, Henderson turned to me.

'Mr Moscowitz,' he told me, 'I'll offer you a carrot and a stick. Take twenty-five hundred dollars, a first-class plane ticket to New York, and the assurance that all criminal charges pending against you will have vanished by the time you arrive home in Brooklyn. Or I'll see to it that the authorities realize that the Feibush Maskovitz hired by the State of Florida is actually Foggy Moscowitz, wanted for child abduction and involuntary manslaughter. I know your real name, you see? I'll secure your extradition to New York, there to stand trial and most certainly go to prison.'

He stood.

'As to the Indians?' He shook his head. 'Roll the dice. I know you have influence, but I have senators. I'm almost certain that your deal with the government will fall apart, and, even if it doesn't, I can make a great legal argument that my company's purchase of the land and oil rights should supersede your control of the swamp. You'll get some land. I'll take the oil and timber. You can keep the mosquitoes.'

He adjusted his coat, nodded to us all, and headed out of the room.

'You forgot about me?' McReedy asked.

Anyone could see that McReedy's most recent shot was going wrong. He couldn't focus, his speech was slurred, and he was on the verge of nodding off.

'You've outlived your usefulness,' Henderson said without turning around. 'I've tolerated you because you're family, but I'm done with you. You couldn't even take care of this Moscowitz problem. I'm done.'

'No you're not!' McReedy stood, unsteadily, and raised his pistol.

Henderson stopped in the doorway, but he didn't even turn around.

'Didn't you think it was a coincidence that you ran into Jody when you left that diner called *Yudda's* just now?' he asked.

In the seven seconds of silence that followed that question, I had time to piece together an unbelievable puzzle.

'You can't be that good,' I said slowly to Henderson.

That made him turn around.

'Oh, but I am,' he said. The sound of his voice was the coldest thing I'd ever experienced in Florida – or anywhere.

'What . . . what are you talking about?' McReedy managed to ask, but he was in bad shape. 'What's going on?'

'Did you run into Jody right when you left Yudda's?' I asked McReedy.

'Yeah,' he said. 'I was going to her place to score, and there she was, right outside. Lucky for me.'

'No,' I corrected him. 'Henderson planned it this way. How he did it, and how he got the timing just right, I have no idea. But he planned to have Jody visit you at Yudda's to give you a little pick-me-up. Only the envelope she gave you, it was wrong. I don't know what it was exactly, but you're in trouble.'

'Bravo, Mr Moscowitz,' Henderson said. 'I can see why Sharon likes you.'

'What are you saying?' McReedy asked me.

But then he dropped his gun on the floor and doubled over.

'Jody gave him . . . what?' I asked Henderson. 'Too much? Something uncut?'

'Roughly five times his usual allotment of heroin,' Henderson said.

McReedy hit the floor with a solid thud.

'That's why Jody came here,' I said to Henderson. 'You called her, told her to meet McReedy, because he'd failed to take care of things for the last time, in your mind, right? So Jody gave McReedy the overdose and skittered up here for the payoff. She wasn't here about her girlfriend at all, or me, or Gerard.'

Henderson shrugged. And then he smiled.

'I think that concludes our business.' He turned again and headed for the elevator.

'Wait,' I called after him. 'How did you do it? How did you work out the timing? I have to know.'

'Sharon was watching at the window of her office,' he said, hitting the button to his elevator. 'When she saw you and Joseph coming, she called me. I had plenty of time to arrange everything – Jody, the police – and now I've managed to stall long enough in this particular meeting to let Sharon get away from the hospital to meet me at my private plane. So, what will it be, Mr Moscowitz? Money and Brooklyn, or policemen and prison? Please make up your mind quickly, I hear my elevator coming.'

I pulled out the police revolver again.

'How about if I just pop you now?' I said.

'Oh for God's sake, what good would that do you?' he answered, impatiently. 'I have people and lawyers who would set my plans in motion even without me, and you'd be a cold-blooded murderer.'

'No,' I corrected him, 'I'm pretty warm right now. First time in a while, actually.'

I pointed the pistol. The elevator doors opened. I aimed. Henderson stepped into the elevator. I felt my finger on the trigger. He smiled. The doors began to close. And I never got a chance to find out if I was the sort of person who could pull a trigger like that, because Philip came up behind me and bopped me on the head so hard that my family in Brooklyn could feel it. I went down. So did the gun. The elevator doors closed shut. And I fell into a deep, black hole.

THIRTY-TWO

I woke up because I heard running water. I was in my own bed in my own apartment – in Fry's Bay, not in Brooklyn. I closed my eyes again because they hurt. It was dark outside and still raining. I lay there for a second. My head hurt like there was a railroad spike in it, right behind my eyes. My neck was stiff.

Then I heard a noise in the room.

I sat up and turned on the lamp beside the bed. If I'd been a little more awake, maybe I'd have been startled to see John Horse sitting on the windowsill.

'John Horse,' I said, my voice sounding groggy. 'Somehow it stands to reason that you're here.'

'Foggy Moscowitz,' he said. 'Somehow I'm not surprised to hear you say that.'

'Philip brought me here?' I asked.

'Yes.'

'Any idea why he bopped me in the head?'

'Do you want some water?' He held out a glass.

I eyed it with understandable suspicion. 'What's in it besides water?'

He smiled and sipped it. 'See? Nothing.'

'No,' I shook my head. 'That's not good enough. I know the sort of thing you're liable to put into your body, and I can't take another confusing encounter with the water people at the moment. I just want to . . . wait. What time is it? How long was I out?'

'Philip brought you down to the Jeep right after he knocked you out. He drove you here. I was waiting. We got you into bed. I went to the kitchen for this water, and you woke up. I'd say you haven't been out for more than half an hour. You have a hard head.'

'Ask anybody,' I said, 'and they'll tell you the same. How did you get to my apartment? How did you even know where it was?'

'I followed you and Philip and Joseph out of the swamp. I was in another Jeep when you came into town,' he said. 'Philip was the only one who knew I was doing that. I did it because I was afraid that something might happen to you. I didn't know what, but I was afraid that you might be hurt. Your address was on your business card, the card you keep in your wallet. I went thought your wallet when you were at my house. I didn't think you would mind, since I was just trying to get to know you better. So that's how I knew where you lived. I came here and I waited. It's a nice apartment.'

'It's a dump,' I argued. 'But the rent is cheap and it's on the quiet side. I like the quiet side.'

'I was sitting in the window watching the rain. You can see the ocean from here.'

'Yeah,' I said, 'that's another nice thing about the place. I like to look at the ocean.'

'I'm glad you're not dead,' he said, and he finished the glass of water.

'Well, when it comes to that,' I said, 'I'm glad you're here, for some reason. Can't imagine why, but I am.'

'You're glad I'm here because I'm comforting,' he said with a big smile.

'You are *not* comforting,' I rejoined. 'You are, what they call, a *trickster figure*, as I have heard it said.'

'What would you know about a trickster figure?' he wanted to know, more than a little amused.

'I know everything,' I said, sitting up. 'My aunt Shayna told me about a trickster tailor in Brooklyn.'

'Tell me about him,' said John Horse.

'Why?' I was trying to get more awake, but I was still feeling like I might conk out again.

'If you tell me about your tailor,' he said, like he was trying to bargain with me, 'I'll tell you what it means that you visited the water people. Aren't you curious about that?'

'That?' I said, shaking my head. 'That was just a wild ride and you know it.'

'No,' he told me very definitely. 'It was a significant experience for both of us. But I won't tell you what it means until you tell me about the tailor.'

'Why?'

'Remember I made you tell me what your favorite Leonard Cohen song was,' he explained to me, 'and when you did, it was actually important?'

I only had to mull this for a second to realize that the song I mentioned, *The Story of Isaac,* could very well be a song about the evil Pascal Henderson. I got that. Plus I figured, what the hell, I couldn't see straight at that moment anyway, so why not indulge the old guy.

'OK,' I sighed. 'A guy comes to a tailor for a nice suit, but the tailor takes forever, and the guy gets drafted, see? In World War Two. He goes off to Europe for three years. He finally comes home to Brooklyn, he goes to the tailor, and the tailor says, "Good, I'm glad you're here. I just finished your suit today." And the guy says, "It took you over three years to make my suit? God made the entire world in seven days!" And the tailor says, "Yes, but look at the shape the world's in, and wait 'til you see what a swell *suit* I made!"'

John Horse didn't laugh.

'You're making the analogy that I do things slowly, like the tailor,' he said very studiously, 'but when I'm done, the work is good, unlike so many things in this world today – so many things are not so good. I like the analogy.'

'Or is it that the tailor is just tricking the guy into waiting forever for something that shouldn't have taken so long at all?' I asked.

'Oh.' He thought about it for a second. 'Yes, that could be it too.'

I got out of bed. I was only seeing double at this point, which was an improvement.

'OK,' I said. 'Do you have any idea why Philip hit me in the head, or not?'

'Don't you want to know about the water people?' he asked.

I sighed. 'First tell me about Philip, OK?'

'He's working with Mister Redhawk right now,' John Horse answered. 'Philip told me that you almost shot Pascal Henderson. That would have undone several years' worth of legal proceedings and behind-the-scenes manipulations. Mister Redhawk thinks that he needs Henderson alive.'

'I might not have shot him.' But even I didn't know what the truth of that was.

I saw that I was still in all my clothes, soaked as they were, including my shoes, which were pretty messy at this point. I was considering changing when a light clicked on in my head.

'Wait!' I said, steadying myself on a convenient bedpost. 'Henderson told us he was going to leave by his own private plane. You said I was only out for a half an hour. It could very well be that he's still at the old airstrip, the only place for private planes to land. He might not have left yet. I mean, look at the weather.'

'The airstrip,' John Horse said, nodding.

There was a WWII era airport close to Fry's Bay. It was abandoned for the most part but, sometimes, small planes landed there in the summer when the rich guys came in for deep-sea fishing. Fry's Bay was a kind of rich man's paradise for deep-sea fishing. Personally, you couldn't get me on a boat that far away from land, but some people liked it.

'Yes,' John Horse confirmed, 'Henderson is probably at the airfield.'

He stood and put on his jacket.

'What are you doing?' I asked.

'I'm going to take you there. I think you're right. I think Henderson hasn't left yet. It's raining pretty hard, and the visibility is terrible. If you aren't going to change, we can go now.'

He headed for the door.

'*Now* you want to take me where I want to go?' I asked, trailing behind him. 'After having me brought here?'

'Philip brought you here. I didn't have anything to do with that. I told you that Philip is working for Mister Redhawk at the moment. I'm not. Mister Redhawk doesn't know I'm here. I'm not working for anybody. I just want to see what's going to happen. I have a feeling it will be surprising, and you're an important part of that, somehow. I can't see if it's all going to work out well or not, but it's going to be entertaining to watch no matter what. And I have a stake in it, of course.'

'The land, the oil, the timber,' I began.

'Yes, yes,' he said, waving his hand like what I was saying wasn't important. 'But I'm looking for something . . . grander than money.'

'Such as?' I asked.

'The arc of justice,' he said. 'Do you know the black man who said, "The arc of the moral universe is long, but it bends toward justice"?'

'No,' I said. 'I don't know the man.'

'It's a good saying, though, don't you think?'

I pondered. I wondered if it was a good saying, or if it actually did harm by giving false hope to the hopeless. Then, out of the blue – because that's the way it happens sometimes, sometimes you get lucky – I realized something important. I realized something so important, in fact, that I almost felt good, which was a relatively unusual phenomenon for me, anywhere, anytime.

'John Horse,' I said, 'I just came up with the greatest idea. I am going to make two phone calls. Then you and I are going to the airfield on the edge of this crummy little town. And then you're going to see something good.'

'What's going to happen?' he asked. He sounded excited, like a kid.

'If everything goes the way I want it to,' I said, 'we can watch the universe get bent in the right direction.'

THIRTY-THREE

The abandoned airstrip looked like something out of a horror film, especially in the rain. There was a single runway, weeds everywhere, and a spooky hangar made mostly out of rust and bad memories. There was no tower, and, if there had ever been any other buildings, they'd have fallen apart long ago. The place was originally constructed as a secret airbase during WWII to fight off the German invasion, but, as it turned out, the Germans didn't make it all the way to Florida, for the most part, so the point was moot. Aside from being used by the aforementioned rich fishermen, and apparently Pascal Henderson, the place was deserted most of the time.

The rain was coming down pretty hard when John Horse and I pulled up to the side of the hangar. Sure enough, there were several cars there, and some lights on inside the hangar.

'This could get dicey,' I said to John Horse. 'You want to wait here?'

'I'm going to go in there with you,' John Horse assured me, grinning.

'You're not afraid someone might shoot at you?' I asked.

'Wouldn't be the first time.' He got out of the Jeep and headed toward the hangar's giant double doors.

I was out of the Jeep and by his side when we walked through the open doorway. All the gang was there. Henderson, Sharon, and Mister Redhawk were seated at the back end of the hangar, a couple hundred yards from the doorway. They sat at a nice little table, sipping tea or coffee out of porcelain cups. Philip and some other guy were standing about thirty feet to their right, beside a very nice airplane – the Dassault Falcon 10, a relatively new private jet. I only knew this because, at one time, Pan Pan Washington and I considered expanding our talents to boosting private planes. Turned out that an airplane, no matter how small it is, does not drive like a car, and the whole resale market was much more difficult. So we nixed the proposition, but not before having done the research. And a Dassault Falcon 10 was very nice. It had the distinction of being the first aircraft ever certified with a Honeywell engine. It wasn't as roomy as the Falcon 20, of course, but you couldn't have everything.

Sharon was the first to see us come into the hangar. I couldn't be certain, but I thought she smiled. Then she touched Henderson's arm. He looked. He sighed. He shook his head. He said something to Mister Redhawk, who turned, shook his head too, and said something to Philip. Philip looked my way, saw me and John Horse, and waved at us like a little kid.

'This is already interesting,' said John Horse. 'Look at that airplane.'

'It's a jet,' I said, waving back at Philip.

Philip was motoring toward us, and Sharon stood up. John Horse and I kept walking toward the back of the hangar.

'I'm glad to see you're OK,' Philip said, real loud. 'I was worried.'

'You hit hard,' I said. 'But I got a hard head.'

'Are you mad at me?' he asked. 'You know I was just doing what Mister Redhawk told me to do.'

'John Horse filled me in,' I told him.

By that time, John Horse and I were halfway into the hanger. That's when I noticed that the other guy in the hanger, the one Philip had been taking with when we'd come in, had a gun in his hand.

Mister Redhawk stood up and headed toward us. Henderson was still seated, and Sharon stayed put as well.

'John Horse,' Mister Redhawk said, but he didn't sound happy.

'Don't worry,' John Horse said, 'I'm not here to disrupt anything. I just came to say goodbye to Pascal Henderson.'

I shoved my hands into my pants pockets to appear casual.

'I've come for other reasons,' I said to everyone, 'but I do not have any intention of shooting Mr Henderson, if that's what you're worried about.'

'But just the same,' Philip said, 'would you mind if I check your pockets?'

'By all means,' I told him. 'I want everyone to feel comfortable.'

I took my hands out of my pockets and let Philip check me out. When he found that I didn't have a firearm, everybody seemed to relax a little.

'Then why are you here?' Mister Redhawk wanted to know.

'Henderson made me an offer back at his place, and I never got a chance to answer,' I said. 'I'd like to speak with him about his deal.'

Mister Redhawk was clearly suspicious of me, but, as luck would have it, Henderson overheard our conversation, and he called to me.

'Of course, Mr Moscowitz, come over,' he told me. 'Sharon likes you, as I've said, and since she's right here, and since you don't intend to shoot me, let's finalize the particulars of our arrangement.'

I looked at John Horse. 'I'm going over to finalize the particulars of our arrangement.'

'I can't wait to see this,' he told me.

We all adjourned to the nice little table in the back of the hangar. Mister Redhawk sat back down in his chair, but he was clearly impatient with my interruption.

'How's your noggin?' I asked Sharon.

'Hurts,' she said.

'How's Joseph?'

'He'll be fine,' she told me. 'Coffee?'

'Absolutely,' I said.

'Is that the only suit you own?' she asked me, shaking her head at my appearance.

'Give me a break,' I whined, 'I've had a rough couple of days.'

Philip pulled up two more chairs to the table, for John Horse and me.

'How much longer do we have to wait, Harvey?' Henderson called out.

Harvey, who was apparently the pilot, put his gun away. 'They said at least another hour. But it's letting up. We could probably try to get away in forty-five.'

'God,' Henderson mumbled, then looked at me. 'How can you stand it here? After New York.'

'Yeah, it's a difficult adjustment,' I admitted, 'but it might be doing me some good. I don't get into nearly as much trouble here as I did in Brooklyn. Of course, I'm not taking into account the past couple of days. I do eat a lot of fresh seafood, which is supposed to be good for your brain.'

'But you want to go back to New York,' he sighed, 'and you want to see if my offer still holds, despite the fact that you menaced me with a pistol.'

'Something like that.'

'Have a seat,' he said.

John Horse and I sat down. Sharon got coffee for me but did not offer any to John Horse, I noticed. In fact, it was like she didn't even see him.

'Now, correct me if I'm wrong,' I began, 'but the deal was five thousand dollars and immunity from any and all prosecution, plus first-class air fare to LaGuardia.'

He smiled. 'Technically inaccurate on all counts,' he told me, amused, 'but I think what you're saying would be satisfactory, with the caveat that once we're done, we're done. Any trouble you get yourself into from now on? That's your problem. This deal only takes care of existing legal troubles, not any future such difficulties.'

I looked at John Horse. 'That's a pretty good deal.'

'It's a *very* good deal,' he agreed.

'I am curious,' Henderson said to John Horse, without actually looking at him, 'as to why you're here.'

'I'm not here,' John Horse insisted. 'Fifteen people in the swamp will tell you that I am in my house there at this very moment.'

'Good,' said Henderson. 'I'd hate to have it reported that you violated the terms of your parole.'

'In fact, the terms of my parole have been satisfied,' said John Horse calmly, 'but thank you for your concern.'

'Why are you here?' Henderson insisted.

'I came to say goodbye to you, Pascal Henderson,' John Horse said plainly. 'I didn't know how that was going to happen, exactly, but I was pretty sure I'd get to do it tonight. Now I'm certain. It's important to say goodbye to the people who are big in your life, when it's their time to go. So I wanted to come . . . and thank you.'

This obviously surprised Henderson, who looked right at John Horse at last.

'Thank me?' he said to John Horse.

'Yes,' John Horse answered. 'I wanted to thank you for standing in my way. I would not have become the person I am today without an adversary as significant as you. How does a man grow strong? He fights adversity. A small amount of adversity gives him a small fight. Fighting you has been like battling an endless pack of wolves . . . in a hurricane. But now, here I am. Sitting across from you at this table. And I am the person that I have become. So I say thank you.'

'Famous Blue Raincoat,' I interjected all of a sudden, without thinking.

All eyes looked my way.

'I just thought of my actual favorite Leonard Cohen song, like you asked me a while back,' I told John Horse. 'It's *Famous Blue Raincoat*. He says to his enemy, "I'm glad you stood in my way". This is the first time, just now, just this second, that I ever understood this lyric.'

'Mazel tov,' said John Horse to me.

'Thank you,' I said right back.

'I have no idea what either of you is talking about,' Henderson snapped.

'You're not supposed to thank an adversary,' Sharon complained.

'What are you supposed to do?' I wanted to know.

'You're supposed to crush him.' She looked at me like I was a dope.

'Exactly,' said Henderson, without a hint of irony.

'Well, that is usually my philosophy,' I said, nodding. 'I fall more into your way of thinking. People like John Horse – and, of course, Leonard Cohen – they're what I would call enlightened human beings. Who can understand what they think?'

'So you accept my deal,' Henderson said. 'Good. My Seminole friends and I are just coming to an agreement as well, and this evening can end on a relatively satisfying note, except for this terrible weather. I had no idea that Florida could get this cold.'

'It'll get colder still before spring,' I said. 'And I agree that this evening will end up being pretty satisfying for most of us. Except, of course, for McReedy. I presume he's dead.'

Henderson only nodded.

'How are you going to manage that?' I ask. 'I mean, there's now a dead guy in your condominium.'

'That?' He laughed me off. 'I have a special cleaning service. He's already gone. Someone will find him in some alley some-where – another junkie dead from an overdose.'

'I think the rain's letting up,' Harvey sang.

I looked out the big hangar doors. It did seem that the rain might be backing off somewhat.

'And, as to our understanding,' Henderson said to Mister Redhawk, 'I can have the papers delivered to you by the end of the week. You'll have your park, I'll have the majority of the oil rights, everything else is split equitably.'

'We still don't quite agree on the percentages,' Mister Redhawk began.

'You wouldn't have *any* percentage if you didn't have some small bargaining chip!' Henderson barked. 'Consider yourself lucky that I've decided it's just too irritating to stay in this place one more night! We're not going to settle anything further; don't press me!'

I turned to John Horse. 'Now, do you think?' I asked.

'Seems right,' he said, nodding.

Harvey the pilot got into the Dassault Falcon 10 and started making preparations for takeoff. Sharon began to gather up some of her things; a purse, a packet of papers, a small overnight bag. Henderson stood and was about to say something when I held up my hand.

I pulled out a notepad from my inner suit coat pocket. I considered, then, how lucky it was that I hadn't changed clothes. I could never have remembered everything I needed to say without my notepad.

'Pascal Henderson,' I said, using the same voice I'd used only twice before in Florida, 'Pursuant to a criminal investigation regarding Florida statutes 794.05 and 800.04: please sit down.'

'What?' he asked me with an equal mixture of amusement and irritation.

'I said sit down, please,' I told him. 'You're under arrest.'

He began to laugh. 'Under arrest? You think you can link me to McReedy's death?'

'I think I could if I had enough time, but that's not the crime in question at the moment.' I flipped my pad. 'You're going to want to hear my little speech. In all my concern for your child, Lynette's little baby, I overlooked something very obvious. I overlooked the fact that my job is to protect *all* children.'

'Protect all children.' He seemed more confused than amused at that point. 'Isn't the child protected by your Indian friends, here?'

'Not that child,' I said, and with no small amount of delight. 'I am referring to another child.'

Henderson turned to Sharon. 'What's he talking about, do you have any idea?'

She just stared. I wondered if she might, at that moment, be figuring out what I had in mind. It had been pretty obvious all this time.

'You had the U.S. Army raid the Seminole compound to get McReedy in 1957, is that correct?' I asked Henderson.

He glared at me. 'When my jet is ready to take off, I'm leaving.'

'I really wouldn't do that. The police are on their way. Not the ones you own, the real ones.' I looked at Sharon. 'The ones you told me to avoid: Baxter and Gordon. Turns out they're not on your father's payroll.'

Sharon looked down.

'What is he talking about, Sharon?' Henderson repeated.

'Math,' I said. 'My job is to protect children. And, if my math is correct, nine months ago it was 1973. Let us say that Lynette was several months old when you had her taken away from her family and put in an orphanage, that would make her sixteen years old when you schtupped her. And that, my friend, is statutory rape in the great State of Florida.'

'What are you talking about?' Henderson mumbled, but the amusement was entirely gone from his demeanor.

'I'm talking about Florida statute 794.05.' I consulted my notepad. 'I quote: "A person twenty-four years of age or older who engages in sexual activity with a person sixteen or seventeen years of age commits a felony of the second degree, punishable as provided . . ." well, a few of the other statutes outline the various punishments. The worst is death, followed by life in prison. The original section, you will be interested to know, was enacted nearly a hundred years ago, to protect children under the age of eighteen. Then, in 1943, it was expanded by section 800.04, which applies to children under the age of sixteen. Either way, you're screwed, if I may use that word. Because we have scientifically verifiable evidence of your crime in the person of Lynette's baby; yours and Lynette's. I checked on this. There are tests they can run to tell with 99% certainty who's the father. And my friend, you're the father. Ergo, you have violated the aforementioned statutes, and I am fulfilling my legally mandated duty as an officer of Florida Child Protective Services.'

'The child he's protecting, you see,' John Horse said calmly, 'is not the baby. It's Lynette.'

'Statutory rape,' said Mister Redhawk, smiling bigger than I would have thought possible. 'How could I not have . . . nice work, Mr Moscowitz.'

'And the thing is,' I went on, 'that I'm legally empowered to enforce these laws, ironically, by virtue of the job that *you* got me. You have to love that.'

'You're a common criminal!' Henderson erupted. 'You don't have any *legal empowerment*!'

'I think Sharon will tell you otherwise,' I allowed. 'When I was hired, they gave me a badge and a lecture about what my job was. I swore an oath. I do have certain limited legal powers. Oddly enough, I take that oath and those powers very seriously. You may be aware of certain motivations I might have for taking this job in the first place, and you think you know me. You think it was all your idea. But it wasn't. It was God's idea.'

'God?' He looked around at all of us, like not one of us was sane. '*God?*'

'Or whatever,' I said, giving him a shrug I inherited from my Aunt Shayna. 'The point is, I took the job for reasons of my own, and I'm feeling pretty good about those reasons right at the moment.'

'Statutory rape?' he said, really loud. 'Are you serious? Is this a joke? The girl is a junkie and a prostitute.'

'Who was sixteen when you abused her.' I looked back down at my notepad, but mostly for effect. 'That's verified by science. And it says here that it's a second-degree felony punishable by death or life in prison. That doesn't sound funny to me.'

'You actually think you can make the slightest case, that the police are going to come and arrest *me*?' he demanded to know.

And right on cue, we hear, way off in the distance, police sirens.

'Yes,' I say. 'I think they are.'

'Well, this is ridiculous,' he said, but he looked less sure of himself than he had all evening. 'I'll just . . . I have the best lawyers in the world. I'll brush this off before it ever comes to court. And you, Mr Moscowitz, you're the one who'll be in prison. Our deal is off! And as far as the Seminoles go? Forget your little park. I'll drill every inch from here to the ocean. There won't be a livable square foot anywhere in that swamp, or this town, or this part of Florida. Let's do some more *math*, shall we? By the end of this year, crude oil will sell at twelve dollars a barrel. If I drill, say, just five hundred wells in the swamp and across that execrable little village, Fry's Bay, and each one produces, let's say conservatively, twenty barrels a day, wait . . . that's over $43,000,000 a year. That's what I get. Moscowitz gets prison. Indians get nothing. I get $43,000,000. So. Are we done here?'

That's when I produced the nice little Swiss Model 210 Sig, Sharon's small but accurate pistol.

'Look what I found,' I said to Sharon. 'Does it look familiar? It's yours. I palmed it neatly when Philip went to frisk me a minute ago. Pretty neat, don't you think? It's just the right size for that! So I guess we're not entirely done here, after all, Mr Henderson.'

'That's what you think,' Henderson said, and then he yelled, 'Start the plane, Harvey.'

'Yes, sir,' Harvey called out, 'but I have to get the tractor to pull it out of the hangar.'

'Start the goddamned engines!' Henderson insisted.

'I can't do that in the hangar, sir,' Harvey yelled back, 'this is a jet. But I'll get the plane out right now.'

Harvey was apparently unaware of the drama unfolding elsewhere in the hangar.

'Right now!' Henderson shouted.

Harvey jumped out of the plane, went to some squat little tractor and fired it up. He backed it right up to the nose of the plane.

Henderson glared at Sharon. 'What are you doing just standing there? Get on the damned plane.'

She seemed confused. Then she looked around the room like she didn't recognize anybody. Then she threw up.

'Sharon doesn't feel well,' I told Henderson.

Harvey hooked up the jet to the tractor thing, and he started to haul the airplane out of the hangar. Outside, the rain was nearly gone, but the sky was still black and the clouds were low.

And the sound of sirens was getting louder.

'I don't think you can entirely prove paternity, by the way,' Henderson said, edging himself around the table. 'I don't admit to being the father of the baby. It's not my child.'

'No, this is what I'm trying to tell you,' I said. 'Besides calling the police, I also called Maggie Redhawk at the hospital. She confirms what I already suspected – that the Seminole tribe has a very good lawyer.'

'We have incontrovertible proof of your paternity, Mr Henderson,' Mister Redhawk said, still seated. 'I, quite naturally, assumed that you'd deny the child if it came to a lawsuit. You

don't think I'd have threatened you if I hadn't had ironclad
evidence, do you? I just hadn't . . . I'd overlooked the obvious
angle of statutory rape. I mean, Lynette seems much older than
she is. That's thanks to you, I suppose.'

'This is ridiculous,' Henderson raved. 'Do you have any idea
who I am?'

Henderson moved all of a sudden like lightning. He grabbed
Sharon and twisted her around, holding her in front of him. He
had his arm wrapped around her throat. She was a little taller
than he was, so it all looked pretty uncomfortable.

'Wait,' Sharon said weakly.

'I'm getting on my private jet,' he told us all, holding Sharon
in front of him like a giant rag doll. 'I have urgent business in
New York. My lawyers will deal with this.'

'Your lawyers are going to have to deal with it in Fry's Bay,'
I told him.

Without much of a thought, I moved pretty quickly toward the
jet. I showed Harvey my gun. He seemed very surprised. The
tractor stopped moving.

Then I shot the front tire of the big jet. It made an ungodly
noise exploding inside the old hanger. Everyone reacted badly,
me included.

My hearing was momentarily blocked.

Henderson was staring like I'd shot his dog. I said to him,
'See? You're not going anywhere. So let go of Sharon and have
a seat.'

My voice sounded funny to me, and there was a definite ringing
in my ears.

Henderson dropped Sharon and started screaming. 'You're all
going to be dead! I've changed my mind! I'm just going to have
you killed!'

The sirens were really loud by then. Henderson was practically
frothing at the mouth. Philip and Mister Redhawk seemed oddly
calm, John Horse was grinning, and Harvey had a sudden emergency and ran to the toilet in the back of the hangar.

Sharon groaned from her spot on the floor. She looked terrible.

'Damn it,' I said. 'I think I just figured out why Sharon's so
sick tonight.'

I put away my pistol and hustled over to her.

'What is it?' Philip said, coming over to the table.

'Sharon,' I said. 'Wake up.'

She didn't move.

'Sharon, what did you do?' I said, a little softer.

I pushed up her sleeves, and I was relieved to see that there are no track marks on her arms. Then I noticed that her nose was bleeding.

I looked up at Henderson. 'Here's what's wrong, I think. You told Jody to prepare a stronger package than usual for McReedy after he failed to ice me. So Jody had some strong stuff in play. But what you didn't know is that Jody and Sharon knew each other – that's my guess. She's always talking about her criminal friends. So let's say that Jody got this strong stuff tonight, and then thought it would be a shame to give it all to McReedy when, if they were careful, they could snort just a little, and get quite a punch. Only for a junkie, *just a little* turns into *just one more* after you've done about six or seven lines. Jody and Sharon did too much. Here's another thing that's your fault, Mr Henderson: your daughter, here, might die. She has to go to the hospital right now.'

'Sharon?' He looked down. 'How would she know Jody?'

'Through you,' I said simply. 'Plus, it's a small town. I'm surprised that I met so many new people in the past couple of days. Fry's Bay, it's really a kind of wonderland.'

The cop car pulled up into the hangar, lights flashing. Two cops got out. They were both in uniform, both in hats, guns in holsters, and almost impossible to tell apart at a distance – or maybe it was just me. All cops looked the same in uniform because I didn't ever look them in the face.

Philip went to stand next to Mister Redhawk. I noticed that his pistol had vanished. I felt it wise to make mine do the same, and it was gone. I was still kneeling beside Sharon.

'Mister Redhawk,' one of the cops said.

'Good evening, Mr Baxter,' he answered.

'Mr Henderson?' the other cop said. 'Would you mind standing up, please?'

Henderson stayed seated.

The cops were sauntering our way very casually. The other one, Gordon, spoke to me over the tabletop.

'Are you Moscowitz?' he wanted to know. 'What are you doing back there?'

'It's my boss, Sharon,' I said. 'She has to go to the hospital.' Both cops moved faster.

'What happened?' Baxter asked.

'She's having a drug reaction,' I said. 'She needs to get to the hospital right away. Can you take her or let us take her in the Jeep and give us an escort or something?'

'What kind of a drug reaction?' Gordon asked.

'Pretty sure she snorted a speedball mix,' I said.

'Got it from Jody,' Baxter assumed.

'That was quick,' I said, unable to hide my surprise at his deductive powers. 'How did you figure that?'

'Jody's in the hospital already,' Baxter said. 'She's seriously messed up. Same deal. Nose bleeding. Quasi-comatose.'

'So can we just get Sharon to the hospital?' I asked again. 'There's a lot that I don't like about her right at the moment, but I don't want her to die.'

And, just at that moment, gunfire exploded in the hangar. Once again the sound was deafening. I peered under the table to discover Harvey, who was not the bland character I had previously taken him for, had a serious automatic rifle leveled in my direction. Although I was lucky to have one policeman and one table between me and the gun, I was still very nervous about my chances, because I saw that the gun was a very pretty AK-47, and the wood was polished to the hilt, which meant that Harvey loved his gun. Which meant he probably knew how to use it. Which was bad news. Guys who didn't know how to use an AK-47 would just point and pull and let the gun do the work. Guys who did know how to use one could put seventeen bullets into your midsection before you could blink twice.

Harvey was planted behind the tractor thing, and everyone else was on the floor, except Henderson. Philip had literally picked up Mister Redhawk and shielded him with his body as they both dived for the space beside the table. The two cops hit the deck, guns drawn, and looked for a shot. John Horse was the most graceful among us. He somehow managed to shove his chair backwards with his heels so that the chair glided across the smooth floor of the hangar, with him in it, almost ten feet away from the table. Then he just sat on the floor behind a large metal cabinet and watched.

Henderson stood up.

'Thank you, Harvey,' he said coldly. 'Can we take off with the front tire like that or will you have to change it?'

'It'd be rough,' Harvey said, still aiming his gun. 'It's possible to take off that way, but it's risky. Better to change the tire.'

Henderson moved quickly to the shelter behind the tractor, beside Harvey.

I saw Baxter inching his way along the floor and I got that he was trying to clear a side shot, but unfortunately Harvey saw it too. Without any warning, Harvey fired two shots. Both hit Baxter, one in the gun arm and one in the opposite leg. Harvey did, indeed, know what he was doing.

Baxter was making a pretty awful noise, and Gordon was cursing up a storm.

Actually, that was a good thing, because it created a sort of sonic cover. It was distracting to hear a man screaming in pain and another man tearing the fabric of human decency with his profanity. At least I hoped it was distracting for Harvey.

I took out the little Sig from my coat as inconspicuously as I could, trying to look like I was ministering to Sharon. Then I calculated my options. Unless I stood up, I couldn't see Harvey. And if I stood up, I'd get shot. Then it came to me: I was just about at tractor tire level, where I was under the table. It came to me to shoot out a second tire. That would be a lot more distracting than the noise of the cops, and I might be able to get off a few shots at Harvey.

I figured about where I'd have to shoot to pop at least one tractor tire. It was going to be riskier than before, of course, because before I just went up to the tire and shot it point blank. To shoot the tractor tire from at least fifty feet away, that would be something that took a little skill and a lot of luck.

So I tried to settle my mind, and my hand. I tried to think of everything Red had ever told me about how to aim with your guts and not with your eyes. How you have to think that the shot's done even before you pulled the trigger. How you had to make your mind understand that the shot was nothing. Plus, I wasn't shooting a guy, which I didn't know if I could actually do or not. I was shooting a tire.

So. I shifted. I sat. I pointed. I breathed. I shot.

The gun went *blam* and, almost at the same time, the tire exploded.

Once again, it was so loud that I couldn't hear anything for a second. I saw, however, that my ploy had worked. Harvey reacted to the noise by pulling up and away from the tractor, and Officer Gordon got him twice out of five quick shots. The AK went clattering to the floor, followed almost immediately by Harvey.

Meanwhile Henderson was also startled and backed away from the tractor. I got myself to my feet as fast as I could and ran like I had a dog chasing me, right toward Henderson. He saw me coming and, for the first time, he looked scared.

That was very satisfying.

'Tell me *one* thing that keeps me from shooting you dead,' I shouted at him as I came roaring down on him. 'Give me *one* reason I shouldn't empty this gun into your guts, you son of a bitch.'

He was backing up fast and making little barking sounds. He eventually got stopped by the wall, but I kept coming. We ended up face to face, with his daughter's little gun jammed into his solar plexus so hard I thought he might stop breathing.

'Can't think of anything?' I whispered.

I made a motion like I was cocking the pistol, although with the Sig, it wasn't really necessary. I did it for effect.

'Our deal!' he snarled. 'I won't tell anyone your real name; they'll never find you. I can do that.'

'Oh, that,' I said, even softer than before. 'I know you won't tell anyone my real name because, as it happens, you don't know it. That name you spewed out, the one you think is my real name? It's one of about seventeen aliases I acquired in Brooklyn as a teen. I have so many names on account of good advice I got back then. See, if they don't know your real name, they can't find you so good. So, no, Mr Henderson, no deal.'

For emphasis I shoved the pistol so far into his guts I could feel his backbone.

Henderson shrieked. Also very satisfying.

Then I heard from behind me, 'All right, Moscowitz. I got it.'

I turned my head a little to see Gordon behind me. He had handcuffs in one hand and his gun in the other.

I paused for just a second to make Henderson think I might just go ahead and pop him as it was, then I backed away slowly, holding the gun out to the side so that there would be no question in Gordon's mind what I was about.

'This pistol,' I said to Gordon, 'belongs to Sharon. You want me to give it back?'

'Just hang on to it for a second,' Gordon said, 'while I finish this up, right?'

'Right,' I agreed.

'Pascal Henderson,' Gordon said, very much like a cop on television, 'you're under arrest for the statutory rape of Lynette Baker, resisting arrest, ordering the shooting of a police officer, attempting to flee, and, if I understand some documents we've just received from the Seminole Tribal Council, land fraud.'

Henderson was momentarily too stunned to say anything.

'Have a look at Baxter, would you?' Gordon said to me. 'Then, if you know how to work it, go to the squad car and call for an ambulance, right?'

I moved instantly while Gordon put Henderson in cuffs. I noticed that Gordon had kicked the AK-47 far away from Harvey, who was unconscious, or dead. Still, I liked to ere on the safe side. I scooted over and collected the rifle, then hurried to Baxter.

Baxter was passed out, but he was very much alive. He had a bad wound in his right forearm and a graze on his left thigh. I ripped up the sleeve of his cop shirt and make a quick bandage out of it for the arm. I couldn't tell if the bullet was still in or not. The thigh was bleeding, but not as bad.

Philip and Mister Redhawk were up and moving. They seemed amazingly calm. Mister Redhawk stopped beside me, but Philip kept going toward his Jeep, with a quick smile and nod in my direction.

'How is he?' Mister Redhawk asked, standing over me and Gordon.

'I'm worried about the arm, but I think he's fine,' I said. 'Are you leaving?'

'Thanks to you,' he answered. 'We won't forget this. I think things are going to be better for you now.'

That was all. He was gone.

I glanced over at John Horse, who was getting himself to his feet as well. 'This turned out even better than I thought it would!' He had a big smile on his face.

'Are you going with Philip and Mister Redhawk?' I asked him. 'Because I think I still have some sorting out to do, and I'd like to talk with you a little bit more, if you wouldn't mind.'

'Oh, no,' he assured me, 'I'm here to be with you. We'll take care of this mess, get everyone off to the hospital or to jail, and then go back to your place and talk, if you like.'

'Good,' I said. 'Now I have to call for an ambulance.'

I headed for the cop car.

'Hey, Foggy,' John Horse called out. 'Do you see which side you're on tonight? Take a look around this place. Do you see what that means?'

I didn't feel like taking a look around because I wanted to call the hospital. But then I realized, just as my hand was on the driver's side door of the cop car, exactly what he meant. I was about to get into a police vehicle willingly for the first time in my life. And I was doing that to call for help for two policemen, and a woman who was my boss and also a person who did me wrong. And that was happening while the baddest of the bad guys got cuffed, primarily on account of me. I was in the process of seeing to it that criminals got arrested and policemen got help. And I thought to myself, *Well, this is certainly a topsy-turvy world.*

THIRTY-FOUR

Ambulances arrived, people departed, and I decided for some reason that I had to go back to my office and finish signing my time card. Funny what gets into a person's head after a series of difficult events; funny what you think might give you the feeling that it was all finally over. John Horse said he'd drive me. We didn't talk much on the way.

The sky was beginning to clear, and every once in a while

you could see a silver moon. The streets were slick with rain, and the occasional neon was splashing around in the puddles.

We pulled up in front of my office building and, before I got out, John Horse spoke up.

'Now,' he announced, all business, 'let's sort out a few things, like you said.'

I stared at him. 'Just like that? No slow cooking?'

'You've had a hard couple of days,' he said. 'I'd imagine you're pretty tired. I thought I would spare you the crafty Seminole schtick.'

I continued to stare for a moment, trying to figure if he was still messing with me or not. He didn't return my stare, so I gave up after a second and went along with him.

'OK,' I mumbled.

'What do you want to know?' He wasn't looking at me. He was looking straight ahead, his hands still on the steering wheel.

'Well, OK, I am curious about something that Mister Redhawk said to me just as he was leaving the airplane hangar,' I suggested.

'What was that?'

'He said, "I think things are going to be better for you now,"' I told him. 'What do you think he meant by that, would you happen to know?'

'If I had to guess,' John Horse answered, 'I would think he meant that Sharon's not going to be your boss anymore. I think that somehow you'll be in charge up there in that little office of yours. That would be better, wouldn't it?'

'You think he can arrange a thing like that?' I asked, uncertain how I felt about it.

'Yes. I've told you already, Foggy,' John Horse said, 'I think you have talents and abilities that you've wasted, or haven't discovered, because of your past. Mister Redhawk agrees with me about that. Now is the time to start using those talents. Now is the time to become the person you really are. And you're not a car thief.'

'What am I?' I asked, mostly to be polite.

I was suddenly feeling completely exhausted. All I wanted to do was go up to my office, sign my time card, declare the case officially finished, and then sleep for a week.

'What did the water people tell you?' he asked softly.

'Oy, again with the water people,' I complained.

'I think you should examine it for just a second,' he said. 'What was the last thing that the water people told you?'

I grumbled, but I could see that I was going to have to humor him. He wasn't going to let it go, for some reason. So I tried to think back to my tea-induced trip. And after a second, there she was: the water girl, in the place under the lake.

'I was telling the water girl how nice it was under the water. She was telling me I had to go back to save children.' I related this begrudgingly, because I was a little embarrassed to be taking it even a little seriously.

'There you go.' He nodded once. 'Right now it looks like you might be a person who saves children, in one way or another. Sounds corny, I know, but that's what you are.'

'Yeah, about that,' I said, unwilling to ponder his suggestion. 'What's going to happen with Lynette and the baby, and also to Sharon, who, after all, is only an older wayward child? And while you're at it, what's going to happen with the Seminole land and the oil rights, really?'

He looked out on to the silvery streets for a moment and then up into the clouds.

'What's going to happen with the moon?' he said.

I sat silently, because I had no idea what he meant.

'The moon?' I asked after a minute.

'What's going to happen with the moon tonight, as the night wears into tomorrow?'

'I guess . . . I don't know, it'll move across the sky, set, and disappear around the other side of the world. But—'

'And what's going to happen with it tomorrow night? The moon. It's going to rise again, and ride across the sky again, and set again. Right?'

'Right,' I answered uncertainly.

'And it doesn't matter if you want it to or not, and it doesn't matter what you do, and it doesn't matter what you hope for or what you wish.' He shrugged. 'That's what's going to happen. It's going to do what it does.'

I blinked.

'All right, I'm going home,' he said. 'You can walk to your apartment from here when you're finished?'

I glared at him for a second, and then let out a slow, patient breath. 'If I don't just curl up on top of my desk and fall asleep, yes – I can walk home from here.'

'You should come and visit me soon,' he said, still not looking at me.

'How would I do that exactly?' I sighed. 'I have absolutely no idea how to get to where you live.'

'Philip will probably drop by to check up on you. He likes you. He could bring you to my house.' He smiled then. 'Isn't it funny that you had to come back to this office, after all that's happened?'

'It's a riot.' I started to get out of the Jeep.

'It's almost like you're already the boss.' He shifted into first. 'Nice to be in charge of your own life for a change, isn't it?'

And just like that, he was gone.

I stumbled a little getting up to the offices and, when I shoved in through the front door, it felt, all of a sudden, very empty. I turned on the humming florescent overhead, and there it was – my plywood desk, the smeared walls, the spattered blond carpet. And, even after all that time in a swamp, a gas-soaked airplane hangar, and several bars, I could still smell the stale cigarette smoke from the previous occupant of my office.

I was aching, wet, freezing, shivering, and about as coherent as a sardine sandwich. So when the phone on my desk started ringing, I was certain I didn't want to answer it. Who, after all, would be calling at such an ungodly hour?

But it wouldn't stop ringing, and so I picked it up at last, with no small sense of déjà vu, since the last time that had happened it had been Sharon on the other end, inviting me into my recent adventures in hell.

'Moscowitz,' I said, but I sounded like an undertaker.

'Oh my God, you're actually there,' the voice on the other end said.

There was a lot of noise and loud music in the background.

'Yes I am,' I affirmed. 'Who is this?'

'It's Gerard,' he said. 'I've been trying to call you. I'm at the club now.'

'Gerard?' I squeezed my eyes shut, trying to focus. 'How did you get this number?'

'You gave me your card, remember?' he said.

'Really? Well, good. Good, then. So. How are you?'

'How are *you* is the question,' he said. 'I wanted to check and see if you were all right.'

'This past couple of days were very strange,' I told him, 'but things turned out all right. How about you?'

'Peachy,' he said, all lit up. 'Remember my telling you about my difficulties with that Jody girl?'

'Yes.' I sobered up just a little.

'Well, problem solved!' he said quite cheerfully. 'And I gather it had something to do with you. She showed up here in our dressing room about an hour ago, looking like hell, and collected her girlfriend – you know, the one who hates me? – They split like they were on fire, packed up everything and told the management they were leaving town for good. Leaving town!'

'Say,' I told him. 'That is news.'

'It is,' he agreed. 'But since they said you had something to do with it, and it sounded, I don't know . . . a little dicey, I thought I would give you a call. I was worried.'

'Thanks, Gerard,' I said, and I meant it. 'It's nice to know somebody was concerned.'

'Well, I'm glad you're all right, that's all,' he said. 'And Jody's gone and taken her filthy drugs with her. Maybe things are looking up around here.'

I thought about that assessment for a moment.

'Maybe they are at that,' I finally told him, and I might have been smiling – it was hard to tell.

We said our goodbyes and hung up. I looked around my crummy little office. Then, although I still couldn't have told you exactly why, I actually filled out my time card. I put it in the outbox and managed my way to the door. When I turned off the light, I could see moonlight slanting hard through the window blinds. I peeked out, and the whole town – the streets and the buildings and the alleyways – were all painted white by the moon, like there was snow everywhere. And then, all of a sudden, for no reason I could figure, I wasn't quite so cold anymore.

31901064605159